INTO

❧ THE ❧

STILL
BLUE

Roar and Liv (Under the Never Sky e-story)

Brooke (Under the Never Sky e-story)

INTO THE STILL BLUE

VERONICA ROSSI

www.atombooks.net

ATOM

First published in the United States in 2014 by HarperCollins
First published in Great Britain in 2014 by Atom
Reprinted 2014

Copyright © 2014 by Veronica Rossi

The moral right of the author has been asserted.

A CIP catalogue record for this book
is available from the British Library.

ISBN 978-1-907411-07-6

Printed and bound in Great Britain by
Clays Ltd, St Ives plc

Papers used by Atom are from well-managed forests
and other responsible sources.

MIX
Paper from
responsible sources
FSC   FSC® C104740
www.fsc.org

Atom
An imprint of
Little, Brown Book Group
100 Victoria Embankment
London EC4Y 0DY

An Hachette UK Company
www.hachette.co.uk

www.atombooks.net

For Michael

1

ARIA

A ria lurched upright, the echo of gunshots ringing in her ears.

Disoriented, she blinked at her surroundings, taking in the canvas walls, the two bed pallets, and the stack of battered storage trunks, finally recognizing Perry's tent.

Pain pulsed steadily in her right arm. She looked down at the white bandage wrapped from her shoulder to her wrist, dread swirling in her stomach.

A Guardian had shot her in Reverie.

She licked her dry lips, tasting the bitterness of pain medication. *Just try it,* she told herself. How hard could it be?

Aches stabbed deep in her bicep as she tried to make a fist. Her fingers gave only the slightest twitch. It was like her mind had lost the ability to speak with her hand, the message vanishing somewhere along her arm.

Climbing to her feet, she swayed in place for a moment,

waiting for a wave of dizziness to pass. She'd come to this tent soon after she and Perry had arrived, and hadn't left since. But she couldn't stay there a second longer. What was the point, if she wasn't getting better?

Her boots sat on top of one of the trunks. Determined to find Perry, she slipped them on—a challenge, one-handed. "Stupid things," she muttered. She tugged harder, the ache in her arm becoming a burn.

"Oh, don't blame the poor boots."

Molly, the tribe healer, stepped through the tent flaps with a lamp in hand. Soft and gray-haired, she looked nothing like Aria's mother had, but they had similar demeanors. Steady and dependable.

Aria jammed her feet into her boots—nothing like an audience to motivate—and straightened.

Molly set the lamp down on a trunk and came over. "Are you sure you should be up and about?"

Aria swept her hair behind her ear and tried to slow her breathing. Cold sweat had broken out along her neck. "I'm sure I'll go insane if I stay here any longer."

Molly smiled, her full cheeks glowing in the lamplight. "I've heard that very comment a few times today." She pressed a rough-skinned hand to Aria's cheek. "Your fever's down, but you're due for more medication."

"No." Aria shook her head. "I'm fine. I'm tired of being asleep."

Asleep wasn't really the right word. For the past days, she had a few murky recollections of surfacing from a black abyss for medicine and sips of broth. Sometimes Perry was there, holding her and whispering in her ear. When he'd spoken, she'd seen the glow of embers. Other than that, there'd been nothing but darkness—or nightmares.

Molly took her numb hand and squeezed. Aria felt nothing, but as Molly probed higher, she sucked in a breath, her stomach clenching.

"You've had some nerve damage," Molly said. "I suppose you're figuring that out for yourself."

"But it'll heal, won't it? Eventually?"

"I care for you too much to give false hope, Aria. The truth is I don't know. Marron and I did the best we could. We were able to save the limb, at least. For a while it looked like we might have to remove it."

Aria drew away, turning toward the shadows as the words sank in. Her arm had almost been removed. Taken off, like some expendable part. An accessory. A hat or a scarf. Had she really come that close to waking up and finding a piece of herself missing?

"It's the arm that was poisoned," she said, tucking it close to her side. "It wasn't much to start with anyway." Her Marking, the half-finished tattoo that would have established her as an Aud, was the ugliest thing she'd ever seen. "Will you show me around, Molly?"

Aria didn't wait for an answer. The urge to see Perry— and to forget about her arm—was overwhelming. Ducking through the tent flaps, she came to a dead stop outside.

She looked up, overcome by the sheer presence of the

3

cave, a hefty immensity that felt both close and everywhere. Stalactites of every size emerged from the darkness above, darkness unlike what she'd experienced in her medicated haze. That had been empty, an absence. This darkness had sound and volume. It felt full and alive, droning low and constant in her ears.

She drew a deep breath. The cool air smelled brackish and smoky, the scents so strong she could taste them.

"For most of us, the darkness is the hardest part," Molly said, coming to her side.

Around them, in neat rows, Aria saw more tents, ragged ghosts in the gloom. Sounds carried from farther off, where torches flickered—the crunch of a cart wheeling over stone, the steady trickle of water, the pleading bleat of a goat—all echoed frenetically in the cave, assaulting her sensitive ears.

"When you can't see more than forty paces off," Molly continued, "it's easy to feel trapped. We aren't, thank the skies. It hasn't come to that yet."

"And the Aether?" Aria asked.

"Worse. Storms every day since you arrived, some right on top of us." Molly threaded her arm through Aria's healthy one. "We're lucky to have this place. Sometimes it's not easy to feel that way, though."

An image of Reverie crumbling to dust came to Aria's mind. Her home was gone, and the Tide compound had been abandoned too.

Molly was right. This was better than nothing.

"I suppose you want to see Peregrine," Molly said,

leading Aria past a row of tents.

Immediately, Aria thought. But she said, simply, "Yes."

"You'll need to wait a little while, I'm afraid. We had word of people entering the territory. He's gone out with Gren to meet them. I'm hoping it's Roar and that he's brought Cinder with him."

Just hearing Roar's name brought a rawness to Aria's throat. She worried about him. She'd only been separated from him for a few days, but it felt like too long.

They came to an open area, wide as the clearing at the heart of the Tide compound. At the center spread a wooden platform surrounded by tables and chairs—all packed with people gathered around lamps. Dressed in browns and grays, they blended into the dimness, but their chatter drifted toward her, their voices tinged with anxiety.

"We're only allowed to leave the cave when it's safe outside," Molly said, noticing Aria's expression. "Today there are fires burning close by and a storm just south, so we've been stuck here."

"It's not *safe* to be outside? You said Perry was out there."

Molly winked. "Yes, but he gets to break his own rules."

Aria shook her head. As Blood Lord, he needed to take risks, more like.

By the stage, people began to notice them. Sun-bleached and salt-scrubbed, the Tides were an aptly named tribe. Aria spotted Reef and a few of his strongest warriors, a group known as the Six. She recognized the three brothers: Hyde, Hayden, and Straggler, the youngest. It didn't surprise her that Hyde, a Seer like his brothers, spotted her first. He lifted a hand in a tentative greeting.

Aria returned a shaky wave. She barely knew him, or any of these people. She'd only spent a few days with Perry's tribe before she left the Tide compound. Now, standing before these almost strangers, she felt a powerful longing to see *her* people, but she didn't. Not a single person she and Perry had rescued from Reverie was there.

"Where are the Dwellers?" she asked.

"In a separate portion of the cave," Molly said.

"Why?"

But Molly's attention had moved to Reef, who left his men and stalked over. In the darkness, his features looked even harsher, and the massive scar that cut from his nose to his ear appeared more sinister.

"You're finally up," he said. His tone made it sound like Aria had been lazing around. Perry cared for this man, she reminded herself. Trusted him. But Reef had never made any attempt to befriend her.

She stared into his eyes. "Being injured is boring."

"You're needed," he said, ignoring her sarcasm.

Molly wagged a finger at him. "No, you don't, Reef. She just woke up and needs a chance to get acclimated. Don't put this on her so soon."

Reef squared his shoulders, his thick eyebrows drawing together. "When should I tell her then, Molly? Every day brings a new storm. Every hour, our food stores dwindle. Every minute, someone else comes closer to going mad inside this rock. If there is a better time for her to know the truth, I'd like to know when it is." He leaned in, a few of his thick braids falling forward. "War rules, Molly. We do what's needed, when it's needed, and right now that means she needs to know what's happening."

Reef's words shook any last wisp of fuzziness from Aria's mind. They brought her back to where she'd been a week ago, alert and tense, a little breathless, with a sense of desperation curling inside her like a stomachache.

"Tell me what happened," she said.

Reef turned his intense gaze on Aria. "Better if I show you," he said, striding away.

She followed him from the gathering area, deeper into the cave, where it grew darker and quieter and darker still, her dread mounting with every step. Molly let out a sigh of exasperation, but she came along.

They wove through the melting formations—a forest of stone that dripped from the ceiling and rose up from the ground, gradually molding together—until Aria walked through a natural corridor. Here and there, the tunnel opened to other passageways, which breathed cool damp drafts against her face.

"Down that way is the storage area for medicines and supplies," Molly said, gesturing to the left. "Everything that's not food or animals. Those are kept in the caverns at the south end." Her voice sounded a little too cheerful, like she was trying to compensate for Reef's gruff manner. She swung the lamp gently as she walked, causing the shadows to tilt up and back along the cramped space. Aria found herself growing slightly light-headed and seasick. Or cavesick.

Where were they taking her?

She had never known darkness like this. Outside there was always Aether, or sunlight, or moonlight. In the Pod, within the protected walls of Reverie, lights always blazed. Always. This was new, this suffocating pool. She felt the pitch black fill her lungs with every breath. She was drinking the dark. Wading through it.

"Behind that curtain is the Battle Room," Molly continued. "It's a smaller cavern where we brought one of the trestle tables from the cookhouse. Perry meets with people in there to discuss matters of importance. The poor boy hardly ever leaves."

Walking silently ahead of them, Reef shook his head.

"I worry about him, Reef," Molly said, with plain irritation. "Someone has to."

"And you think I don't?"

Aria worried too—more than either of them—but she bit her lip, leaving them to argue.

"Well, you're good at hiding it, if so," Molly shot back. "All you seem to do is lecture him about what he's doing wrong."

Reef glanced over his shoulder. "Should I start slapping him on the back and telling him he's wonderful? Will that do us any good?"

"You could try it once in a while, yes."

Aria stopped listening to them. The hair on her arms lifted

8

as her ears latched onto new sounds. Moans. Whimpers. Sickly sounds that swept toward her through the tunnel. A chorus of need.

She broke away from Molly and Reef, clutching her wounded arm to her side as she rushed ahead. Rounding a bend in the corridor, she arrived in a large, dim cavern, lit along the perimeter by lamps.

Spread across the floor on blankets lay dozens of people in varying states of consciousness. Their faces were ghastly white against their grays—the same clothes she'd worn her entire life until she'd been cast out of Reverie.

"They took ill immediately after you all arrived," Molly said, catching up to her. "You went to Perry's tent, and they came here, and that's how it's been. Perry said this same thing happened to you when you first came out of Reverie. It's the shock to your immune systems. There were inoculations onboard the Hover you arrived in. A supply for thirty people—but there are forty-two here. We administered equal amounts to everyone, at Perry's request. He said it's what you'd have wanted."

Aria couldn't respond. Later, when she could think clearly again, she would recall Molly's every word. She'd consider the way Reef watched her with his arms crossed, like this was her problem to fix. Now she moved further inside, her heart stuck in her throat.

Most of the people she saw were still as death. Others shook with fever, their complexions sallow, almost green.

She didn't know which was worse.

She searched the faces around for her friends—Caleb and Rune and—

"Aria . . . over here."

She followed the voice. A pang of guilt hit her when she spotted Soren; he hadn't come to mind. Aria stepped past the quaking bundles, kneeling at his side.

Soren had always been so burly, but now the thickness in his shoulders and neck had deflated. Even wrapped in a blanket she could tell. She could see it in his hollow cheeks and sunken eyes, which were heavy, half-lidded, but focused on her.

"Nice of you to come by," he said, clearly more lucid than the others. "I'm a little envious you got private accommodations. Pays to know the right people, I guess."

Aria didn't know what to say. She couldn't absorb this level of suffering. Her throat was choked with it. Tight with the need to help. To change this somehow.

Soren blinked tiredly. "I can see why you love the outside," he added. "It's mega champ out here."

2

PEREGRINE

Y ou think it's Roar and Twig?" Gren asked, pulling his horse alongside Perry's.

Perry inhaled, searching for traces of the riders who'd been spotted earlier. He smelled nothing but smoke.

Ten minutes ago he'd left the cave, eager for fresh air. For light and the feeling of openness and movement. What he'd gotten was a thick gray haze from the morning's fires blanketing everything, and the stinging sensation of the Aether like soft pinpricks over his skin.

"I'd be surprised if it was someone else," he replied. "Hardly anyone besides me and Roar knows this trail exists."

He had hunted these woods with Roar since they were kids. They had killed their first buck together not far from here. Perry knew every bend on this path, which cut through land that had once been his father's, then his brother's, and then—half a year ago when he'd become Blood Lord—his.

It had changed, though. In the past months, Aether storms had started fires that sheared through the hills, leaving wide, charred stretches. The temperature was too cold for late spring, and the smells of the wood were different too. The scents of life—earth, grass, and game—seemed buried beneath the acrid stench of smoke.

Gren tugged his brown cap down. "What are the odds they have Cinder with them?" he asked, a note of desperation bleeding into his voice. Cinder had been kidnapped while under Gren's watch, and he hadn't forgiven himself.

"Good," Perry said. "Roar always comes through."

He thought of Cinder, of how weak and frail the boy had been when he'd been taken. Perry didn't want to think about what was happening to him in Sable's and Hess's hands. They had joined forces, Horns and Dwellers, and abducted Cinder for his ability to control the Aether. He was key to reaching the Still Blue, it seemed. Perry just wanted him back.

"Perry." Gren reined in his horse. He angled his head, turning to better catch sounds with his keen ears. "Two horses. Riding hard right toward us."

Perry couldn't see anyone yet as he scanned the trail ahead, but it had to be them. He whistled to let Roar know he was there. Seconds passed as he waited for Roar's answering call. None came.

Perry cursed. Roar would have heard and whistled back.

He swept his bow off his shoulder and nocked an arrow, his gaze never leaving the bend in the path. Gren drew his

12

bow as well, and they fell silent, bracing for anything.

"Now," Gren murmured.

Perry heard the horses thundering closer. He drew his bowstring back, aiming at the trail, as Roar tore around a stand of birches.

Perry lowered his bow, trying to sort out what was happening.

Roar approached at a gallop, his black mount kicking up clods of dirt. His expression was focused—cold—and it didn't change when he spotted Perry.

Twig, one of the Six like Gren, rounded the bend behind him. Like Roar, he rode alone. Perry's hope of getting Cinder back crashed.

Roar rode hard until the last moment, and then checked his mount sharply.

Perry stared at him, unable to speak, the silence stretching between them. He hadn't expected to look at Roar and think *Liv*, though he should have. She had belonged to Roar, too. The loss landed like a blow to Perry's stomach, as hard as it had days ago when he'd first learned.

"Good you're back safe, Roar," he said finally. His voice sounded strained, but he got the words out at least.

Roar's horse stamped in agitation, tossing its head, but Roar's gaze held steady.

Perry knew that hostile look. It had just never been directed his way.

"Where have *you* been?" Roar asked.

Everything about that question was wrong. The accusing tone in Roar's voice. His implication that Perry had failed in some way.

Where had he been? Looking after four hundred people who were withering away in a cave.

Perry ignored the question, asking his own. "Did you find Hess and Sable? Was Cinder with them?"

"I found them," Roar said coldly. "And, yes. They have Cinder. What are you going to do about it?"

Then he put his heels to his horse and rode away.

They returned to the cave without a word. The awkwardness clung to them, as dense as the smoke hanging over the woods. Even Gren and Twig—best of friends—said little to each other, their usual banter banished by the tense mood.

The hour of silence left Perry plenty of time to remember the last time he'd seen Roar: a week ago, in the eye of the worst Aether storm he'd ever been in. Roar and Aria had just come back to Tide territory after spending a month away. Seeing them together after weeks of missing Aria, Perry had lost his mind and attacked Roar. He'd swung his fists, assuming the worst of a friend who had never once doubted *him*.

Surely that contributed to Roar's dark temper, but the real cause was obvious.

Liv.

Perry tensed at his sister's memory, and his horse shied beneath him. "Whoa. Easy, girl," he said, settling the mare.

14

He shook his head, streaked at himself for letting his thoughts slip.

He couldn't let himself think about Liv. Grief would make him weak—something he couldn't afford with hundreds of lives in his hands. It would be harder to stay focused with Roar back, but he'd do it. He had no choice.

Now, as he took the switchback trail down to the protected cove below, he caught sight of Roar up ahead and told himself not to worry. Roar was his brother in every way except by blood. They'd find a way past a fight. Past what had happened with Liv.

Perry dismounted on the small beach, staying behind as the others disappeared into the dark cleft that led into the belly of the mountain. The cave was his personal torture, and he wasn't ready to return to it yet. When he was in there, it took every bit of his concentration to quell the panic that tightened his lungs and stole his breath away.

"You're claustrophobic," Marron had told him yesterday. "It's an irrational fear of being trapped in close spaces."

But he was also Blood Lord. He didn't have time for fear, irrational or otherwise.

He drew a breath, savoring the outside air for a few moments longer. Afternoon ocean breezes had blown away the smoky haze, and for the first time that day, he could see the Aether.

The blue currents rolled across the sky, a tempest of luminescent, twisting waves. They were fiercer than ever—more violent than even yesterday—but something else caught his

15

eye. He saw tinges of red where the Aether churned most intensely, like hot spots. Like the red of sunrise, bleeding through the crest of a wave.

"Do you see that?" Perry said to Hyde, who jogged out to meet him.

One of the best Seers in the Tides, Hyde followed Perry's gaze, his hawk's eyes narrowing. "I see it, Per. What do you think it means?"

"Not sure," Perry said, "but I doubt it's good."

They fell quiet for a few moments before Hyde broke the silence.

"I wish I could see the Still Blue, you know?" His gaze had moved to the horizon, across endless miles of ocean. "It'd be easier to take all of this if I knew it was there, waiting for us."

Perry hated the defeat that gathered in Hyde's temper, a flat, stale scent like dust. "You'll see it soon," he said. "You'll be the second to see it."

Hyde took the bait. He grinned. "My eyes are stronger than yours."

"I meant Brooke, not me."

Hyde shoved him in the shoulder. "That's not right. I have twice her range."

"You're a blind man compared to her."

Their debate continued as they headed into the cave, Hyde's temper lifting, just as Perry had hoped. He needed to keep morale up, or they'd never get through this.

"Find Marron for me, and get him to the Battle Room,"

he told Hyde as they stepped inside. "I need Reef and Molly there as well." He nodded to Roar, who stood a few paces away, staring across the cave with his arms crossed. "Get him water and something to eat, and have him join us right away."

It was time for a meeting, and Roar had information about Cinder, and Sable and Hess. In order to reach the Still Blue, Perry needed Dweller ships—he and Aria had taken one from Reverie, but it wouldn't carry enough people—and he also needed a precise heading or the Tides wouldn't go anywhere.

Cinder. Hovers. A heading.

Three things, and Sable and Hess had them all. But that was going to change.

Roar spoke with his back still turned. "Perry seems to have forgotten that I can hear his every word, Hyde." He turned to face Perry—and there was that dark stare again. "Whether I want to or not."

Anger washed over Perry. Nearby, Hyde and Gren tensed, their tempers spiking red, but Twig, who'd been with Roar for days, moved first.

He dropped the horse lead in his hands and darted to Roar, taking a fistful of his black coat. "Come on," he said, giving Roar a nudge that was almost a shove. "I'll show you the way. Easy to get lost around here till you get used to it."

When they'd left, Gren shook his head. "What *was* that?"

Answers flipped through Perry's mind.

Roar without Liv.

Roar without a reason to live.

Roar in hell.

"Nothing," he said, too rattled to explain. "He'll cool off."

He headed for the Battle Room as Gren went to tend to the horses. Anxiety built inside him with every step he took, pressing on his lungs, but he fought against it. At least the darkness of the cave didn't bother him, as it did most everyone. By some twist of fate, his Seer eyes saw even better in low light.

Halfway there, Willow's dog, Flea, charged up, jumping and barking like he hadn't seen Perry in weeks. Talon and Willow arrived right behind him.

"Did you find Roar?" Talon asked. "Was it him?"

Perry grabbed Talon, holding him upside down, and was rewarded with a belly laugh. "It sure was, Squeak." Roar had shown up—in appearance, at least.

"And Cinder, too?" Willow asked, her eyes wide with hope. She had grown close to Cinder. She was just as desperate to get him back as Perry.

"No. Just Roar and Twig so far, but we'll get him, Willow. I promise."

Despite his assurance, Willow let loose an impressive stream of curses. Talon giggled and Perry laughed too, but he felt sorry for her. He scented the way she hurt.

Perry set Talon down. "Do me a favor, Squeak? Check on Aria for me?" She'd been drifting on pain medication since they'd arrived at the cave, the wound in her arm refusing to heal. He went to see her whenever he could, and spent every night with her in his arms, but he still missed her. He couldn't wait until she woke.

"Sure!" Talon chirped. "Come on, Willow."

Perry watched them dash away, Flea loping after them. He had expected the cave to frighten his nephew, but Talon had adapted—all the kids had. The darkness inspired them to play endless games of hide-and-seek, and they spent hours on adventures exploring the caverns. More than once, Perry had heard kids in hysterics over the echoing of sounds—some best left unheard.

He only wished the adults had the same spirit.

Perry stepped into the Battle Room, nodding to Marron. The ceiling was low and uneven, forcing him to duck as he made his way around the long trestle table. He fought to keep his breathing steady, telling himself the walls weren't caving in; it only felt like they were.

Roar had arrived before him. He leaned back in his chair, his boots kicked up on the table. He held a bottle of Luster, and he didn't look up as Perry entered. Bad signs.

Bear and Reef nodded at Perry, in the midst of a conversation about the red flares that had appeared in the Aether. Bear's walking stick rested lengthwise on the table, spanning the distance occupied by the three men. Whenever he saw that cane, Perry remembered dragging Bear from the rubble of his house.

"Any idea why the color is changing?" Perry asked. He took his usual seat, with Marron on his right and Reef on his left. He felt strange sitting across from Roar, like they were adversaries.

Candles burned at the center of the table, the flames steady and perfect; there were no drafts back here to make them flicker. Marron had ordered rugs hung along the perimeter to create false walls and the illusion of a real room. Perry wondered if it helped the others.

"Yes," Marron said. He began twisting a gold ring around his finger. "The same phenomenon happened during the Unity. It signaled the onset of constant storms. They held for thirty years in those days. We'll see the color continue to change until it's entirely red. When that happens, it will be impossible to go outside." He pursed his lips, shaking his head. "We'll be confined here, I'm afraid."

"How long do we have?" Perry asked.

"The accounts from those days vary, so it's difficult to say precisely. It could be as long as a few weeks, if we're lucky."

"And if we're not?"

"Days."

"Skies," Bear said, propping his heavy arms on the table. He let out a loud breath, setting the candle flame trembling in front of him. "Only *days*?"

Perry tried to digest that information. He had brought the Tides there as a temporary shelter. Promised them it wouldn't be forever—and it couldn't be. The cave wasn't a Pod like Reverie, with the capability to sustain itself. He needed to get them out of there.

He looked at Reef, for once craving his advice.

But then Aria stepped into the chamber.

Perry lurched to his feet so fast that his chair fell backward. He took the ten paces to her in a flash, bumping his head on the low ceiling, knocking his leg into the table, moving with less coordination than he had in his entire life.

He pulled her close, holding her as tight as he could while being careful about her arm.

She smelled incredible. Like violets and open fields under the sun. Her scent set his pulse racing. It was freedom. It was everything the cave wasn't.

"You're awake," he said, and almost laughed at himself. He'd been waiting to talk to her for days; he could have done better.

"Talon said you'd be here," she said, smiling at him.

He ran his hand over the bandage on her arm. "How do you feel?"

She shrugged. "Better."

He wished it were really true, but the dark circles under her eyes and the pallor of her skin told him otherwise. Still, she was the most beautiful thing he'd ever seen. Easily.

The room had fallen quiet. They had an audience, but Perry didn't care. They'd spent a winter apart while she'd been at Marron's, and then another month when she'd gone to Rim with Roar. The week they'd spent together at the Tides had been made up of stolen moments. He'd learned his lesson. He wouldn't waste another second with her.

He took her face in his hands and kissed her. Aria made a small sound of surprise, and then he felt her relax. Her

21

arms came around him, and what started as a brush of their lips became deeper. He gathered her close and forgot everything, everyone except her, until he heard Reef's gruff voice behind him.

"Sometimes I forget he's nineteen."

"Oh, yes. Easy to do." The gentle reply could only be from Marron.

"Not now."

"No . . . certainly not now."

3

ARIA

Aria blinked at Perry, a little overwhelmed.

Their relationship had just made a definitive shift to public, and she was unprepared for the wave of pride that swept through her. He was hers, and he was incredible, and they didn't have to hide, or explain, or be apart anymore.

"We probably should get started with the meeting," he said, smiling down at her.

She mumbled her agreement and forced herself away from him, trying not to look as staggered as she felt. She spotted Roar standing on the other side of the table, relief snapping her back to the present.

"Roar!" Aria rushed to his side, wrapping him in a half hug.

"Easy, there," he said, frowning at her arm. "What happened?"

"Oh, this? I got myself shot."

"What did you go and do that for?"

"I wanted some sympathy, I guess."

It was their usual way with each other, teasing and light, but Aria studied him as they spoke, and what she saw brought a twist to her heart.

Though he sounded like himself, Roar's eyes had lost all their humor. They were heavy with sadness now—a sadness he carried everywhere. In his smile. In the drape of his shoulders. Even in the way he stood, weight to one side, like his entire life was out of balance. He looked as he had a week ago, when they'd floated down the Snake River together: heartbroken.

Her attention moved past him to Marron, who made his way toward them and smiled expectantly, his blue eyes alert and lively, his cheeks ruddy and round—the very opposite of Roar's hardened planes.

"It's so good to see you," Marron said, pulling her close. "We've all been worried."

"It's good to see you too." He was soft, and he smelled so good, like rosewater and woodsmoke. She held on to him a moment longer, remembering the months she'd spent in his home over the winter after learning that her mother had died. She'd have been lost without his help.

"Aren't we in the middle of a crisis, Aria?" Soren walked in with his shoulders back and his chin tipped up. "I swear that's what you said five minutes ago."

The expression on his face—arrogant, annoyed,

disgusted—had been hers six months ago when she'd first met Perry.

"I'll get rid of him," Reef said, rising from his chair.

"No," Aria said. Soren was Hess's son. Whether he deserved it or not, the Dwellers would look to him as a leader, along with her. "He's with me. I asked him to be here."

"Then he stays," Perry said smoothly. "Let's get started."

That surprised her. She'd worried about Perry's reaction to Soren—the two had despised each other at first sight.

As they settled around the table, Aria didn't miss the dark look Reef cast her way. He expected Soren to disrupt the meeting. She wasn't going to let that happen.

She sat next to Roar, which felt both right and not, but Perry already had Reef and Marron at his sides. Roar slouched in his chair and took a long pull from a bottle of Luster. The action struck her as angry and determined. She wanted to lift the bottle from his hands, but he'd had enough taken away from him.

"Hess and Sable have almost every advantage, as you all know," Perry said. "Time is against us too. We have to move on them quickly. Tomorrow morning, I'll lead a team to their camp with the aim of rescuing Cinder, securing Hovers, and getting the exact heading for the Still Blue. In order to plan the mission, I need information. I need to know what you saw," he said to Roar, "and what you know," he said to Soren.

As he spoke, the Blood Lord chain winked at his neck

25

and candlelight glinted on his hair, which was pulled back but coming loose in pieces. A dark shirt stretched across his shoulders and arms, but Aria could easily recall the Markings it concealed.

The rough-edged hunter with the fierce glare she'd met half a year ago was almost gone. He was confident now, steadier. Still fearsome, but controlled. He was everything she'd expected him to become.

His green eyes flicked to her, holding for an instant like he knew her thoughts, before moving to Roar beside her.

"Whenever you're ready, Roar," he said.

Roar answered without bothering to sit up or project his voice. "Hess and Sable joined up. They're on the plateau between Lone Pine and the Snake River, right out in the open. It's a big camp. More like a small city."

"Why there?" Perry asked. "Why gather forces inland if the Still Blue is across the sea? What are they waiting for?"

"If I knew any of those things," Roar said, "I'd have said so."

Aria's head snapped to him. On the surface his appearance verged on boredom, but his eyes held a predatory focus that hadn't been there moments ago. He gripped the bottle of Luster tightly, the lean muscles in his forearms taut.

She looked around the table, picking up other signs of tension. Reef sat forward, his gaze boring into Roar. Marron darted a nervous glance at the entrance, where Gren and Twig stood, looking very much like guards. Even Soren had picked up on something. He looked from Perry to Roar, like he was trying to figure out what everyone knew that he didn't.

"Anything else you do know that you'd like to share?" Perry said calmly, like he'd missed Roar's biting comment completely.

"I saw the fleet of Hovers," Roar answered. "I counted a dozen like the one outside on the bluff and other kinds of smaller craft too. They're lined up on the plateau outside this segmented thing that's coiled up like a snake. It's massive. . . . Each unit is more a building than a craft."

Soren snorted. "The segmented, coily thing is called a Komodo X12."

Roar's dark eyes slid to him. "That's helpful, Dweller. I think that cleared it up for all of us."

Aria looked from Soren to Roar, dread moving like ice through her veins.

"You want to know what the Komodo is?" Soren said. "I'll tell you. Better yet, how about you take these rugs down and I'll draw some stick figures on the cave wall for you? Then we could have a séance or a sacrifice or something." Soren looked at Perry. "Maybe you could supply some drums and half-naked women?"

Aria had some experience handling Soren, and was prepared. She turned from Perry to Marron. "Would drawings help?" she asked, fighting Soren's sarcasm with directness.

Marron leaned forward. "Oh yes. They'd help immensely. Any specifications you can provide with respect to the Hovers' speed, range, cargo capacity, weaponry. Onboard supplies . . . Truly, Soren, anything would be very useful. We'd know which craft we need. We could prepare better. Yes, drawings and any other information you can recall. Thank you."

Perry turned to Gren. "Bring paper, a ruler, pens."

Soren looked from Marron to Perry to Aria, his mouth gaping. "I'm not drawing anything. I was *joking.*"

"You think our situation is a joke?" she said.

"What? No. But I'm not helping these Savag—these people."

"They've been taking care of you for days. Do you think you'd be alive if weren't for *these people*?"

Soren looked around the table like he wanted to argue, but said nothing.

"You're the only one who knows the Hovers," Aria continued. "You're the expert. You should also tell us everything you know about your father's plans with Sable. Every one of us needs to know as much as possible."

Soren scowled. "You're kidding me."

"Didn't we just agree this wasn't a laughing matter?"

"Why should I trust them?" Soren asked, as if there were no Outsiders there.

"How about because you don't have a choice?"

Soren's furious gaze went to Perry, who was actually watching *her*, his lips pressed together like he was fighting a smile.

"Fine," Soren said. "I'll tell you what I know. I intercepted

28

one of the comms between my father and Sable before Reverie . . . fell."

Reverie hadn't just fallen. It had been deserted. Thousands of people had been abandoned and left to die—by Soren's father, Hess. Aria understood why Soren might not want to bring attention to that fact.

"Sable and a few of his top people have the coordinates to the Still Blue memorized," he continued. "But there's more to it than just knowing where it is. There's a barrier of Aether at sea somewhere, and the only way to the Still Blue is by breaching it. Sable said he'd found a way through it, though."

The chamber fell silent. They all knew that *way* was Cinder.

Perry rubbed his jaw, the first trace of anger appearing on his face. Across the back of his hand, Aria saw the scars Cinder had given him, pale and roped.

"You're sure Cinder's there?" he said, turning to Roar. "You saw him?"

"I'm sure," said Roar.

Seconds passed.

"Do you have nothing more to add, Roar?" Perry asked.

"You want more?" Roar drew himself up. "Here's more: Cinder was with the girl named Kirra, who was here at the compound, according to Twig. I saw her take him into the Komodo thing. You know who else is there? Sable. The man who killed your sister. The ships we need are also there, since I'm assuming the one outside isn't going to carry us all to the Blue. It looks to me like they have everything and we have nothing. There it is, Perry. Now you know the situation. What do you recommend we do? Stay in this miserable pit and talk some more?"

Reef slammed his hand on the table. "Enough!" he bellowed, pushing up from his chair. "You cannot speak to him that way. I won't allow it."

"It's grief," Marron said softly.

"I don't care what it is. It doesn't excuse his behavior."

"Speaking of excuses," Roar said, "you've been looking for a way to come after me for a while now, Reef." He stood and spread his hands. "Looks like you've got it."

"This is exactly what I'm talking about," Soren said, shaking his head. "You people are animals. I feel like a zookeeper."

"Shut up, Soren." Aria rose to her feet and took Roar's arm. "Please, Roar. Sit down."

He jerked away. Aria flinched as pain ripped through her, and she pulled in a hissing breath. She'd reached for Roar with her good arm, but his sharp movement had given her a jolt, igniting a hot flare in her wounded bicep.

Perry shot out of his chair. "Roar!"

The room fell quiet in an instant.

Aria's arm trembled, pressed against her stomach. She forced herself to relax. To hide the waves of pain that tore through her.

30

Roar stared at her in silent mortification. "I forgot," he said under his breath.

"I did too. It's all right. I'm fine."

He hadn't meant to hurt her. He never would. But still no one moved. No one made a sound.

"I'm *fine*," she said again.

Slowly, the attention of the room shifted to Perry, who was glaring at Roar, his gaze burning with rage.

4

PEREGRINE

Anger made Perry feel strong and clear-headed. Sharper than he'd felt since he stepped into the cave.

He drew a few breaths, forcing his muscles to loosen. To let go of the drive to attack.

"Stay," he said, looking from Roar to Aria. "Everyone else, leave."

The chamber emptied in a rush, Reef quelling Soren's objections with a few firm pushes, Bear last to step outside. Perry waited for the knock of his walking stick to fade away before he spoke. "Are you hurt?"

Aria shook her head.

"*No?*" he said. She was lying to protect Roar, because the answer was obvious in her braced stance.

She looked away, her gaze falling to the table. "It wasn't his fault."

Roar scowled. "Really, Perry? You think I'd hurt her? On *purpose*?"

"You're out to hurt at least a few people. I'm sure of that. What I'm trying to figure out is how wide you're casting the net."

Roar laughed—a bitter, clipped sound. "You know what's funny? You, acting so superior. What I did was an accident— what about you? Which one of us spilled his own brother's blood?"

Anger washed over Perry. Roar was throwing Vale's death in his face. A low blow—the lowest—and totally unexpected.

"I'm warning you this once," Perry said. "Don't think you can say or do anything to me because of who you are. You can't."

"Why? Because now you're Blood Lord? Am I supposed to bow to you, Peregrine? Am I supposed to follow you around like your six loyal hounds?" Roar tipped his chin toward Perry's chest. "That piece of metal has gone to your head."

"It better have! I swore an oath. My *life* belongs to the Tides."

"You're hiding behind that oath. You're hiding *here*."

"Just tell me what you want, Roar."

"Liv is dead! She's *dead*."

"And you think I can bring her back? Is that it?" He couldn't. He would never see his sister again. Nothing would change that.

33

"I want you to do *something*. Shed a damn tear, to start with! Then go after Sable. Cut his throat open. Burn him to ash. Just don't keep hiding here under this rock."

"There are four hundred and twelve people under this rock. I'm responsible for *every one*. We're running out of food. We're running out of options. The world outside is burning, and you think I'm *hiding*?"

Roar's voice dropped to a growl. "Sable *murdered* her! He fired a crossbow at Liv from ten paces. He—"

"Stop!" Aria yelled. "Stop, Roar. Don't tell him this way. Not like this."

"He put a bolt through your sister's *heart*, and then stood there and watched the life pour out of her."

The instant Perry heard the word *crossbow*, his body went rigid. He'd known that Sable had killed Liv, but not how. He didn't *want* to know. Images of Vale's death would haunt him for the rest of his life. He didn't need nightmares of his sister, pierced through the heart by a piece of wood, as well.

Roar shook his head. "I'm done." He didn't say it, but *with you* echoed in the beat of silence that followed.

He made his way out but turned to add, "Keep acting like it didn't happen, Peregrine. Carry on with your meetings, and your tribe, and everything else, just like I knew you would."

When he was gone, Perry gripped the chair in front of him. He lowered his gaze to the table, staring at the grain of the wood as he tried to slow his racing pulse. Roar's temper had brought a fine, charred scent to the chamber. It felt like breathing soot.

In more than ten years of knowing each other, of spending every day together, they'd never fought. Never like this, in earnest. He'd always counted on Roar, and he'd never expected that to change. He had never imagined that with Liv gone, Roar might be lost to him too.

Perry shook his head. He was being stupid. Nothing would sever their friendship.

"I'm sorry, Perry," Aria said softly. "He's hurting."

He swallowed through a tight throat. "I got that." The words came out sharp. But Liv was his *sister*. The last of his family, except for Talon. Why was she worrying about Roar?

"I only meant that he isn't acting like himself. It may seem like it, but he doesn't want you as an enemy. He needs you more than ever."

"He's my best friend," he said, lifting his gaze to her. "I know what he needs."

Aside from Liv and Perry—and now Aria—Roar had only ever loved one other person: his grandmother. When she'd died years ago, he'd stormed around the compound for a month before settling down.

Maybe that was what Roar needed. Time.

A lot of it.

"You don't know what it was like, Perry. What he went through in Rim, and afterward."

Perry went still, blinking at her in disbelief. He couldn't stand to hear that right now. "You're right," he said, straightening. "I wasn't there when Liv died, but I should have been. That was our plan, remember? We were going to go together. As I recall, you and Roar left without me."

Aria's gray eyes widened in surprise. "I had to go. You'd have lost the Tides otherwise."

He needed to leave now. Frustration and anger still roiled inside him. He didn't want to take that out on her. But he couldn't stop himself from replying.

"You made that decision on your own. Even if you were right, couldn't you have told me? Couldn't you have said something, instead of leaving without a word? You vanished on me, Aria."

"Perry, I was . . . I didn't think you . . . I guess we should talk about this."

He hated to see the small line between her eyebrows, hated to see her hurting because of him. He should have never opened his mouth. "No," he said. "It's done. Forget it."

"Obviously, you haven't."

He couldn't pretend otherwise. The memory of walking into Vale's room to find her gone still played in his mind. Whenever he left her side, a flicker of fear taunted him, whispering in his ear that she might disappear again—though he knew she wouldn't. It was an irrational fear, as Marron had said. But when had fear ever been rational?

"It'll be morning before long," he said, changing the subject. They had too much else to consider to dwell on

36

the past. "I need to get organized."

Aria's eyebrows drew together. "*You* need to get organized? So *you're* going this time?"

Her temper cooled by the second. She thought he was leaving her. That he was getting back at her for leaving him by going without her tomorrow.

"I want us both to go," he rushed to clarify. "I know you're hurt, but if you feel well enough, I need you on this mission. You're as much Dweller as you are Outsider—we'll be facing both—and you've dealt with Hess and Sable."

There were other reasons. She was clever and tenacious. A strong Aud. Most importantly, he didn't want to say goodbye to her in the morning. But he didn't say any of those things. He couldn't bring himself to open his heart only to have her choose not to be with him once again.

"I'll go on the mission," Aria said. "I already planned to. And you're right. I am hurt. But I'm not afraid to admit it."

Then she was gone, taking all the air and light in the cavern with her.

5

ARIA

Aria returned to the Dweller cavern.

Work would help her sort through her anger and confusion. It would help her forget the sound of Perry and Roar shouting at each other. Maybe, if she busied herself enough, she'd even get the words *You vanished on me, Aria* out of her head.

Molly moved amid the sickly bundles that stretched back into the darkness. Some of the Dwellers seemed to be stirring now, and a few of the Tides were helping Molly tend to them. Blond hair in the distance caught her attention. She spotted Brooke carrying a jug of water from one person to another.

Aria knelt by Molly. "What's she doing here?"

Molly drew a blanket over a young girl. "Ah," she said, looking up and seeing Brooke. "You two didn't get off to a good start, did you?"

"No . . . but only one of us is responsible for that."

Molly pursed her lips. "She knows she treated you poorly, and she's grateful to you for bringing Clara back. This is her way of showing it."

Brooke must have felt their attention because she looked over, her blue eyes moving from Aria to Molly. Aria saw no apology in them. No gratitude.

"Interesting way of showing it."

"She is trying," Molly said. "And she's a good girl. She's just had a tough stretch."

Aria shook her head. Weren't they all having a tough stretch?

She settled to work, delivering water and medicines to the Dwellers who had stirred. She knew every one of them, but some better than others. Briefly she spoke with a friend of her mother's, aching for Lumina, and then checked on Rune, Jupiter, and Caleb. Her friends were still barely conscious, but just being near them felt good, nourishing a part of her that had been dormant for months.

Gradually, Perry and Roar faded from her thoughts. Even the pain in her arm did. She immersed herself in work until she heard a pair of familiar voices.

"Can I get some water?" Soren asked. He was sitting up and looked healthy enough to get his own water, but the meeting earlier had drained the color from his face.

Brooke knelt and shoved the jug at him.

"Thanks," Soren said. He took a slow drink, his gaze never leaving Brooke. Then he grinned and handed the water back. "You know, you're really pretty for a Savage."

"Three days ago you vomited all over my sleeve, Dweller. That wasn't pretty." Brooke stood, moving to the next patient.

Aria fought back a laugh. She remembered that Brooke and Liv had been close friends. How was Brooke coping? Grief simmered right on the surface with Roar. On his face, in his voice. Where was it in Brooke?

For that matter, what about Perry?

She sighed, looking around her. Would she really contribute to the mission tomorrow with her arm the way it was? Did the Dwellers need her to be here for them? The real source of her apprehension, she knew, was Perry.

How were they supposed to get past the hurt she'd caused him when he wouldn't even discuss it?

The ring of a bell echoed into the cavern.

"Supper," Molly said.

It didn't feel like suppertime. Without the sun, it could've been morning or noon or midnight. Aria let out another slow breath, rolling back her shoulders. She'd been helping for a few hours.

After Brooke and a few others left, Molly came over. "Not hungry?"

Aria shook her head. "I don't want anything." She wasn't ready to see Perry or Roar again. She'd grown tired. Her arm ached. Her heart ached.

"I'll have something sent over for you." Molly patted her shoulder and left.

When Aria went to check on Caleb again, she found him waking. He blinked at her in confusion. His red hair, a few shades deeper than Paisley's, was matted down with sweat. Fever had left his lips chapped and his eyes glazed.

He took a slow, artist's perusal of her face. "I thought you'd be happier to see me."

She knelt beside him. "I am, Caleb. I'm really happy to see you."

"You look sad."

"I was a minute ago, but now I'm not. How could I be, now that you're with me?"

He smiled softly, and then his gaze drifted around the cavern. "This isn't a Realm, is it?"

She shook her head. "No. It's not."

"I didn't think so. Who would want to come to a Realm like this?"

She sat, resting her hands on her lap. A knot of pain throbbed deep inside her right bicep. "They wouldn't . . . but it's all we have."

Caleb's gaze came back to her. "I'm sore everywhere. Even my teeth hurt."

"Do you want something? I can get you medicine or—"

"No . . . just stay." He gave her a shaky smile. "Seeing you is good. It's making me feel better. You've changed, Aria."

"Have I?" she asked, though she knew she had. They used to spend afternoons cruising the art Realms. Seeking out the best concerts, the best parties. She barely recognized the girl she used to be.

41

Caleb nodded. "Yes. You have. When I get better, I'm going to draw you, changed Aria."

"Let me know when you're ready. I'll get you some paper."

"Real paper?" he asked, brightening. Caleb had only drawn in the Realms.

She smiled. "That's right. Real paper."

The spark of excitement left his eyes, his expression turning serious. "Soren told me what happened. About Ag 6 . . . and Paisley. Have you forgiven him?"

Aria glanced toward Soren, who had fallen asleep nearby. She nodded. "I had to, to get you out. And Soren has DLS—a disease that makes him volatile. But he's on medications to control it now."

"Are we sure they work?" Caleb said, with a weak smile.

Aria smiled. If he was making jokes, he couldn't feel that terrible.

"He wasn't the reason Pais died," Caleb said. "It was the fire that got her that night. Not him. He was crying when he told me that. I never thought I'd see Soren cry. I think . . . I think he blames himself. I think he stayed and helped us get out of Reverie because of that night."

Aria believed it because it was true for her as well. She'd brought Paisley to Ag 6. Because of that night, she'd never again leave someone she loved in need, if she could help it.

Caleb squeezed his eyes shut. "Pain is such a pain, you know? It's very taxing."

She knew. Aria lay down, settling in beside him, feeling like she'd found part of herself. She saw her past in Caleb. She saw Paisley and the home she'd lost, and she never wanted to forget them.

"Not exactly the Sistine Chapel, is it?" she asked after a while, staring at the jagged shapes that pierced down from the darkness.

"No, it's rather purgatorial," Caleb said. "But if we squint really, really hard, we could imagine it otherwise."

She pointed with her good hand. "That big one there looks like a fang."

"Mm-hmm. It does." Beside her, Caleb scrunched his face. "Over there. That one looks like a . . . like a fang."

"And just to the left? Fang."

"Wrong. That is clearly an incisor. Wait, no . . . it's a fang."

"I've missed you, Caleb."

"I've mega missed you." He peered at her. "I think we all knew it was going to come to this. Everything started to change after that night. You could feel it. . . . But you're going to get us out of here, right?"

She stared into his eyes, finally clear about where she was needed. She'd do more good on the mission than she would here, regardless of her arm or any lingering tension between her and Perry.

"Yes," she said. "I am." She told him about Hess and Sable, and about the mission she'd be part of in the morning.

"So you're leaving again," Caleb said when she'd finished. "I guess I'm all right with that." He yawned and rubbed his left eye, where his Smarteye would have been, then smiled tiredly at her. "The Outsider you were with when we left Reverie—is he the reason you were sad?"

"Yes," she admitted. "What happened was my mistake, mostly. A few weeks ago, I was trying to protect him, and . . . I ended up hurting him instead."

"Tricky, but I have an idea. When I fall asleep, go find him and apologize." He winked at her. "Mostly."

Aria smiled. She liked that idea a lot.

6

PEREGRINE

Have you chosen your team?" Reef dropped more kindling onto the fire, coaxing the flames to life. "Who are you taking tomorrow?"

Perry rubbed his jaw, watching as the rising firelight brought his friends out of the darkness. The rest of the Six emerged. Molly and Marron, too.

It was late—hours after supper—but he had chosen fresh air over sleep. They followed him outside, one and then two and then eight of them, settling in a circle on the small beach. His closest friends, except Roar and Aria.

Now he saw Reef's question in all of their eyes. Perry had considered the team he'd take for tomorrow's mission, and he was sure about his choices, but he expected them to raise some debate.

"Everything here will be fine while you're away," Marron said, picking up on his hesitation. "No need to worry."

"I know," Perry said. "I know it will be."

Before he left, he would give the Blood Lord chain around his neck to Marron, entrusting the Tides to his care once again. No one was better suited to look after them.

Perry leaned back, his gaze moving south to a knot of Aether—a storm heading their way. The red flares were mesmerizing. They could have been beautiful.

Looking at Reef, he forced himself to say what needed saying. "You're staying here." He found the rest of the Six. "All of you are."

"Why?" Straggler said, straightening. He was still shorter than Hyde and Hayden, who slouched at his sides. "Did we do something wrong?"

"Shut up, Strag," Gren called across the fire.

"You shut up," Straggler shot back. "Perry, no one would fight harder for you than us. Who could be *better*?"

Hyde smacked his brother on the head. "Be quiet, you idiot. Sorry, Per. Go on. . . . Where did we fail you?"

"You didn't, but this isn't a straight fight. We won't stand a chance if we try to meet Sable and Hess head-on."

"Then who are you taking?" Strag asked.

Here goes, Perry thought. "Roar," he said.

Silence fell over the group, amplifying the snap of the fire and the crash of the waves.

Marron spoke first. "Peregrine, I don't think that's a good idea, considering the way the two of you have been since he came back. Not to mention the loss you've both suffered."

Perry had never understood that phrase *not to mention.* It

was mentioned. Liv was suddenly there, in the cool ocean air. In the tumbling waves. In the monster waking inside his mind and clawing at the walls of his skull.

He dug his fingers into the sand, squeezing until his knuckles ached. "Roar is the right man for it."

Silent and lethal, Roar was the closest thing he had to an assassin. He also had the fine, perfect features of a Dweller. He could pass for an Outsider or a Mole, which made him versatile—a good thing, as they'd form a plan of attack once they could assess the Komodo more closely.

"Who else?" asked Reef tightly.

"Brooke."

Gren's mouth fell open and Twig made a choking sound, which he camouflaged by clearing his throat. No secrets here; they all knew Perry's history with Brooke.

As far as appearances went, Brooke had the same advantage as Roar. Men nodded yes first and listened second when she spoke, and that might prove useful. She was as strong a Seer as the brothers, a better shot, and levelheaded in tough situations. A few weeks ago, when the Tide compound had been raided, she hadn't made a single misstep. They'd been through some bumps, but Perry needed her.

"And Aria?" Marron asked, his voice rising at the end.

"Yes."

He didn't miss the stunned looks traded across the flames. Everyone knew she was injured. Everyone knew they'd fought. Or argued. Or whatever that had been. The Battle Room had lived up to its name today.

"I'm taking Soren, too," he said, forging ahead. "He's the only one who can fly the Hover. He's the only one who can get us there quickly. You said we might only have days, Marron. I can't waste time traveling to the Komodo on foot or horseback."

Perry saw no way around it. He needed speed. He needed the Hover. As much as he wished otherwise, that meant he needed Soren.

"Just so I don't mistake you," said Reef, "these are the people you're taking *with* you? You believe this group—the five of you—will come together as a team?"

"That's right," Perry said.

"You're betting our lives on that?" Reef pressed.

Perry nodded. "Sable and Hess have all the brute power. Force won't work against them. We need to be small and sharp. We'll have to pierce like a needle to have any chance."

Quiet settled over the group again, a few anxious glances turning south. Perry listened to the surf as their tempers drifted toward him, carrying disbelief and anxiousness and outrage.

The silent roar of the Tides.

When Perry stepped into his tent, he found Talon still awake.

"What are you doing up, Squeak?" he asked, setting his bow and quiver against the trunks. It had to be well past midnight.

Talon sat up and rubbed his eyes. "I had a nightmare."

"Hate those." Perry unbuckled his belt and dropped it aside. "What are you waiting for?" he said, climbing into bed. "Get on over here."

Talon scrambled to his side. He thrashed around, his knobby knees banging into Perry's ribs for a few minutes before he finally settled down.

"I miss our house," he said. "Don't you?"

"Yes," Perry said, staring up at the canvas above him. More than anything, he missed the gap in the loft's timbers. For years he'd been too tall to stretch out fully in that loft, but he hadn't cared. He'd loved falling asleep with his eyes on a little piece of the sky.

He bumped Talon's arm playfully. "This isn't so bad though, is it? You and Willow don't seem to mind it."

Talon shrugged. "Yeah. It's not bad. Willow said that Molly said that you're leaving tomorrow to get Cinder. Why do you have to go, Uncle Perry?"

There it was. The real reason Talon couldn't sleep.

"Because Cinder needs me, just like you did when you were in Reverie. And I need a few things from the Dwellers that'll help us get to the Still Blue."

"If you don't come back, I'll be alone."

"I'm coming back, Talon."

"My dad's gone. My mom and Aunt Liv—"

"Hey." Perry propped himself on an elbow so he could look at his nephew's face. He searched for a little of himself or Liv, but all he saw—from Talon's serious green eyes to his dark curls—was Vale. He couldn't fault Talon for being afraid. But there was no way he'd fail his nephew. "I'm coming back. All right?"

Talon nodded, the gesture a little dismissive.

"Do you know what happened between me and your father?" The words came out before Perry could stop them. They hadn't spoken about Vale yet. About how Vale had sold Talon, his own son, to the Dwellers for food. Brooke's sister, Clara, too. Unforgivable. But then Perry had killed Vale—also unforgivable. He knew that act would haunt him forever.

Talon lifted his small shoulders. "I was sick. He sent me to the Dwellers to get better. When I was, you came to get me back."

Perry studied his nephew. Talon knew more than he was letting on. Maybe he was saying what Perry wanted to hear, or maybe he wasn't ready to talk about it yet. Either way, Perry wasn't going to push. It wouldn't get him anywhere. Talon didn't just look like Vale. He was as hardheaded and tight-lipped too.

Perry lay back down, resting his head on his arm, and flashed on his argument with Aria. Maybe he did have something in common with his nephew after all.

"You think there are places to fish in the Still Blue?" Talon asked.

"Sure. I bet there's lots of places to fish."

"Good, because Willow and I found some night crawlers today. *Eleven* of them. *Huge* ones. I have them in a jar."

Perry tried his best to focus as Talon prattled on about

50

bait, but his eyes grew heavy. He'd just closed them when he heard the shift of canvas.

Aria stepped into the tent and froze, squinting to see them in the darkness.

"We're here," Perry said. It was the only thing that came to mind. He hadn't expected her, but a wave of relief swept through him at the sight of her.

"Hi, Aria," Talon said, all chirky and bright.

"Hi, Talon." She bit her lip, glancing at the tent flap behind her. "I just came to . . . I was going to . . . I guess I'll see you later?" Her voice rose at the end, like a question.

Perry didn't know what to do. Talon lay curled at his side—Aria's spot for the past few nights. He couldn't send his nephew away, but he didn't want her to leave, either.

"You don't have to go," Talon said. He hopped over Perry, to his right side. "There's room."

"Great," Aria said, and slid in on Perry's other side.

For a long second, Perry couldn't believe she was right next to him. Then he became intensely aware of everything about her. The weight of her arm resting on his chest. The chill her clothes held from the cave. The violet scent he loved.

"You're quiet," she said.

Talon giggled. "Because he likes you. Don't you, Uncle Squawk?"

"I do." Perry peered down and found Aria looking at him. She smiled, but concern shadowed her eyes. "Did you know that?"

"Even though I vanished?" she asked, using his word from earlier.

"Yes. Of course . . . I'll always . . . like you, Aria." He grinned, because he sounded like a fool. He loved her—down to his soul—and he was going to tell her sometime. But not with Talon's knee digging into his kidney.

Aria smiled. "I'll always *like* you too."

The way she said it, the way her temper opened up, he knew she'd read his mind and felt the same way. Her lips were close. He pressed a kiss to them, though he wanted more, everything she'd give him.

That sent Talon over the edge. He lost it, his torrential giggles infectious, pulling them all in.

A full hour passed before the tent fell quiet again. Perry was covered in legs and arms and blankets, so hot that sweat dampened his shirt. The shoulder he'd dislocated a month ago ached beneath the weight of Aria's head, and Talon was snoring right into his ear, but he couldn't remember the last time he'd felt so good.

Being with the two of them reminded him of the first time he ever shot a bow. Like he had discovered something that was new, but that already fit him perfectly.

He stayed awake as long as he could, savoring it. Then he closed his eyes and surrendered to sleep.

7

ARIA

Hovers.

They weren't her favorite things in the world.

Aria stared up at the Belswan, taking in its liquid shape. Eighty feet from nose to tail, the cargo craft still managed to look sleek. The exterior was smooth and opalescent, like blue pearl, the coloration lightening gradually toward the front, like the tip of the craft had faded in the sun, exposing the transparent glass beneath. The tip, of course, was the cockpit.

"Perfection," Caleb said reverently. He was still weak, but he'd insisted on coming outside to see her off. They stood on the bluff above the cave as Aria waited to leave on the mission. "Flawless design and craftsmanship. It's like Gaudí created a modern ship."

Aria shook her head. "It *is* beautiful." But that didn't mean she liked it. Only a week ago, she'd stood in the cockpit of this very craft watching Reverie collapse before her eyes. Months earlier, she had been thrown from a Hover onto the hard desert outside Reverie and left to die.

This time would be better. How could it not be?

"Where is everyone?" she asked, scanning the small crowd around her.

A few of the Tides had come to send them off. Willow stood with her grandfather, Old Will, while Flea trotted around, sniffing busily. Reef and a couple of the Six were there, along with others she didn't know, but so far she was the only member of the team to show.

Despite having slept against Perry all night, she still felt their argument weighing on her. He wouldn't talk about how she'd hurt him, and he wouldn't talk about Roar or Liv.

It felt like a lot. A lot to go unsaid.

"They're just a little tardy," said Caleb. "They'll be here."

"They'd better hurry."

With a thick layer of fog cloaking the coast, she couldn't see the red flares that had everyone worried, but she heard the storm they'd been anticipating. The distant shriek of the funnels sent a shiver through her.

Five miles away, she guessed. They needed to leave soon.

"See?" Caleb said. "Here comes Soren . . . and *Jupiter*?"

Soren crested the switchback path that climbed up from the beach, his closest friend at his side. Jupiter walked with an amble that matched his leisurely personality. Today he appeared mellower than usual, having just emerged from days of fever. Like Soren, he carried a bag over his shoulder.

"What is this?" Reef grumbled. "Someone explain to me why there's another one of them now?"

Aria felt Caleb tense at her side. He was one of "them" too.

Soren stopped in front of Reef and lifted his chin. "This is our second-in-command, Jupiter," he said importantly.

Jupiter flipped his shaggy hair out of his eyes. It felt strange to see him outside the Realms. Even stranger to see him without drums and his bandmates. "Hey, Aria and Caleb. And, uh . . . hello, Outsiders."

"No," Reef said. "Not hello. You can leave, Dweller. You're not part of the team."

Jupiter's eyes went wide, but Soren held his ground.

He crossed his arms. "If Jupiter goes, I go."

"Done," said Reef. "Good-bye to you both."

"Can any of you fly a Hover?" Soren asked, looking around him. "I didn't think so. We *can*. Isn't that what we need? A way out of here? And I want equal representation on this pathetic team."

"Equal?" Reef said. "There are forty Dwellers in that cave. You are one tenth our count."

"We speak technology, which makes our tenth a hundred times more valuable."

A few paces away, Twig turned to Gren. "So are they more valuable or are we?"

"I don't know," Gren answered. "I'm lost."

"Get in there, Jupiter," Aria said, gesturing to the Belswan.

A dozen heads whipped to look at her. No one stared more intently than Reef.

"Soren has a point," she said. "It's smart to bring someone else who can fly the Hover. We should have an alternate pilot in case something incapacitates him during the mission."

Soren's expression went from smug to shocked as he realized what she'd said.

Reef's face underwent the same transformation, in reverse. He broke into a wide grin, tipping his head at her in a gesture of respect.

"Don't just stand there," he said to Soren and Jupiter. "Your first-in-command just gave an order. Load up."

Aria hugged Caleb, promising she'd see him soon, and boarded with them.

The bay doors opened to the cargo hold, a wide, bare space that stretched across the middle of the Hover. She moved to the cockpit at the front with Soren and Jupiter, who dropped into the two seats and immediately began to argue about which button controlled what.

It didn't inspire confidence.

Leaning against the threshold, she watched them while keeping her ears tuned for Perry and Roar.

She wasn't worried about bringing Jupiter. He was harmless, and she liked the idea of having another Dweller on the team. The more they could integrate, the better.

But Soren was another matter.

Could she trust him? He had come through for her with Talon. But then he'd also attacked her in Ag 6. And she'd trusted his father, Hess, and look where that had gotten her. Then there was Soren's attitude and his history with Perry. The only thing he really contributed were his piloting skills, and those were shaky.

Soren sensed her watching him and broke off with Jupiter. "What?"

"Are you ready?" she asked.

His lip curled up—a dead giveaway that he was nervous. "What kind of question is that? Is there a way to prepare for this that I'm unaware of?"

"You'll do fine. You've flown it already. Just don't crash."

She caught him by surprise. His smirk softened into a more natural smile. "I'll try not to."

Aria heard Perry walk up behind her. His hand settled on the small of her back.

"Get this ship moving, Soren," he said, over her shoulder. "Put us ahead of that storm."

Through the windshield she saw that the fog had begun to burn off, revealing a patch of sky to the south. There, the Aether wheeled in spirals, a sight both terrifying and familiar. The red flares were brighter than she'd expected, shocking as fresh blood. Seeing them stole her breath away.

"I was just waiting for you to show up, Outsider," Soren said.

Perry had already left, heading back into the cargo hold, leaving a fading warmth where his hand had rested.

Soren's mouth pulled into a sneer. "Aria, please explain to me how you can—"

"I'm not explaining anything to you, Soren," she said, and left.

She knew what he was going to say. Perry had shattered Soren's jaw that night in Ag 6. She knew he found the idea of her and Perry together repulsive.

At the far end of the cargo hold, she saw Perry duck through the door that opened into a stowage room. Earlier, when she'd first arrived on the bluff with Caleb, she had left her things in the supply lockers back there. She'd found food, medicine, and camping supplies, along with a small kitchen. Most importantly, the room stored their weapons.

An entire wall of lockers contained pistols, stun guns, bulkier weapons she suspected were for long-range, and other arms used by Guardians. Perry's and Brooke's bows would be added as well, along with a few full quivers.

A packed arsenal, but it didn't feel like enough. Together, Sable and Hess had at least eight hundred people. She'd seen Hess's forces as he'd fled Reverie. He'd taken all the Guardians, choosing soldiers over regular civilians. But Sable worried her even more. Maybe he didn't have the technological prowess Hess had, but he was cunning and completely ruthless.

They were facing the most capable fighters from both worlds. To succeed, they'd need much more than the weapons stored in the back.

The engine thrummed to life, startling her. She pulled one of the jump seats down from the wall and sat, drawing the thick harness straps over her shoulders.

Brooke came in from outside, followed by Roar. Aria heard them walk up the ramp and into the hold, but she didn't look up. With only one hand, snapping the heavy closure of the harness was impossible. She fumbled with it, trying not to scream.

Roar knelt in front of her. "Do you really need help or are you just trying to get my attention?"

"Very funny."

He buckled the harness, hands quick and sure; then he looked up, staring at her thoughtfully.

His eyes were bloodshot, and fine dark stubble covered his cheeks. It wasn't him. Unlike Perry, Roar didn't like scruff. He looked like he hadn't slept in a week. Like he'd never sleep again. The sorrow in his eyes seemed to go on forever.

"It'll heal, Ladybug," he said.

Roar was always giving her nicknames. *Ladybug* had come just over a week ago. They had been on a boat together, moving down the Snake River, when the ship's captain had called her that. With this memory came others that made her stomach clench. Roar with tears running down his face. Roar unspeaking, buried under thick layers of grief.

He was speaking now. He was a dark, shifting force. Would *he* ever heal?

Aria rested her hand on his, wanting to say something that would help. Wanting him to know that she loved him and was sorry about the tension between him and Perry.

Roar's mouth lifted, a flicker of a smile that didn't reach his dark eyes. "Got it," he said.

He had listened to her thoughts and heard everything.

Her gaze moved over his shoulder. Perry stood by the entrance to the cockpit watching them, his expression unreadable. Roar turned and they froze, locked in a hard stare that had no place between friends.

A prickling feeling crawled up Aria's spine. Somehow she felt like a barrier between them, and that was the last thing she ever wanted to be.

Buckled in the seat on the opposite wall, Brooke watched Perry watch Roar. The cargo doors closed with silent finality, and the sound of Soren and Jupiter's bickering over the Hover's controls grew louder, breaking the quiet spell that had trapped them.

Roar moved to the cockpit to guide them back to where he'd seen the Komodo. Perry followed, watchful and focused.

Soren lifted the Belswan off the ground with a stomach-dropping lurch.

Across the cargo hold, Brooke scowled. "I thought he could fly this thing."

"He can fly it," Aria said. "Landing is the problem."

Brooke gave her an appraising look. Aria met it evenly, trying not to wonder what Perry had seen in her. What he'd acted like with her. She had no reason to be envious. She didn't want to be.

"Roar said you met Liv," Brooke said.

Aria nodded. "I knew her only for a few days, but . . . I liked her. Very much."

"She was my best friend." Brooke glanced toward the cockpit. "We were like them."

Perry and Roar stood inside, leaning against either side of the access opening. From her angle, she could only see half of each of them, and the open space between.

They were so different, inside and out, but they stood exactly the same way. Arms crossed. Ankles crossed. Their posture somehow both relaxed and alert. It was as close as they'd come to each other since Roar's return.

"Like how they *used* to be," Brooke amended.

"Has this ever happened before?"

"Never. And I hate it."

Incredible. They actually agreed on something.

Aria rested her head against the wall and closed her eyes. The Hover hummed along, and the journey had turned smooth, but she knew it wouldn't last.

A team, Reef had called them earlier. But they weren't. Not even close.

They were six people with at least a dozen different agendas between them.

It didn't matter. It *couldn't* matter.

They needed to rescue Cinder. They needed a heading, and they needed Hovers to reach the Still Blue.

Her eyes fluttered open, finding Roar.

They needed revenge.

8

PEREGRINE

Soren set the Belswan down in a clearing with a distance of about ten miles between them and the Komodo. They decided to hike to a vantage point and observe from a safe distance.

Perry asked Roar to watch over the Belswan. Someone needed to guard it, and Perry needed Brooke for her eyes.

Roar agreed with a shrug, and Jupiter offered to stay as well. Perry waited outside, hoping Soren would stay too, but he emerged from the Belswan, jogging down the ramp behind Aria and Brooke.

Soren still wore his pale gray Dweller clothes, which would make him stand out like a whale in the woods, and he had a forty-pound pack taken from the supply room slung over his back.

Perry shook his head. "We'll be back by tonight. You know that, right?"

Soren shot him a seething look and marched on.

They climbed to a cluster of stone outcroppings at the top of a hill. The spot would give them plenty of cover. Most importantly, it offered a clear view of the valley. The Komodo itself lay hidden behind a small slope in the distance. Hess and Sable would surely have sentinels posted along that ridge, and possibly also a patrol.

Perry sat beside Aria on the same rock, settling in to watch. They planned to assess their options from afar before moving closer.

They'd left the Aether storm behind at the coast, and the Aether flowed more calmly here, rolling in waves instead of turning in whirlpools. He didn't see the red sparks, but he had a feeling he would soon. Thick clouds drifted across the sky, casting wide shadowed patches across the plateau, and he smelled rain coming.

"What was it your father used to say about patience?" Aria said after a little while.

Perry smiled. "It's a hunter's best weapon," he said, happy she remembered something he'd told her months ago. But her temper was low and cool, at odds with her lighthearted comment.

"You all right?" he asked.

She hesitated, the shadowed look in her eyes reminding him of their argument. "I'm fine," she said, a little too brightly. She tipped her head. "But Soren might need some help."

Perry saw him and laughed. Soren had gutted his bag,

emptying all its contents. Supplies spilled everywhere around him, and he was looking through a pair of binoculars, searching the distance.

"Perry, due east," Brooke called from behind them.

He searched the low hills there. A Hover like the one that had taken Talon skimmed over the plateau.

Soren shot to his feet in excitement. "That's a Dragonwing. Fastest Hover in existence."

"It's circling," Brooke said. "It's following a specific route around the Komodo."

"A patrol," Perry agreed.

They kept up their surveillance into the afternoon as massive thunderheads moved in, clotting the sky. The patrol followed the same route every two hours. Armed with that information, they returned to the Belswan and gathered in the cargo hold to discuss their options.

"We can't outrun a Dragonwing," Soren said. He rapped his knuckles twice on the metal floor of the Belswan. "Not with this slug."

At the center of their circle was a light stick from the Belswan's supplies. Perry turned the dial down to limit its brightness. In less than five minutes, the glaring light had given him a headache.

"A Dragonwing is built to do two things," Soren continued. "One, catch anything it wants, and two, destroy it. If they're running patrols, then they're ready for us. At the very least it means they haven't forgotten we're out here. There's no way we can get close without drawing them into a fight. If that happens, we're done for. We'd be annihilated. Wouldn't we, Jup?"

Jupiter startled, surprised to hear his name. Then he nodded. "Definitely. Very annihilated."

"Twig and I got close," Roar said. He stood away from the group, alone by the open bay doors, his dark clothes blending into the darkness. "It's not hard to do on foot."

A gust of cool air blew into the Hover. It smelled more like rain by the hour.

"You want to go on foot?" Soren said. "All right, we could try that. We could run up and throw spears at the Komodo's steel walls. Wait. Do you guys have any of those catapult things? Those are champ."

Roar shrugged—he couldn't care less about Soren's comment—but Aria winced.

Perry remembered her making similar biting comments when they'd first met. That felt like a long while ago, though it'd only been half a year.

"What do you recommend, Soren?" he said tightly. He had far less tolerance for Soren than Aria did.

"I recommend we get a Hover. There's no way we're breaking into the Komodo without one. And I mean a Dragonwing, not this flying heap. But I hate to break the news to all of you: there's *no way* we're getting one."

"There are a bunch of Dragonwings outside the Komodo, aren't there?" Brooke said. "We could divide up. Some of us could distract the patrol and give the rest of you a chance to get close to the fleet on foot."

Soren snorted. "You can't just walk up and take a Hover-craft. And a distraction would never work. Any disturbance on a routine patrol would get reported back to the command leader at the Komodo. If you create a diversion, you're basically putting everyone on high alert."

"What if we contact them first?" Aria said.

"And say what? Our feelings were hurt when you tried to kill us?"

Perry leaned forward, forcing himself to ignore Soren. "What are you thinking?" he asked Aria.

"That we're approaching this the wrong way," she said. "We have to get way ahead of them." She looked at Soren. "Can you hack into their communications from this ship?"

"Honestly, Aria, sometimes I feel like you don't even know me."

"Answer," Perry snapped.

"Yes. I can." Soren looked at her. "For the last time, hopefully: I can hack *anything.*"

Aria smiled. "Perfect."

9

ARIA

er plan was this: they would transmit a false message to the Dragonwing, sending the patrol on a mission to assist a downed Belswan—which they would pretend to be.

If the order came from a Dweller commander, Aria reasoned, the pilots would have no reason to check it. When the patrol unit came to assist, they'd walk into an ambush. Aria and Perry would have their team waiting, ready to overpower the crew. They'd take over the patrol ship and then return to the Komodo disguised as the regular team.

It was the same way she'd entered Bliss when she'd been searching for her mother. She'd put on a Guardian uniform and walked right in.

Why fight the enemy when you could fool them?

"I like it," Roar said, when she'd finished explaining. "It's a damn good plan."

Aria caught his eye and smiled in thanks.

"It would get us close," Perry said, nodding. "Closer than any other option we have."

Aria looked at Soren, who stared into space, lost in thought. She wondered what he thought of the plan most of all.

"It all depends on you," she said. "The only way it'll work is if you break into the Komodo's communications system."

Soren looked at her and nodded. "I can do it. No problem."

She never doubted it. For all the trouble he was, Soren had one skill she could always count on. In a way, it was what had started everything.

Soren stood. The glazed look in his eyes was gone, replaced with fevered anticipation of the challenge. "I'm going to run a basic vulnerability analysis to get a look at the Komodo's attack surface."

Aria had no clue what that meant. Judging by the blank faces around her, she wasn't alone.

Soren rolled his eyes and wiggled his fingers in the air. "You know. Feel the security system up a little to see what I'm dealing with."

A laugh burst out of Jupiter, but he muffled it when Perry stood.

"Uh, sorry," Jupiter said.

She'd forgotten how commanding Perry could be. How he could quiet people with a look when he chose to.

"Get to work, Soren," he said, and then turned to Brooke and Roar. "Let's start outside. I want a full sweep of the terrain. If we're going to draw them to us, I want to be in the strongest position possible."

Brooke looked at Soren and wiggled her fingers in the air, parroting his gesture. "That means we're going to feel up the surrounding area a little, Dweller. See what we're dealing with."

Soren's eyes never left Brooke as she grabbed her bow and headed outside with Perry and Roar.

"What was her name again?" he asked when she was gone.

Aria stood, trying to hide a smile. "Laurel," she answered on a whim. Soren irritated everyone else. Let him be on the receiving end for once. Inspired, she added, "I think she likes you, Soren."

Then she jogged outside.

Perry was buckling a black belt with a Dweller pistol in the holster. He seemed comfortable with carrying the weapon, though he'd held it for the first time only a week ago. His bow and quiver also rested at his feet. Aria smiled to herself. Instead of choosing a weapon from her world or his, he'd decided to take both.

"Do you need me?" she said. She could scout as well as Roar and Brooke, who had already disappeared into the darkness.

Perry looked up. His hair was tied back with a leather strip, but a piece fell forward, a blond wave coming to rest at his eyebrow. "You want the truth?"

Aria braced herself for a comment about her arm. "Always."

"That's my answer. But it's probably better for you to keep

an eye on things here." He grinned, sweeping his bow and quiver over his shoulder. "I'd do it, but I'm worried my fist might find Soren's face."

As she watched him walk away, she tried to shake off the feeling that he'd left too quickly. He'd just said he needed her always. Why couldn't she focus on that?

When he reached the edge of the woods, she called out, "Be careful."

She knew he would be. It was just a way to stall. To feel close to him a little longer.

He looked back, still walking, and pressed a hand to his heart.

In the cockpit, Soren had put on his Smarteye.

"I brought it out of Reverie," he said. "Thought it might come in handy."

She leaned against the threshold and pursed her lips, disliking his choice of words. If something *handy* was useful, what did that mean for her, with her lame hand?

Soren mistook her expression, thinking she objected to his use of the Smarteye. "I don't *need* it or anything. But I can work ten times faster with it."

"I know," she said, dropping into the other seat. "It's fine. Use whatever you have to."

Aria watched him for a while. Soren alternated between periods of inward focus when he was working through the Smarteye and bursts of frantic swiping at the commands on the Belswan's controls. He was completely different when he

71

had a task in front of him, a puzzle to solve.

She stared through the windshield at the trees tossing back and forth as anxiety began to build inside her. There were dangers in those woods. Bands of violent drifters. Aether storms that struck suddenly. She couldn't get the image of Perry with his hand over his heart out of her mind.

Restless, she left the cockpit and rummaged in the rear storage room for field meals—prepackaged rations. Aria took spaghetti for herself and Jupiter, and tossed a meat loaf pack to Soren.

Then she sat at the top of the ramp, where she'd be able to see Perry, Roar, and Brooke when they returned. The trees swayed and creaked as the wind rose.

"These woods look so strange," Jupiter said, joining her.

"That's because they're real."

Jupiter flicked his head to the side, tossed his shaggy hair out of his face. "Right . . . that makes sense."

As they fell into silence, she found herself straining to see into the darkened woods. Why hadn't they come back yet?

She ate slowly, though her stomach rumbled. The pain in her arm had intensified, leaving her a little nauseous, and eating with her left hand took longer. The food, which only tasted slightly better than dirt, didn't help matters.

Jupiter finished before she did and found two twigs to use as drumsticks. "So, are you still singing?" he asked as he tapped a rhythm against the ramp.

"Not very much. I've been a little preoccupied."

Aria recognized the beat of the song "Winged Hearts

Collide"—Roar's favorite by the Tilted Green Bottles—but she had no urge to sing. The metallic clatter rattled in her ears. She felt like those twigs were banging against her brain, and now she couldn't stop thinking about Roar and worrying about him.

"That's too bad. Your voice is the best."

"Thanks, Jup."

Jupiter broke rhythm, pausing to rub his eye as though looking for the Smarteye that was no longer there. "You think Rune is all right? Caleb and the rest of everyone?"

She nodded, thinking of Molly. "They're in good hands."

Aria heard herself and winced. Was every stupid expression about stupid hands?

"You know, Beethoven?" Jupiter said. "He was deaf—mostly deaf or something—and he had to hear through percussion and conductivity and stuff. I just keep thinking about him, you know? If he was able to do that, then I should be able to figure this out."

"Figure what out?"

"Not having the Realms anymore. I keep trying to fraction. I keep thinking my Smarteye is malfunctioning, and it's kind of like I've gone deaf. Like there's this huge missing piece. Then I remember this is all we have. Real is all that's left."

"It'll get easier."

Jupiter stopped drumming. "Sorry. I didn't mean to complain or sound ungrateful or anything."

"Ungrateful?"

73

"You saved my life."

"You didn't sound ungrateful. And you don't owe me anything. You don't have to act a certain way."

Anxiety bled through her words. She'd meant to reassure him, but it sounded like she was scolding him. She looked down, hiding her grimace, and caught movement at the edge of her vision.

The fingers of her injured hand were twitching. She'd had no idea.

She tried to make a fist, hoping this meant she was healing. Instead of her fingers curling, they stopped moving. Her hand wasn't even part of her.

Tears blurred her vision, and she didn't think.

She jumped up and ran down the ramp, plunging into the night.

10

PEREGRINE

Perry had almost reached the Belswan when he spotted Aria running toward him.

In an instant he had his bow off his shoulder, an arrow nocked and ready, as he scanned the woods for an attack. For fire. Dwellers. Anything.

"What is it?" he asked as she ran up.

"I don't know," she said, breathless, her pupils dilated, her temper frantic. She held her arm against her stomach. "Nothing."

Her gaze darted past the trees. Over the rocky ground. Everywhere except at him.

Perry pulled his bow back over his shoulder and slipped the arrow back into his quiver. He let out his breath, his fear seeping out of him. "What's going on?"

She shook her head. "I said nothing. Just forget it."

"You're not telling me the truth."

Her eyes snapped up. "Maybe not, Perry, but what about you? You won't talk about Liv. You won't talk about Roar or about us. You say what happened in the past doesn't matter, but it does to me. By not talking, you're keeping *yourself* from me. How is that any worse than lying?"

He nodded, finally understanding. He could fix this. They could.

She blinked at him, shocked. "Are you . . . are you *smiling*?"

Her eyes began to fill, so he hurried to explain. "I'm smiling because I'm relieved, Aria. A minute ago I thought your life was in danger, but you're safe. You're right here, and we're together. That feels a lot better than me worrying about you, or missing you because you're hundreds of miles away."

"Just because we're together doesn't mean everything is *fine*."

He couldn't agree with that. Being with her was all he needed. They'd work out all the rest. But he saw that it was different for her. "Then tell me how to make it right. That's all I want to do."

"You have to talk to me. We have to tell each other the little things, the bad things. Maybe they'll hurt for a while, but at least they won't become big things. If we don't, we're just going to keep hurting each other. And I don't want to do that anymore."

"All right. I swear to you, from now on I'll talk. You'll get tired of hearing my voice. But I think you should be the one to start." He wasn't the one with tears in his eyes.

"Right now?"

"Brooke and Roar aren't back yet. We have some time."

Aria shook her head. "I don't know where to start. It was one thing at first, but now it feels like everything." The wind swelled, blowing her hair into her face. She pushed it away. "We haven't fixed anything, Perry. Reverie is gone. We had to leave all those people behind, and you had to leave your house, and I liked that house. I wanted to sleep with you in the loft and watch the Aether through the crack in the roof—how you told me you loved to do? We never had a chance to do that. We won't ever be able to."

She lifted her injured hand. "And there's this. I was just figuring out how to fight; now it doesn't work. I couldn't buckle the belt in the Hover. I can't even tie my hair back." She tucked the arm to her side again. "Cinder is a prisoner. Liv is gone. Roar is . . . I don't know . . . I don't know how to help him. I don't know what's happened to the two of you—and then there's *you*. I hurt you when I left, and I'm so scared that I damaged us—"

"You didn't."

"Then why won't you talk about it?"

Pressure built inside his chest, quickening his pulse. It was the same trapped feeling he got inside the cave, and it reminded him of how he'd felt when he'd walked into Vale's room and found her missing. He'd carried that pressure around until the moment she'd come back.

"I want to forget it happened. I need to, Aria. You were poisoned right in front of me. You almost died. For a while there . . . I thought you'd really left me."

"I left *for* you, Perry."

"I know. I know that now. It hurt both of us, but we got through it. And we're not damaged because of it. We're stronger."

"We are?"

"Sure. Look at us. We're surviving our first fight . . . or second."

Aria rolled her eyes. "This isn't a fight and neither was yesterday."

He smiled. "Now you're scaring me."

She laughed. It was a sparkling sound. A burst of brightness in the quiet of the woods. For the first time since he'd seen her running toward him, he relaxed.

Aria still held her hand against her side. He wanted to take it and kiss each one of her fingers, but he didn't want to chance making her feel worse about her injury.

He stepped around her.

"Perry, what are you—"

He held her shoulders, keeping her from turning. "Trust me."

He swept her hair behind her shoulders, feeling her tense in surprise. Then he combed it back with his fingers. He loved her hair. Black as onyx, steeped in her violet scent. Heavy as a blanket in his hands.

Reaching up, he tugged off the leather strap he'd used to pull his own knots back earlier, and tied her hair at the base of her neck.

"Is that what you wanted?" he asked.

"It's, um . . . much better."

Bending, he kissed the smooth skin just beneath her ear. "How's this?"

"I don't know. . . . Try again?"

He smiled and wrapped his arms around her, gathering her close. Ahead of them, the lights from inside the Hover filtered through the trees—her world, blending with his. "You really want me to talk?"

Aria leaned back, letting him take her weight. "Yes."

"You're going to hear a lot about my favorite subject."

"Hunting?"

He laughed. "No." He slid his hands to her hips, feeling muscle and solid bone, and then back up, over the curve of her waist. "Not hunting." Every part of her drove him mad, and he told her so, whispering in her ear as she rested against him.

When she turned sharply to the woods, he knew she'd heard Roar and Brooke. It was time to go back, but he held on, keeping her there just a little longer.

"What brought you out here, Aria?" he asked.

She looked up, right into his eyes. "I needed to find you."

"I know," he said. "The second I left you, I felt the same way."

They returned to the cargo hold to listen to Soren's assessment.

Perry sat with Aria, Brooke, and Jupiter, while Roar stood off in the shadows again.

Soren planted his feet wide and locked his hands behind his back, letting out a self-important sigh as he scanned their faces. He acted as though he were going to address a crowd of thousands instead of the five of them.

"First, I want to say that it's a real shame none of you are smart enough to appreciate what I've done here. To put it in simplistic terms, which you may or may not comprehend, I essentially hit a bull's-eye."

Perry shook his head. Every single thing Soren did chafed him, but Aria seemed unruffled.

"What did you find out?" she asked.

"That I'm unstoppable. And indispen—"

"*Soren.*"

"Oh, you mean about the plan? We're all set."

Aria looked at Perry in surprise. Soren had only been at work for two hours, maximum.

"Let's run through it," Perry said.

"It's *ready*," Soren insisted. "Let's get this going. Every minute we spend sitting here, we're taking a chance they'll find us out."

Perry rubbed his chin, studying Soren. Scenting his temper. Something didn't feel right. While still in Reverie, Soren had begun an experimental treatment to control his moods. Supposedly there was no risk of him becoming violent anymore, but anger lurked behind his obnoxious comments. Perry questioned his frame of mind, and his allegiance, even if Aria didn't.

Had Hess really betrayed Soren—his *son*? Given Perry's

own experience with Vale, he knew betrayal was possible within families. But maybe there was something more. Was Soren leading them right into the jaws of the enemy? Into a trap?

Roar spoke from the shadows. "I'm with the Dweller."

Jupiter shrugged. "I am too?"

"Aria and I decide how this goes," Perry said.

"Why?" Soren barked. "I hacked the system. I'm the one flying this ship. I'm doing everything. What are *you* doing? Why aren't *you* taking orders from *me*?"

"Because you're scared," Perry said. Might as well put it out there now, before they went any further. As a Scire, he seldom manipulated people, poking at the fears revealed through their tempers. But if Soren was going to break, Perry wanted it to happen here, not during their mission. So he pressed again.

"You don't know what you want. Do you, Dweller? Are you going to turn your back on us the first chance you get? Are you taking us in to impress your father? To get back on his good side?"

Soren went very still, the veins at his neck swelling. "Just because of your weird mutation, don't think you know what's in my head. You don't know anything."

"I know what side I'm on. I know I can handle pressure."

Perry's words hung in a beat of silence. He'd gone right to Soren's weakness, but it was the truth: Soren's control was brittle, and Perry had proved it.

Soren cursed and lunged forward. "Stupid Savage! I

should have killed you. You should be dead!"

Perry shot to his feet, yanking Aria behind him. Roar drew his blade, but Brooke was closer. She stepped in and pulled an arrow from the quiver at her back.

"Go ahead," she said, pressing the steel tip into Soren's chest. "Take another step, Dweller. I'm already tempted."

Soren's glare shifted away from Perry. He raked his eyes down Brooke's body and said, "I'm tempted too. Anytime, Laurel. Just say the word."

For a long moment, no one moved. Perry knew he wasn't the only one grasping for some clarity on what had just happened.

Then Brooke said, "Who the hell is *Laurel*?"

Behind him, Aria let out a chirp of laughter, and suddenly Perry understood.

Roar sheathed his knife, glancing at her. "And you call me wicked."

A scarlet blush crawled up Soren's neck. "You're all crazy," he growled. "Every one of you!"

Aria slipped past Perry. "I want to see what you set up, Soren. Show us?" She headed into the cockpit, denying him the opportunity to brood or argue by pulling him with her.

Nicely done, Perry thought. She had gotten them exactly what they needed, a run-through of the plan, and it would give Soren a chance to recover his confidence by showing them the work he had done.

"Brooke," Perry said as the others filed into the cockpit.

"Thank you."

She paused, setting her bow and quiver against the wall. "You'd have done the same for me."

Perry nodded. "I might have drawn blood, though," he said.

Brooke's smile was a quick flash, but genuine. She glanced into the cockpit. "I miss her, Perry . . . . don't you?"

Liv. "Yes," he said.

Brooke waited for him to say something more. What was there to say? What did she and Roar and Aria want from him? He couldn't change his sister's death. If he let himself feel it, the crack that ran through his heart would widen. It would break him, and he couldn't break. Not here. Not now.

"Do you think it's easy for me and Roar?" Brooke asked.

"No." He tipped his chin toward the cockpit. "We should get in there."

Brooke shook her head, disappointed. "Fine," she said, and stepped into the cockpit.

Perry didn't follow her. He leaned against the wall of the Hover, pressing his thumbs to his eyes until he saw red spots instead of Liv with a crossbow bolt in her heart.

They spent the next hours considering every angle of their plan, talking every scenario through as the night wore on. Roar yawned, then Jupiter, and then they were all yawning, fighting sleep. Everyone knew their role, but Aria wanted them to suit up and walk through their parts—a good idea considering Jupiter's and Soren's inexperience.

They found Guardian suits inside the storage lockers. Aria and Brooke grabbed theirs and left, taking turns in the cockpit for privacy.

It took Perry ten seconds to figure out that none of the suits would fit him. He swung open another locker, searching for more, and found a large black vinyl bag. He'd just grabbed the handle, noting its heaviness, when Soren spoke at his back.

"That's an inflatable boat, Outsider. And if that's what you're wearing, I'm out of this operation." He snorted. "Can't you read? It says so right there in huge letters. 'Motorized Ship, Small.'"

Perry stuffed the bag back into the locker. It took all his self-control not to rip the metal door off and slam it across Soren's face.

"Here you go, Perry," Jupiter said, his mouth lifting in an apologetic smile. He tossed a folded bundle. "Extra large."

Perry caught it and pulled his shirt off.

Soren made a sputtering sound behind him. "Are those tattoos *permanent*?" he asked, gaping. His attention shifted to the panther Marking covering Roar's shoulder. Soren opened his mouth to say something else but reconsidered.

He was scared of Roar, which was wise. Roar could be ruthless and deadly. Perry had seen that side of him plenty of times. Lately, it felt like that was the only side he saw.

Roar looked over at Perry, his gaze cold and dark, though his temper flared crimson.

Normally, Roar would have made a crack about Soren, but things were anything but normal. He shut the locker in front of him and left.

The Guardian uniform felt light and tough as Perry pulled it on, the material cool and faintly reflective. He'd never thought he'd have to dress like a Mole. The men who had taken Talon had worn suits like this, as had the Guardians who'd shot Aria in Reverie. Perry expected to hate the garment for that reason, but he was surprised to find that he liked the way it felt, like he'd donned the protective skin of a snake.

He didn't miss Aria's double take as they filed out of the Hover. He grinned, feeling a little self-conscious—and more than a little streaked at himself for caring what she thought when there were more important things to worry about.

Outside, leaves rolled across the clearing in waves, carried on gusts. Rain clouds knitted tightly across the sky, casting the night in a darkness so impenetrable that Brooke and Aria jogged back into the Hover for light sticks.

Though the Aether wasn't visible, Perry could sense it prickling on his skin. He wondered if the currents were coiling into funnels behind those clouds, and if the red flares had appeared. Would they see a rainstorm *and* an Aether storm in the morning?

Brooke and Aria returned, and they all took their positions. Soren and Jupiter stayed by the Belswan with Aria. Brooke, Perry, and Roar waited in the woods, ready to surround the Dragonwing as it came to the rescue. When Perry signaled, they moved in and rehearsed how they would overpower the Guardians, down to who would speak and what they'd say.

They spent time coordinating how to take down the Guardians unharmed. A regular Dragonwing crew consisted of four men, trained pilots all, and they'd need every one of them in order to steal Hovers from Sable and Hess.

Four pilots meant four Belswans. Added to the one already in their possession, they would have enough capacity to carry all the Tides to the Still Blue.

"No bloodshed," Perry said, after they'd run through every detail a few times. "We do this just as planned."

Agreement all around. Nods from everyone.

They'd done all they could do.

They were ready.

11

ARIA

"So . . ." Soren waved a shaky hand at the pilot seat. In his other hand, he gripped the Smarteye tightly. "I'm going to sit so we can get started and everything."

"Go ahead," Aria said.

"Thanks." Soren dropped into the chair, and his leg began to bounce.

Last night during rehearsal, he'd been calm. *Everything* had been calm. But now, rain pelted the windshield of the cockpit. Outside, in the gray early morning, the trees tossed back and forth and the wind howled through the bay doors.

It wasn't an Aether storm, but it was enough to make Aria's stomach buzz with nerves.

"Let's get this going," Perry said.

Roar and Brooke had taken their positions outside, waiting for the mission to begin.

They weren't altering their plan because of the storm.

Aria had really never understood rain until she'd come to the outside. In the Realms, it was poetic. Ambience for a night with friends in a mountain cabin. For a day studying in a café. But in the real, it streamed into your eyes and chilled your muscles to the bone. It had a biting side, and they hoped the Guardians who came in the Dragonwing would be thrown off because of it.

"I'm ready," Soren said. "It's all set. I did this in Reverie once. Remember, Jup?"

In the other pilot seat, Jupiter sat up, almost straightening out of his usual slouch. "Yeah, I remember. You got us out of history exams that one time."

Soren's lip curled. "Right . . . exams."

Aria wondered if he was thinking what she was: how terribly *far* they had come from school. From hours in the lounges of Reverie, studying and fractioning in the Realms.

"Once I hack into their system," Soren said, "I'll be traceable. I'll throw every obstacle I can at them, but that's when the clock starts running."

He had already told them this. There were three components to the mission. First, a breach of the Komodo's security system, which he'd handle alone. This would bring the patrol to them, setting up the takeover of the Dragonwing—the second step. Last, disguised as Guardians, they would enter the Komodo itself.

In the worst-case scenario, the security system breach would be discovered while they were inside extracting Cinder, but Soren predicted they would have two hours before that happened. If they followed the plan, they'd have plenty of time.

"We know, Soren," Aria said. "If we're going to intercept this patrol, we have to start now."

He nodded, the color leaving his face. Aria watched his grip on the Smarteye ease. Then he brought the device to his face with visible effort and placed the clear patch over his left eye.

One second passed. Two. Three.

Soren tensed, his fingers digging into the armrests. "I'm in." He sat up, his shoulders rolling with a small shudder, his knee still bouncing up and down. "Here we go. Where are you? Where am I? Where are you? Where am I?"

Soren's chant stopped when an image appeared, floating in the air before the front windshield.

It was an avatar of him from the waist up, the image three-dimensional but translucent, the likeness complete down to the thin scar on his chin. Down, even, to an almost exact replica of the clothes he wore—the clothes they all wore: a pale gray Guardian flight suit with blue reflective stripes along the sleeves.

There was no context to the image. No room or cockpit. Soren's avatar floated in midair like a ghost.

"Oh, come on," Soren said, running a hand over his head. "My hair looks better than that. The approximation algorithms the military uses are really substandard," he muttered as he entered a series of commands into the Belswan control panel.

Aria had never seen anyone so focused and manic at the

same time. Perry watched in silence, but she wondered what he scented in Soren's temper.

"Sorry you can't stay, Soren," said Soren, "but I'll see you later, handsome."

The three-dimensional avatar blurred and flattened like it had been pressed between glass. Another figure expanded and sharpened before them: Hess, lifeless, staring straight ahead.

Hess was fuller in build than Soren, with a chiseled face and sleek, combed-back hair. Only his eyes, dull and sunken, revealed the decades between him and his son.

Soren sat motionless in the pilot's seat, staring at his father's avatar. Hess had left him behind in Reverie. He had to be thinking about that now.

Aria licked her lips. Her stomach was already in knots and they'd just gotten started.

Perry caught her eye and gave her a slight nod, like he knew the words on the tip of her tongue.

"Keep going, Soren," Aria said quietly. "You're doing fine."

Soren seemed to collect himself. "I know I am," he said, though his voice lacked its usual bravado.

Hess's avatar came to life. His shoulders lifted—the same small shiver Soren had done moments ago. Soren controlled it now. He would use the avatar like a puppet, directing it through the Smarteye.

"Always wanted to be just like you, Dad," he said under his breath. "I'm linking into the Komodo's system."

His fingers glided over the Belswan's controls, effortlessly controlling the avatar and the Hover's instrumentation. This was his language, Aria thought, as surely as singing was hers.

In front of the windshield, a transparent screen flickered up, divided into three segments. Hess occupied the center. The screen on the right contained a combination of maps, coordinates, and scrolling flight plans, all lit in neon blue. The left-hand screen showed a cockpit like the Belswan's, but smaller. It was the inside of the patrolling Dragonwing—the ship they intended to commandeer.

Four Guardians in flight suits and helmets sat in two rows.

Hess—or rather, Soren as Hess—spoke right away, the avatar suddenly brimming with an authoritativeness Aria knew well. "Patrol Alpha One Nine, this is Commander One, over."

He paused, waiting for the information to make an impact. And it did.

The Dragonwing crew exchanged worried looks. Commander One was Consul Hess. They were receiving a direct message from the very top.

The Guardian at the comm responded. "Alpha One Nine, copy. Over."

They'd bought it. Aria let out her breath and sensed Perry relax beside her.

"Alpha One Nine," said the Hess avatar, "we picked up a distress message from a downed Hover, three—no, make that *four*—minutes ago on your incoming. Does anyone want to tell me why you're not responding?"

Soren played his father perfectly, uttering the words with simmering condescension and barely contained hostility.

"Negative on the message, sir. We didn't receive it. Over."

"Stand by, One Nine," Hess said. Soren kept the transmission running, letting the Guardians observe Hess as he turned, bellowing to a control room that wasn't there, that would be nothing more than a figment of everyone's imagination. "Somebody get him the coordinates. Now, people. My son is on that ship!"

"Your son, sir?" said the Dragonwing pilot. Surely he knew that Soren had stayed behind in Reverie as it crumbled, but that didn't mean Soren hadn't survived—or that Hess wouldn't welcome him back.

Hess turned to an imaginary underling and said, "Have his hearing checked when he gets back. And if those coordinates aren't up in—"

The screen with the flight plans blinked. New information trickled down—maps, diagrams of the Belswan, coordinates—all running like fluorescent raindrops from top to bottom.

Hess leaned forward, looking into the camera eye. "Listen closely. I want everyone on that ship here in one hour. If you fail me, don't bother coming back. Acknowledge, Alpha One Nine. Over."

Aria barely heard "Affirm, sir" before the image of Hess disappeared.

Soren had cut off the comm. He rocked back against the pilot seat, breathing fast, his chest rising and falling. "My father is an orangutan's ass," he said after a moment.

No one disagreed. That seemed to deflate him, though the words had been his own. He pressed his eyes closed, wincing, before he returned to the controls, powering the Belswan down completely.

The darkness in the cockpit startled Aria, even though she had expected it. Small rivers of rainwater flowed down the windshield.

Aria clicked on a flashlight, the beam illuminating Soren's face.

"See?" he said, through clenched teeth. "Easy."

So far, Aria thought. It would only get more dangerous.

They left the cockpit and hurried to the bay doors. As she jogged outside, the rain slapped her shoulders and face and pounded against the ramp, raising a riotous clatter.

Beneath the back end of the Belswan, Brooke and Roar fed green branches to a fire partially covered by a field tent and hidden beneath the tail end of the Hover. The effect was convincing: billows of smoke curled around the tail of the Hover, obscuring it and giving the appearance of wreckage.

A thick waft drifted past, and Aria turned away, stifling a cough into her wet sleeve.

"I should be in front," Soren said, jogging up beside her. One minute outside, and she was already soaked. "I should be the first contact point."

Perry shook his head. "No. We stick to the plan."

Soren wheeled around, facing Perry. "You saw how

93

nervous the Guardians were. It'll make it worse if they don't see me right away."

"Wrong, Dweller. You're the asset. They'll expect your position to be protected, which is by the ramp *like we planned*."

"He's right, Soren," Aria said.

They each had parts to play in the mission, based on their strengths. Perry, Roar, and Brooke knew how to stay calm in life-and-death standoffs, and their Senses would bring obvious advantages. They were best suited to engage the Guardians first.

"It's a rescue," Soren pressed. "They're not going to expect—"

"Stay here!" Perry snapped, fury sparking in his eyes. "Don't move from this spot, or I swear I'll break your face again."

He glanced at Aria, a quick flash of green, and then he jogged away, small eruptions of water punctuating every step. He was so tall—so noticeable—but in seconds he melted into the woods along the edge of the clearing. Brooke and Roar followed. All three disappeared into the rain-blurred shadows beneath the tree cover.

"Who does he think he is?" Soren said.

"He's the blood ruler person," Jupiter said.

"Quiet!" Aria said, scanning the hills in the distance. Her ears tuned to a sound through the hissing rain. A drone like bees. Through a scrim of smoke and rain, she spotted a luminous dot moving across the hills. A point, like a blue flare, streaked toward them.

The Dragonwing.

It cut through the air like a blade, the sound of its engine growing louder as it neared. Louder and louder, until she wanted to clamp her hands over her ears.

Wind and rain whipped into her face. Aria flinched and turned to the side to shield herself. She blinked, clearing her eyes, and the ship was suddenly there, floating in place just a hundred paces away.

Her gut twisted at the sight. Beside her, Jupiter took a step back and Soren cursed under his breath. Sleek and compact, gleaming like a drop of moonlight, the Dragonwing Hover looked like raw speed.

As she watched, landing gear hatched from the craft's belly and then gracefully settled onto the rain-soaked grass.

The bay doors slid open, and three Guardians jumped to the ground, landing with a splash.

Only three. That meant one crew member had stayed inside.

She shifted on her feet, her pulse hammering. They'd practiced what to do in this scenario. It would increase the risk—for Perry especially—but they were ready. They could do this.

The Guardians wore lightweight suits and helmets with goggles, just like them. One of the men stayed by the craft, while the other two crossed the clearing toward Aria. They came forward cautiously, their guns sweeping the terrain for danger or any sign of threat.

When a red light moved across her chest, everything took

on a faraway quality, distant and slow. The sound of the rain fading. The fat drops pelting her shoulders disappearing. Everything receded except the seed of pain inside her bicep.

"Hands up! Hands in the air!" yelled one of the men.

At her sides, Soren's and Jupiter's hands lifted. Aria glimpsed curled fingers in her peripheral vision and realized her hands were up too. She didn't feel any pain in her bad arm. She hadn't even realized she had that range of motion.

In the distance, Roar emerged from the woods and moved toward the Guardian posted by the Dragonwing, approaching from behind, as stealthy and purposeful as a panther.

She saw a blur of movement as he closed in, slamming into the Guardian with so much force that she jerked back and felt the wind rush out of her own lungs.

In an instant, Roar had the man on the ground. He jammed a knee into the Guardian's spine, pressing a compact Dweller gun to his head.

Soren gasped, feral energy vibrating off him. She had seen Roar's efficient ruthlessness before, but Soren hadn't.

Perry darted out of the woods, passing Roar and diving into the Dragonwing. Then Brooke emerged and took her place behind the two Guardians who continued their careful approach, unaware of their fallen teammate at Roar's feet.

"Put your weapons down!" Brooke yelled, raising a gun. The two men spun and froze as they saw her. Aria drew her pistol from a concealed holster. It felt awkward handling the weapon with her non-dominant hand, but she doubted she'd need to use it.

The four Guardians had been neutralized: Perry would have the man inside the Hover handled. Roar had taken care of the Guardian outside the craft. She and Brooke had the two in the clearing.

Everything was under control. Just like they planned.

Until Soren reached behind his back and drew a gun.

~ 12 ~

PEREGRINE

Perry crashed into the Dragonwing's cockpit, spotting his target, the Guardian who'd stayed behind, in the pilot seat.

The man grabbed for the gun at his belt. His hand never touched the weapon.

Perry jammed his knee into the Guardian's face. Not the blow he'd intended, but the space was tight. He caught the slumping Guardian by the collar and dragged him to the bay door, tossing him out into the rain, where he landed a few paces from Roar's man.

Perry jumped down from the Dragonwing. He didn't need to say a word to Roar, who knew exactly what to do.

"I got it, Perry. Go," Roar said before his feet even hit the mud.

Perry sped past him, running toward Brooke. Across the flooded field, smoke still spewed from beneath the tail of the Belswan. He was struck by how small Aria, Soren, and Jupiter looked against the Hover. Brooke stood halfway across the field, between the two Hovers, pointing a gun at the pair of Guardians she'd surprised from behind.

The two men still held their guns as they assessed the situation. Perry watched them consider their overpowered teammates lying in the mud at Roar's feet. Then Brooke and Aria, both with guns. And finally him, jogging up.

The Guardians had no options. They would recognize that and yield. They should've already seen that by now, but something didn't feel right.

Perry was twenty paces away from Brooke when he spotted the gun in Soren's hand.

"You heard her!" Soren screamed at the top of his lungs. "She said put your weapons down!"

The Guardians looked from Brooke to Perry to Soren, their movements jerky. They drew together, back to back, their guns raised.

"Do it!" Soren screamed.

They will, Perry wanted to shout. *Give them a chance and they'll do it!*

He bit back the words. Panic fed panic. Yelling would only make matters worse.

Soren's arms straightened, his gun swinging between the Guardians. "I told you, *weapons down!*"

A single *pop* broke into the air, muffled by the patter of the rain but unmistakable.

Soren had fired. He jolted back, absorbing the recoil.

An instant later, shots exploded into the air as the Guardians fired back.

Brooke cried out as she dropped to the ground. Aria, Soren, and Jupiter scattered, running back to the Belswan.

Every muscle in Perry's body wanted to sprint toward them, but he threw himself down. Wet earth coughed as bullets struck around him. He rolled, splashing through rainwater. In the middle of a field, there was nowhere to find cover.

The shots stopped, the drone of the rain filling the quiet. He lifted his head. The Guardians were running for the woods.

The shorter man of the two turned as he fled, unleashing a barrage of shots at Roar, who crouched by the Dragon-wing.

Roar launched himself beneath the craft, disappearing to the other side.

More gunshots. Whistling overhead on a path to Aria. Slapping the mud by Perry's arms.

Ignoring them, he brought his gun up, everything he knew about shooting falling into place. He relaxed his muscles, letting the bones in his arms support the weapon. Then he aimed and let out his breath, firing two shots. Adjusting slightly, he found the next man and squeezed the trigger twice again.

They were clean shots, all. Kill shots.

The Guardians went sprawling just before the tree line.

Perry leaped up before they'd fallen to the earth. Scrabbling for a foothold in the thick mud, he half sprinted, half slid to the Belswan, one thought blaring in his mind. One person.

"I'm fine," Aria said as he reached her.

He took her by the shoulders and looked her over anyway. Head to toe. Toe to head. She was all right. He waited for the relief to set in, but it wouldn't.

"Perry, are you?" Aria asked, her eyes narrowing.

He shook his head. "No."

A wailing sound pulled his attention away. Nearby, Jupiter clutched his thigh as he writhed in agony on the ground. Brooke knelt beside him. Blood poured from a cut high on her scalp, running down one side of her face.

"It's nothing, Perry," she said. "Just a graze, but he's worse. They got him in the leg."

Aria moved to Jupiter's other side. "Let me see, Jup. Calm down and let me see."

Perry glanced across the field. Roar stood by the Dragonwing, over the bodies of the other two Guardians. Perry whistled, and Roar looked up. He shook his head, and Perry understood. Roar had shot them. He'd needed to. The instant Soren's gun went off, there'd been no other possible outcome.

Perry's vision began to tunnel, his rage focusing on one point. Wheeling, he snatched Soren up by the collar. "What's wrong with you?" he yelled.

"They weren't putting down their guns!"

Soren struggled, but Perry held him fast. "You didn't give them a chance!"

"Yes, I did! How much time does it take to lower a gun? An hour?" Soren stilled, no longer fighting against Perry's grip. "It was only supposed to be a warning shot! I didn't know they'd shoot back!"

Perry couldn't respond. He wanted to break Soren's jaw again. Prevent him from ever speaking another word. "I should have finished you off the first time, Dweller."

Roar jogged up. "We need to move, Perry. Time's running."

"You're going back," Perry said, releasing Soren with a shove. "You're out of this."

Soren was a danger. There was no way Perry would take him into the Komodo now.

"Oh yeah? Who's going to fly the Dragonwing for you?" Soren tipped his head to Jupiter. "Him? I don't think so. Who's going to get you to Cinder inside the Komodo? You think you're just going to stumble up to him, Savage?"

"I should've learned to fly Hovers," Aria said.

Her tone was wry, but her temper was ice. Controlled. Perry drank it in, letting it take the edge off his own anger.

"We have to bring him, Perry," she said. "The Guardians are all dead. Jupiter and Brooke are hurt. If Soren doesn't come, it's over."

Perry looked at Soren. "Get in the Dragonwing and wait there. Don't even blink without telling me first."

Soren marched away, grumbling. "I'm blinking, Savage. I'm doing it right now."

"Soren," Roar called. When Soren looked back, Roar

flung his knife into the air. The blade spun end over end, heading right for Soren, who yelped and dodged aside.

It missed him by a hair, as Roar had surely intended. Roar never missed.

"Are you insane?" Soren yelled, his face turning red.

Roar jogged over and calmly picked up his knife, but he sheathed the blade with a vicious thrust. "That's how you do a warning shot."

Perry watched them walk to the Dragonwing. Same direction, twenty paces between them. Then he carried Jupiter into the Belswan, setting him down in the pilot seat.

Aria had already boarded the ship. She tied a tourniquet around Jupiter's leg. Then she wrapped a bandage around Brooke's head as she relayed instructions to Brooke for treating Jupiter's wound. Anticoagulant. Pressure. Pain medication. Everything was in the kit at her feet.

Jupiter rambled, asking over and over if he was going to die. The blood from his leg mixed with the rainwater on the floor of the craft. From what Perry could tell, the shot had only hit muscle, the bullet cutting through cleanly. As gunshot wounds went, it was a good one, but Jupiter blathered on until Aria put her hand over his mouth, silencing him.

"Pay attention," she said. "You need to fly this Hover, Jupiter. Get back to the cave. Brooke knows the way. They'll take care of you there."

"We'll get there," Brooke said, smiling. "Don't worry about us. Go. And good luck."

"You too, Brooke," Aria said. "Be safe." Then she darted out of the cockpit.

Perry caught her at the top of the ramp. A sheet of rain fell across the opening, blocking the outside like a waterfall. He grabbed her by the hips, afraid of hurting her arm—and that was the problem right there.

Four dead. Two injured.

And they hadn't even reached the Komodo yet.

"Aria, that was too close—"

"I'm going with you, Perry," she said, spinning to face him. "We're getting Cinder back. We're getting Hovers, and then we're going to the Still Blue. We started this together. That's how we're going to finish it."

~ 13 ~

ARIA

With Soren piloting the Dragonwing, they sped through the lashing rain toward the Komodo, their breaths loud and ragged in the quiet of the cockpit. They were a quartet of pure stress, each of them fighting to regain focus.

Aria pressed her back into the seat. The ride was jarring, almost violent compared to the Belswan, as though this craft had to fight to reach its greater speeds. She felt every small jostle in her throbbing arm.

Soren and Roar sat in the two anterior seats, commander and pilot. She and Perry sat in the seats behind them.

Half an hour ago, four men had been in these same spots. Her seat still held the warmth one of them had left behind. It seeped through her clothes to her legs and her back. She was cold, trembling and soaked, but that warmth—the final echo of a man's life—made her want to crawl out of her skin.

Was it her fault? She hadn't pulled the trigger, but did that matter? Her eyes moved to Soren's back. She had brought him to the Tides. She had trusted him.

Beside her, Perry sat rigidly. He was muddied, bloodied, and intent, his stillness contrasted by the rainwater dripping steadily from his hair. He'd been against Soren from the beginning, Aria thought. Should she have listened to him?

She turned her focus back to the windshield. Trees blurred past, the hills where the Komodo was stationed drawing closer at an astonishing rate.

"Five minutes out," Soren said.

Five minutes until they reached the Komodo. They were heading right into the dragon's lair—and there were two dragons.

She pictured Hess, who was so quick to disregard human life. *Travel safely, Aria,* he'd said, before he dumped her out to die. He'd done the same to the thousands of people he left in Reverie. He'd told them he was going to fix everything; then he'd abandoned them in a collapsing Pod.

If Hess was a killer, then Sable was a murderer. The act was personal with him; he'd looked into Liv's eyes when he'd fired the crossbow at her.

Aria bit her lip, an ache building in her throat for Perry. For Roar and Talon and Brooke. She was stupid to think this way right now, but grief was like the mud that covered them. Messy. Quickly spreading everywhere, once it found a way in.

"I'm going to learn how to fly these too," Perry said, his voice low and deep. "So I can race you."

His green eyes held a smile, a trace of good-natured competitiveness. Maybe he really did want to fly Hovers. Or maybe he knew exactly what to say to calm her down.

"You're going to lose to her," Roar said from the front seat.

He was teasing, Aria thought, but Perry said nothing back, and every second that passed in silence made Roar's comment seem less friendly.

To her relief, Soren broke the silence. "I pulled up the last five flight plans and I don't see any deviation. I'll extract voice samples from those missions, change them up and graft everything together. That will get us through the protocols and make everything seem routine. They won't notice a thing."

They had planned this part earlier, knowing that even alive, the Guardians could jeopardize the mission over a live comm. Soren would splice the recordings of the now-deceased Guardians and reuse them in order to continue their façade. The Realms—their entire life once—had become a weapon, helping them uphold the image of a normal patrol.

Was Soren telling them all of this again, waving his contributions in the air, as a way of apologizing?

Aria cleared her throat. She played along, asking for more information that they already knew. They needed to band together. Now.

"And when we get there?" she asked.

"All covered," Soren said. "I've got it right here."

He pushed a few buttons. A diagram of the Komodo appeared on a transparent screen, just as it had in the Belswan. The Komodo looked like a spiral made of individual units that could link and unlink, like old-fashioned train cars. Each segment was capable of breaking off and becoming individual, or self-determining, as Soren said during their run-through. Each unit could travel or fight in its own right.

In its stationary state, the Komodo coiled like a snake, following the same principle that had been utilized in Reverie's design. The outer units were defensive and supportive. The inner three, at the center of the coil, were highest security, highest priority. They housed the most important figures.

"My father and Sable will be in these central units," Soren said, highlighting them. "My guess is Cinder's in there too."

They were risking their lives on that guess.

"The landing port is on the south end of the compound right here," Soren said, illuminating that portion on the diagram. "The central-corridor access is on the opposite side, the north end. That's where we want to go. It'll take us right to the inner units of the Komodo without having to move through the entire thing."

"You'll get us into that corridor?" she asked.

"It's secured, no question, but I'll try to hack the codes when we get there. I tried earlier, but there's no way to do it unless I'm on-site."

"What if you can't hack them?"

"Then we go to the loud plan. Explosives."

Soren spoke without his usual bragging tone. He had made a mistake, and he knew it.

She glanced at Perry, hoping he sensed it too. But he seemed deep in his own thoughts.

"Three minutes," Soren said as they crested hills that had seemed far away just moments ago.

A jolt of adrenaline shot through her. There, sitting at the heart of a plateau, was the Komodo.

Aria sensed the gradual descent of the Dragonwing as Soren counted down the last two minutes. Her pulse sped up as they approached the rows of Hovers lined across the plateau. She saw ten Belswans. Twice as many of the smaller Dragonwings. Just eight days ago, these same craft had been inside a hangar in Reverie.

Soren flew the Dragonwing toward a runway—a stretch of dirt that cut through the center of the fleet. At the far end, through curtains of thick rain, the south side of the Komodo hulked, dark and imposing.

The Dragonwing gave a gentle lurch as it touched down. A few Guardians exited the Komodo and jogged toward them on the runway.

"They're just coming to check the Hover," Soren said, answering the question on all their minds. "Don't worry. Standard postflight procedure. Get your flight helmets on. When the doors open, go straight to the Komodo. I'll handle the ground crew and catch up to you. Oh, and try to act like you've been here before."

Aria glanced at Soren. As difficult as he was, they couldn't have done this without him.

She pulled a helmet on. It was too big and smelled faintly of vomit and rancid sweat.

She left the cockpit, forcing herself to straighten her arm despite the pain that bloomed in her bicep. She needed it to look normal.

"Here we go," Soren called, just before the bay doors opened.

A gust sent rain spraying into her visor.

Aria jumped down, followed by Roar and Perry. Her legs felt heavy as she hit the mud, the drop bigger than she'd expected. She flew forward, lurching a few steps before finding her footing again. Both Perry and Roar reached out, but she straightened and ignored them. She doubted Guardians went around catching each other's stumbles.

Behind her, Soren talked to the ground operators, his voice loud and confident, like he knew everything about everything.

Through her rain-pelted visor, she saw Hovercraft looming all around her, sleek and silent. Even with Roar and Perry at her sides, she felt exposed. Like the huge ships were an audience, watching her as she walked by.

The Guardian suit was water-repellent, but sweat rolled down her spine and over her stomach, causing the uniform to cling to her anyway.

With every step, the Komodo seemed to grow larger. So large that she questioned how it could ever be mobile. As she neared, she glimpsed massive, spiked wheels—each one several feet high. She'd been thinking of it as a snake because of its coiled structure, but now she thought *centipede*.

Two Guardians stood beneath a small overhang, manning the entrance. They wore weapons like the ones that had put a hole in her arm and in Jupiter's leg. To either side of the entrance, she saw black-tinted windows.

Was anyone watching them? Hess? Sable? How well could they see through the pouring rain?

Soren brushed past her and jogged up the ramp, past the Guardians, and into the Komodo without breaking his stride. The men at the door barely nodded in acknowledgment as Aria, Perry, and Roar followed.

Inside, a steel corridor stretched to the left and right, hardly wide enough for two people to stand shoulder to shoulder. Aria's breath came in gasps as they jogged right, Soren leading the way.

Ten minutes ago he'd almost compromised the entire mission; now he was in charge, following a schematic of the layout on his Smarteye.

Aria grabbed Perry's arm, slowing him. Slowing them all. They were too noisy. Too obvious. Perry, Roar, and Soren had substantial builds. She was probably running with five hundred pounds at her sides at least, and the Komodo felt it. They were creating a small earthquake in the corridor, the floor shaking, reminding her this wasn't a fixed structure.

They passed two doors. Three. Five.

Soren led them into the next one—an equipment room. Rows of flight suits like theirs lined the far end. Helmets. Weapons in narrow storage lockers.

Soren ran to a locker and rifled through it. He came up with a small, stubby black gun with a thick barrel. "Grenade launcher," he said. "For the loud plan."

They left their flight helmets, taking fresh weapons. Perry pulled a length of rope across his shoulder, and they filed back out to the corridor, Soren leading the way once again. He set a quick pace, just short of breaking into a run as he navigated through the twisting corridors.

Aria worried that every turn they made now was a turn they'd have to make *again* in order to get out of there.

Voices carried to her ears, coming from somewhere behind her. Aria locked eyes with Roar, who'd also heard. Someone was approaching. They'd avoided other people so far, but their luck had run out.

Roar whistled softly. Up ahead, Perry spun, reacting instantly. Together they moved toward the voices, so swift and close that Aria felt a rush of air as they passed her; then they turned the corner and disappeared.

Aria forced herself to keep going with Soren—to reach the central corridor—despite the desperate pull to go after them.

She picked up the pace, glancing back once more, and ran right into Soren's chest. Aria bounced away, stunned.

Soren stood with his arms crossed, a smile on his face. "Intense, isn't it?"

"Why are you stopping?" she asked, dread knotting inside her. He was *enjoying* this.

"We're here." Soren tipped his head toward a heavy door with a darkened access panel at its side. "This is it."

The door itself was unmarked and not at all like what she'd expected of the gateway to the most secure areas of the Komodo.

Then it hit her. Behind that door, she'd find Cinder.

And Hess.

And Sable.

Soren knelt in front of the panel. He cracked his knuckles and coaxed it to life with a tap, then expertly moved through screen after screen of security interfaces.

Watching him, she was reminded of Ag 6. Of the night he'd done this months ago. In a flash she remembered Soren's hand, crushing her throat. Aria shook away the memory and listened for footsteps in the corridor—or for Roar and Perry. She heard only the soft buzz of the overhead lights.

"Hurry, Soren," she whispered.

"Do I need to explain why that's not helpful?" he said, without looking up from the panel.

Her eyes went to the grenade launcher at his belt. *Quiet plan,* she prayed. *Break the codes. Please let the quiet plan work.*

The security panel flashed green. Relief flooded through

her, but it was short-lived. She glanced down the corridor. Where were Perry and Roar?

Soren peered up at her. "Not that I'm trying to rush you," he said, "but we have sixty seconds before this door closes. What do you want to do?"

PEREGRINE

Keeping close to walls, Perry rushed toward the sound of approaching voices, Roar half a step ahead of him.

With any luck, whoever was around the corner would turn back or head into one of the chambers that split off the corridor. But as he and Roar hurried down the hall, they didn't pass any other doors—that meant no other outlet.

Roar glanced back, shaking his head. He must have realized the same thing: they were on a collision course.

Voices came into focus: a male, saying something cutting about Dweller food. A female, laughing in response.

He knew that laugh. It turned his veins to ice.

Roar surged forward, covering ten paces in total silence. He dropped to a knee at the bend in the corridor. Perry took a defensive position a few feet behind him, his gun aimed and ready. A half a second later, the man appeared, still talking as he rounded the corner.

He wore clothes customary to the Horn tribe—a black uniform with red stag horns on the chest. Roar kicked his leg out, sweeping the man's feet from beneath him. Roar didn't waste an instant. He pounced and slammed the soldier's head against the floor.

The girl who followed wore the same uniform, the black cloth setting off hair as red as sunset.

Kirra.

Perry grabbed her before she could react, trapping her against the wall. He clamped one hand over her mouth, the other around her neck. She didn't fight, but her eyes went wide, her temper jagged and blue with fear.

"Make a sound, and I'll crush your throat. Understand?"

Perry had never hurt a woman before, ever, but she'd betrayed him. She'd used him, and taken Cinder.

Kirra nodded. Perry released her and tried not to see the red marks his fingers had left on her cheeks. Behind him, Roar dragged the fallen man back by the arms.

Back . . . back where? There was nowhere to hide.

"Hi, Peregrine," Kirra said, a little out of breath. She licked her lips, struggling to regain her composure.

Two weeks ago, for about half an instant, he'd considered kissing those lips. He'd been insane then, rejected by his tribe and Aria. Missing Liv and Talon. Kirra had kicked him at the lowest point in his life. She'd almost destroyed him.

"You saved us a lot of trouble," she said. "We were going to come for you."

Perry didn't understand. Why did they want him? He

pushed away his curiosity. "You're going to help me find Cinder and Sable."

"Why Sable?"

"The Still Blue, Kirra. I need a heading."

"I know the coordinates. I could get you there." She narrowed her eyes. "But why should I help you?"

"Do you value your life?"

She offered a wry smile. "You won't hurt me, Perry. It's not in you."

"I have no problem with it," Aria said.

Perry turned to see her jogging toward them, a pistol in her good hand. "Bring her, and hurry," she said, meeting his eyes. "Soren has the door open."

He ushered Kirra through the entrance to the central corridor. Roar lifted the fallen man over his shoulder. He rushed through the door just as it slid closed.

They'd made it. They were another step closer.

"Who's *she*?" Soren asked.

"I'm Kirra."

Aria raised the pistol. "Hi, Kirra." She nodded to the man over Roar's shoulder. "Tell us where to dump him."

Kirra's cheeks flushed, her temper heating. "In there. It's a utility room. No one will find him until tomorrow."

Quickly, Roar disposed of Sable's man.

"Now Cinder," Perry said to Kirra.

"This way." She led them down the hall, this one made of black rubber panels, more a tube than a corridor.

"Time, Soren," Perry said.

117

"One hour."

They were at the halfway mark. An hour ago Soren had posed as Hess and sent the false message to the Dragonwing. In another hour that security breach would be discovered.

"Cinder's in here," Kirra said, stopping at a door. "There should be four other people inside. One Guardian by an observation room at the far end. Three doctors."

Soren made a face, looking from Aria to Perry. "Am I the only one wondering why she's helping us?"

"She's telling the truth," Perry said. He scented it—and that was all he needed to know. They needed to find Cinder and get out of there.

Roar moved to the door, ready to be on point. Despite their falling-out, every move Roar made was exactly what Perry wanted—exactly how they'd always fought and hunted. Reading each other's minds, no need for words.

Perry pushed Kirra to Soren. Then he nodded at Roar, who slipped inside. Perry followed right after. They took swift control of the room. Roar overpowered the Guardian with a burst of speed, stripping the man of his weapon and pinning him to the ground.

A wall of glass divided the room into two chambers. In front of the windows was a line of desks and some medical equipment with monitoring screens. Three doctors in white coats stood there—all frozen in shock.

Looking for security cameras or alarms, Perry never broke his stride as he crossed to the windows of the observation room.

Inside, Cinder lay strapped to a hospital bed, his eyes half open, skin as pale as the sheet that covered him.

Perry fired at the hinges until the door popped loose; then he tore it open and rushed to the bed.

"Cinder."

A thick, chemical scent came from the various bags and tubes that fed into Cinder's arms. Perry had barely drawn a breath, but already his throat felt scraped raw by the strong scents.

"Perry?" Cinder rasped. When he blinked, Perry only saw the whites of his eyes.

"Right here. I'm going to get you out of here."

Perry pulled out the wires and tubes attached to Cinder. He tried to be gentle, but his hands—usually steady—were shaking. When Cinder was free, Perry lifted him up, his gut twisting at the weight in his arms—too little, too light. Not enough for a boy of thirteen.

In the other room, Soren and Roar finished binding the doctors to chairs with rope. By the door, Aria had a pistol trained on Kirra.

They rushed out to the central corridor, retracing their steps as they headed back to the south end of the Komodo. Perry carried Cinder, and Roar shepherded Kirra along.

"Soren, we need pilots," Aria said.

It was the only missing piece, but Perry's instincts told him to abandon that part of the plan.

"Seriously? You think I can find four pilots right now?" Soren said in disbelief.

Perry caught Aria's eye. "We'll have to figure it out later."

"I'm setting off the alarms," Soren said as they passed the equipment room from earlier.

Within seconds, the wail of sirens exploded into the air. This was part of their strategy for leaving. The alarms would signify a breach on the Komodo's north side, where they'd just been. They hoped the diversion would draw attention away from the Hover they were about to steal on the south side.

As they reached the heavy double doors that led outside, Soren stopped short. He cast an anxious look behind him. "My father's in here somewhere."

"Soren, you can't go back," Aria said. "You have to fly us out of here."

"Did I say I wouldn't? I just thought I'd see him. I thought—"

"Think later." Perry handed Cinder to Soren and moved to the doors. Not sure what they'd run into outside, he drew his gun and nodded to Roar. "Go. I'll cover you."

Roar released Kirra. "No. I'm staying here."

For a moment, Perry couldn't make sense of what Roar said. Then he scented Roar's temper, scarlet, burning, blood-thirsty, and knew he hadn't misunderstood.

"I'm not leaving," Roar said. "I'm not going until I've found Sable and watched him die. If I don't end this, he'll come after Cinder again. He'll come after you and me until we stop him. You have to cut off the head of the snake, Perry." Roar pointed down the corridor. "The snake is in there."

Perry couldn't believe what he was hearing. They were seconds away. *Steps* from making a clean escape. "This is about revenge and nothing else. Don't act like it isn't."

Roar spread his hands. His pupils were wide, flashing with feral energy. "You're right."

"You won't change anything by going in there. You'll only get yourself killed. I'm ordering you, Roar. I *command* you as your lord, and I'm asking you as your friend: don't do this."

Roar replied as he backpedaled, retreating into the hall. "I can't let Sable get away with it. He has to pay. And I'm already dead, Perry."

Then he spun and rushed back into the depths of the Komodo.

~ 15 ~

ARIA

Aria sprinted after Roar.

She didn't know how she planned to stop him. By talking to him? He wouldn't listen. By force? He was stronger. She only knew she couldn't let him go. She wouldn't let him face Sable alone.

Perry knocked into her shoulder, shooting past her. He thundered down the hall, gaining on Roar with every step. He'd knock Roar out and it would break her to help him, but she would. No matter what, they couldn't leave Roar here.

Perry had almost reached Roar when he came to a sudden halt. Instinct speared through her. Her muscles locked and she came to a shuddering stop, confused until she saw the corridor beyond them fill with Guardians.

They aimed weapons at Perry and Roar, shouting, threatening, unleashing a barrage of loud demands.

"Down, down, down! Weapons on the ground now!"

Aria drew her gun as she saw five, six Guardians, and still more filing into view. Too many of them. They were trapped. The realization crashed through her.

Then she saw Roar leap at the man closest to him.

Perry followed in the next instant and suddenly it was chaos, a jumble of limbs, swinging and kicking.

She raised her pistol, searching for a clear shot, but the corridor was so narrow and she was using her left hand. She couldn't risk hitting Perry or Roar.

Three men pinned Perry to the floor—she couldn't even see him—but she heard him.

"Go, Aria! Get out of here!" he yelled.

Then Roar exploded from of the mob with two men at his back. They pulled Roar up by the arms and shoved him against the wall. Roar's forehead struck the steel with a sickening crack.

One of the Guardians pushed a gun under his jaw, yelling at Aria. "You shoot, I shoot!"

Perry was still yelling for her to leave but she never would. Even if she'd wanted to, she couldn't.

Behind her, the red-haired girl, Kirra, stood by the exit. She'd gotten hold of the stocky grenade launcher Soren had taken earlier. Smiling, she pressed it to his temple while he stood helpless with Cinder in his arms.

A crackling, static sound made Aria whirl back. A Guardian tugged Perry to his knees, twisting his arm behind him. Another man jammed a stun-baton into his ribs.

Perry's eyes rolled back, and he thudded to the floor.

The man turned the baton on Roar, who jolted and slumped against the wall, then collapsed next to Perry.

All the shouting in the corridor quieted. Aria heard nothing as she stared at Roar and Perry, both lying motionless. Deathly still. She was overcome by the urge to fraction. To leap into the dark frigid waters of the Snake River. Anything that would take her someplace that wasn't *here*.

"It's over, Aria," Soren said. "They got us. It's over."

His voice startled her. She came back to herself, aware she still stood there, her pistol trained on the man with the baton.

How long had she been that way? A while, she realized. Long enough for Guardians to be pressed together on their knees and stomachs, all pointing guns at her.

Waiting.

She uncurled her fingers and let the weapon fall.

～ 16 ～

PEREGRINE

Perry woke to the sound of Kirra's voice.

"Pere-grine . . ." She drew his name out in a sing-song.

He struggled to clear his vision. To figure out where he was.

"Can you see me?" Kirra leaned down. Close. Closer, until her face was the only thing Perry saw. She smiled. "I'm so glad you're here. I hated the way we parted."

He had hated everything before that—every second he'd spent with her. He wanted to tell her so, but he couldn't speak.

Everything seemed slow and loud, and like he was seeing it through warped glass. Kirra's lips looked too thin. Her face too long. The freckles on her cheeks and nose drifted over her skin. Then they spread across her face and over her scalp, darkening, turning deep red, and suddenly she wasn't Kirra anymore.

She was a fox with black shining eyes and needle-sharp teeth.

Panic surged through him. He tried to lift his head, his arms, but his body wouldn't respond. His limbs were leaden. He couldn't even blink.

"You knew I was at the Tides on orders, didn't you?"

It was Kirra's voice, from the fox. From the animal's flashing eyes.

"Sable sent me to get Cinder, but I didn't expect you to become such a distraction. We were just getting to know each other, too. But I always do what Sable says. So should you, by the way. I mean that. I don't want to see you hurt, Perry."

The fox turned away. "Can he hear me, Loran? He seems so *far*."

"I can't hear if he's hearing, Kirra," answered a deep voice. "That's beyond even my ears."

"Are the drugs necessary? He's already tied down to the cot. I can't even scent his temper." The fox disappeared, moving out of Perry's line of sight. "Where are the Mole doctors? Sable isn't going to like this either."

Perry heard a door open and close, and then the sound of Kirra's voice fading.

Above, exposed wires and pipes crisscrossed the metal ceiling. They wavered, like he was seeing them beneath water.

He could do nothing else, so he began at the left corner and worked his way right, memorizing every turn and every bend.

Time passed. He knew because Kirra returned.

"That's better," she said, smiling. She sat on the edge of his cot, her hip against his forearm. She was herself again—no more fox.

"I had the Dwellers lower the dosage," she said. "You're welcome."

Perry could blink now. His mind felt less clouded than earlier, and he could track Kirra's movement with his eyes. Still, he couldn't move his limbs, and he badly wanted to take his arm away from Kirra's hip.

She glanced over her shoulder. "He looks better. Doesn't he, Loran?"

The man who stood by the door was lean, his nose and eyes slender and hawk-like. His black hair showed no hint of graying, but he had a competent, seasoned bearing. Perry guessed the soldier to be in his forties. The stag horns at his chest were sewn in silver thread instead of the customary crimson, likely indicating a high rank in Sable's forces.

"Much," responded the man.

One word, but it carried hefty sarcasm.

Kirra turned back to Perry. "You came so close to getting away this morning. I thought you were going to do it. And I was so looking forward to being your prisoner." She smiled, moving closer. "Oh, your friend? He's the Aud who left with

Aria, isn't he? You didn't tell me he'd be so nice to look at. Though he doesn't compare to you." Her gaze raked over his body. "In case you're worried about him, you shouldn't be. He's locked in a holding cell. With Aria."

Perry knew her games. She took his insecurities and hung them on a line, exposing each one.

"Bet you wish you had depended on the right people. That seems like a recurring problem in your life."

Perry swallowed, his throat as rough and dry as bark. "I never trusted you, Kirra."

She blinked at him, her smile widening at hearing him speak. "I know. You see me for who I am. That's why I like you so much. You know the truth but you still don't hate me. Well, that and you look delicious. More so when you're moving, but—"

She quieted when the door slid open and hopped off the cot.

The man who entered was average in build, with closely shorn dark hair and eyes the color of water. A sparkling Blood Lord chain hung at his neck, the sapphires and diamonds bright against a trim dark coat.

Sable.

Fury crashed over Perry like a tidal wave. He wasn't prepared to see his sister's killer. He hadn't expected the rage that tore through him. He wanted to rip Sable's eyes from his head. Break his fingers off and snap his bones into pieces. But trapped in his body, paralyzed, the urge had nowhere to go. It pounded inside his skull, shaking loose memories of Liv.

His sister came alive in his mind. Tossing her hair over her shoulder as she laughed. Tickling Talon until tears ran down his face. Punching Roar in the arm over some joke they'd shared.

His mind felt so weak; he couldn't push the memories away. To his horror, the pressure of tears built behind his eyes.

"Kirra, you can leave now, please," Sable said calmly. "Loran, bring me a chair, and then you can leave as well."

They did as instructed. Perry waited for Sable to come to the chair by the cot, to begin whatever he had planned.

He didn't.

With every passing moment, Perry's anxiety built. The drugs were still in him, slowing his thoughts and making his blood feel thick. He couldn't fight his emotions. He felt his control over reality slip as horrible images flipped through his mind. Bleeding wounds. Burnt flesh and poisoned veins, each one worse.

He'd almost forgotten Sable until the Blood Lord spoke.

"Your temper is faint, but what I can scent is truly extraordinary. Unfortunately, I don't think I'm entirely responsible. The drug you've been given has mild psychotropic effects. I can't imagine you're enjoying that very much. Hess's idea, not mine. It was intended to demoralize you. I told him it wasn't necessary, but your near success on this mission embarrassed him. Personally, I was impressed by what you almost accomplished. I've been looking around. I know what you did wasn't easy."

Perry forced himself not to respond. He wouldn't give Liv's killer the courtesy of his words.

Sable came to the cot and stood over him. Once again his eyes captured Perry's attention. Clear, but ringed in dark blue, they studied Perry with a mixture of cold calculation and amusement. "I'm Sable, by the way."

He pulled the chair closer and sat down, crossing one leg over the other. "It seems inevitable that you and I should meet, does it not?" he said. "I knew your father, your brother, and your sister. I feel as though everything has led to this. To us.

"I don't think your father thought much of me, though," Sable continued casually, as though they were old friends. "We met years ago, when we still had tribal gatherings. Jodan was reserved and quiet around strangers, not unlike yourself, but Vale and I got on much better.

"Your older brother was cunning and ambitious. I enjoyed the time we spent together when he came to negotiate for your sister's hand. We had many long conversations during his stay in Rim. . . . Quite a few of those were about you."

Perry gritted his teeth until they hurt. He didn't want to hear this.

"Vale expressed serious concerns about you. He feared you'd try for the Tides' chain, so he asked me to take you into my house as part of the arrangement we were making for Olivia. He wanted you gone, Peregrine. And I accepted. People who inspire fear are my very favorite kind. I was eager to meet you. But later, Vale wrote and said he'd made other arrangements for you. We both know where that led."

Sable looked up to the ceiling and drew a deep breath through his nose. The chain at his neck glinted with gemstones—nothing like the crude metal of the Tides' chain. Of *his* chain.

"I would have done the same to Vale had I been in your circumstance," Sable continued. "Betrayal is unacceptable. In fact, I *have* done the same thing, which brings me to your sister. Olivia."

Before he could stop it, a gurgle bubbled in Perry's throat.

Sable's eyebrows rose. "Fresh wound? It is for me, too." He nodded, quiet for a moment as his eyes took on a distant look. "Liv was sublime. Ferocious. Being around her was like breathing fire. I want you to know that I treated her well. I wanted only the best for her. . . ."

He shifted in his seat and leaned closer. "You're very easy to talk to. I don't just mean because you're a good listener."

At first Perry thought he was joking, but Sable's expression was pensive and relaxed.

"You're a Scire, and a Blood Lord," he continued. "You understand my position like no one else can. You know how hard it is to find trustworthy people. How *impossible* it is. People will turn on each other for the smallest reasons. For a meal, they will toss a friendship aside. For a warm coat, they will stab each other in the back. They steal. They lie and betray. They lust for what they can't have. What they do have isn't enough. We are weak, wanting creatures. We are never satisfied."

131

Sable's gaze narrowed. "Do you scent it as often as I do? The hypocrisy? The lack of basic decency? It's unbearable. I get so tired of it. I know you agree."

"I don't," Perry said. He couldn't hold his tongue any longer. "People are imperfect, but it doesn't mean they spoil like milk." His voice came out hoarse and quiet, nearly inaudible.

Sable studied him for long moments. "You're a hatchling still, Peregrine. You'll agree with me in time." He pressed a hand to the gold horns at his chest. "*I* don't lie. When I told Liv I would give her the world, it was the truth. I had planned to do it. And then I came to know her better and I *wanted* to do it. I would have given her anything she asked for, if only she'd been loyal.

"I knew about your friend. Roar. Your brother told me about them when we made the deal. When Olivia came to me months late, months after the time Vale and I had agreed upon, I knew why. I have Auds listening for me everywhere. I have Seers hidden in every patch of forest, acting as my eyes. But Liv came to me nonetheless. She chose *me* and she told me so. I told her she needed to be absolutely certain. I told her she couldn't go back once she decided. She swore she wouldn't. She promised herself to me."

Sable leaned closer, lowering his voice. "I am an honest man. I've been told you are as well. I expect the same from others. Don't you? Is that too much to ask?"

Don't answer, Perry told himself. *Don't argue. Don't speak. Don't give him what he wants.*

Sable sat back and unfolded his legs, a satisfied smile

spreading over his face. "I enjoyed this very much. I'm already looking forward to our next conversation—which we'll have soon."

Standing, he moved to the door, his smile vanishing and his eyes as cold as death. "You know, Peregrine, you weren't the only one double-crossed by Vale. Your brother promised me a bride, but he sold me a whore."

~ 17 ~

ARIA

I want to see my father!" Soren yelled at the door. "Tell him I want to see him!"

He'd been doing the same thing, on and off, for over an hour.

They were locked in a small room with two iron bunk beds bolted to the floor, outfitted with nothing more than thin mattresses. On the far end was a closet barely large enough to house a toilet and sink.

Sitting beside her, Roar looked like he was seconds away from attacking Soren. A purple welt had risen over his eye, where he'd struck the wall earlier.

Finally, Soren turned to face them. "No one's listening," he said.

"He's only figuring that out now?" Roar muttered.

"Who are you to talk, Outsider? You're the one who—"

"Shut your mouth," Roar said through clenched teeth.

"*Me?* We're in here because of you."

"Soren, just drop it," Aria said.

"You're defending him?"

"We need to stay focused on getting out of here," she said. "Your father will talk to you. He'll come. When he does, you need to negotiate with him. Find out where Cinder and Perry are—"

Her voice broke on Perry's name, so she stopped and pretended she'd finished her thought.

Soren plopped down on the opposite bunk, letting out a frustrated sigh. Guardians had confiscated his Smarteye, and his clothes were caked with dirt from their muddy skirmish with the Dragonwing pilots.

Aria stretched out her legs, staring at her own filthy pants. The rainwater had dried from the lightweight material, but she still felt uncomfortably chilled and out of sorts. Hours had passed since Perry had been dragged away unconscious. She felt his absence everywhere, in her skin and deeper, in her muscles and bones.

"You want me to negotiate with my father." Soren gave an exaggerated nod. "Right. That'll work. Remember your little meetings with him? Coffee in Venice? Tea in Japan? You've seen him way more than I have. And he isn't exactly rushing to see me, is he, Aria?"

"He's your father. He wanted you to leave Reverie with him."

He snorted. "He also left my friends to die. What do you want me to say to him, anyway? 'Sorry we hacked your security system, impersonated you, took your Hovercraft, and killed a few of your soldiers, but can you please let us go?'"

"One more word, Dweller, and I will hurt you." Roar's voice was low and full of deadly warning.

Soren went still, the smirk fading from his face. He shook his head and lay back with a thump on the cot.

"Miraculous," Roar said under his breath. He drew his knees up and cradled his head in his hands, tugging at his hair.

Watching him, Aria saw her own frustration. How much longer would they be there? What did Hess and Sable have planned for them? Marron had said that in days, Aether storms might be constant and everywhere. Was that happening now on the outside? Every second they remained trapped in this small room robbed them of their chance for survival.

Her gaze fell to her injured arm, resting on her thigh. There had to be a way out of this. She just needed to figure it out.

"Soren," she said after a while.

"What?" he said wearily.

"When Hess comes for you, tell him I want to see him too."

Some time later, she woke curled on her side on the hard mattress. Roar stood in the middle of the room, staring vacantly into space as his hand worked an invisible blade. Aria had seen him do that a hundred times with steel flashing at his fingertips—a habit he had when he was restless. Now there was nothing but air.

Soren was gone.

Roar stilled when he saw her, embarrassment flitting across his handsome face. He sat opposite her and crossed his arms. "You were right. An hour ago, Guardians came to take Soren to Hess." Roar tipped his head to the door. A plastic bottle and two trays rested on the floor. "They brought food. I was going to wake you, but you looked like you needed sleep. Also, it looks terrible."

Aria sat up, her muscles stiff, her mind groggy. "How long was I out?"

"A few hours."

She hadn't meant to sleep, but the pain in her arm was exhausting, and it'd been more than a day since she'd rested. Her eyes had slammed closed as soon as she'd laid her head down.

"Did you eat?" she asked. Both trays looked untouched.

Roar shrugged. "I would take a bottle of Luster right now. Nothing else."

She studied him, gnawing her lip. Roar had always been lean, but lately his cheekbones looked sharper, and deep shadows welled beneath his eyes.

She had no appetite either, but she grabbed the water and joined him on the same bunk. After taking a long drink, she handed it to him.

"That's not Luster."

"Just drink it."

Roar took it and drank.

"Why did they take him? Why Perry and not us?"

"You know why, Aria."

She didn't like his dismissive tone. Worse, she didn't like the confirmation of her worries.

Hess and Sable had taken Perry because of his connection to Cinder. They planned to use him somehow.

Roar said nothing more. As the moments passed, she felt him retreat. Aria picked at the crusted mud on her uniform, hating the silence that stretched and stretched, with nothing but the sound of their breathing.

Quiet was right on Perry. Not on Roar.

But she didn't break their silence either. She didn't want to blame him for their capture, like Soren, and if she spoke, she might.

Roar set the water jug on the floor. "Have I ever told you about the time Liv and Perry and I went to look at some horses for Vale?" he said, sitting back again.

"No," she said, a lump rising in her throat. He was talking, which she wanted. Sharing a story about Liv and Perry as he'd done countless other times. But those times, Liv had been alive. "You haven't told me that story."

Roar nodded. "It was a few years ago. Some traders came down to the Shield Valley with horses from the north. Vale sent us to have a look. Liv and I were seventeen, Perry a year younger."

He paused, scratching the dark stubble on his chin. Aria didn't know how he managed to sound so normal. Nothing about this story, or this place, or their situation felt normal.

"We never actually saw the horses. We hadn't been at the traders' camp for an hour when a band of dispersed showed up. A group like the Six. Hard men who'd cut you down just for looking at them the wrong way. We tried to steer clear of them, but it turned out we were all waiting to see the horse master.

"These men recognized Liv right off. They knew she was Vale's sister, and they started taunting her and saying these lewd things . . . awful things. It wasn't like Liv to keep quiet, or Perry for that matter. It especially wasn't like me, but they outnumbered us three to one. Perry and Liv held their tongues, but after about ten seconds I'd heard enough. I felt like I was going to lose my mind if I didn't do something.

"So I went after one of them, and pretty soon it was me against nine. Perry and Liv jumped in, of course, and for a little while there we were all in a nice knot until it got broken up. Liv and I came out of it with a few scratches, but Perry's nose was gushing blood and he'd broken a finger or two. So we thought. They were too swollen to tell. He'd also sprained an ankle and suffered a gash on his forearm."

The muscles in Roar's neck rolled as he swallowed. "Seeing him roughed up like that was as bad as hearing those things about Liv. Worse, because it was my fault. He got hurt because of me."

Finally, Aria saw the point of the story. Roar was scared. He feared Perry would be hurt because of him. Because he'd chosen to hunt Sable down instead of escape when they had the chance.

She wanted to tell him that Perry would be all right, but she couldn't. She was too nervous. Too scared herself that Perry *wasn't* all right.

Instead she said, "I feel like every story you tell me, he gets his nose broken."

Roar raised an eyebrow. "You've seen it, haven't you?"

"I have." Aria hugged her legs, ignoring the pain that pulsed in her right arm. She pictured Perry's expression as he'd put his hand to his heart. "I should thank you. I like his nose the way it is." In fact, she loved it.

"You can thank me if we get out of this."

"*When* we get out of this."

Roar frowned. "Right . . . when."

The door hissed open. They shot to their feet.

Three of Sable's men stepped inside. Two had the Horns symbol emblazoned in red on their black uniforms, but the third man, who carried himself like a leader, wore a uniform with silver horns. All three carried Dweller pistols in holsters at their belts.

"Turn around and put your hands behind your backs," said one.

Aria didn't budge. She couldn't look away from the oldest soldier—the silver-horned one. She recognized him as the man who'd been sparring with Liv in the courtyard in Rim when they'd first arrived.

She shook away the memory. "Where are you taking us?

140

Where are Peregrine and Cinder?"

The soldier's eyes narrowed thoughtfully, as though he was trying to recall where he'd seen her before. Then his gaze dropped to her injured arm, tucked to her side. His appraisal was intense and it unnerved her, making the blood pound in her ears. She sensed Roar's tension beside her. He was holding his breath, and she wondered if he remembered the Horn soldier too.

"I have orders to take the two of you to Sable," said the older soldier at last. "I'm authorized to use whatever force necessary to carry out that directive. Is that clear?"

"I can't put my hands back," Aria said. "I was shot a week ago." Just imagining the pain she'd feel made her head spin.

"What do you want to do, Loran?" asked one of the other soldiers.

"I'll watch her," the senior soldier replied.

Loran. Aria recognized the name. That day in the court-yard, Liv had shouted it just after she'd soundly defeated him.

Roar's hands were tied in front of him with plastic cuffs. Then Loran took her by the left arm and yanked her into the corridor.

18

PEREGRINE

The ceiling was different. No more pipes and wires.
It was the first thing Perry noticed when he opened his eyes. The second was the prickling sensation of the Aether, deep in the back of his nose.

Cinder.

Perry turned and saw him in the next bed. Cinder lay strapped down by thick plastic cuffs, his eyebrows knitted in concentration like he'd been willing Perry to wake up. He was dressed in a loose gray shirt and pants, and tubes fed liquid into his arms.

Perry wanted to shoot to his side, but bindings held him down as well; he couldn't move an inch.

Cinder licked his cracked lips. "You came here for me?"

Perry swallowed. His throat ached fiercely. "Yes."

Cinder winced. "Sorry."

"No . . . don't be. I'm sorry I didn't get you out of here."

Every word took effort. The scent of the medicines hung heavily in the room. Perry tasted the chemicals on his tongue. He felt sluggish and slightly dizzy, but the urge to move, to get off the cot and stretch his muscles, overwhelmed him.

Cinder fell silent, his breath wheezing, his eyelids drifting closed for a few seconds.

"I tried too," he said, finally. "To get out of here, I mean. But they're giving me this medicine. It makes me so weak, and I can't call the Aether. I can't reach it. . . . I don't feel very well."

Perry glanced at the long glass wall that divided the room in two. It looked almost exactly like the room where he'd found Cinder earlier, except larger. The other side was empty—just a long table and a dozen chairs.

"We'll find another way out of here."

"How?" Cinder asked. "They're doing the same to you."

He was right. Perry couldn't help anyone in his condition.

"Was Willow . . . was she . . . has she said anything about me being gone?" Cinder asked. "Forget it. I didn't mean to ask that. I don't want to know," he added in a rush.

"She's said a lot, Cinder. Too much, actually. She took up cursing the day you were taken. Nobody can get her to stop. She's got Talon swearing too. . . . I think . . . I think even Flea is barking swear words. Probably it'll be that way until we get you home.

"Molly misses you, and so does Bear. Gren feels terrible Kirra's men got past him. He's told me so a dozen times, and he's told Twig and the rest of the Six a hundred times more than that. . . . That's how it is. Everyone misses you. Everyone wants you back."

The effort of saying so much gave Perry a pounding headache. He wanted Cinder to smile, though. Now that Cinder did—a shaky, teary grin—Perry felt tears well in his own eyes.

"I liked being there, with the Tides."

"You're one of us."

"Yeah," Cinder said. "I am. Thanks for coming for me, even if it didn't work."

Perry smiled back. "Sure . . . glad to be here."

That got them both laughing—or hacking and coughing in an attempt at laughter that was probably the sorriest sound ever made.

The doors in the other room slid open, and they fell silent.

Hess entered with Soren and took a seat at the table.

Others entered behind them. There, escorted under guard, he saw Roar and Aria.

19

ARIA

Aria stared at the black glass. She couldn't see him, but she knew Perry was on the other side.

"What's going on, Hess?" she asked.

Hess folded his hands on the table and ignored her.

Her captor, Loran, dragged her to the table. "Sit." He pushed her into a chair and ordered Roar to take the seat on her other side. Aria sensed Roar's focus on her and realized she was breathing quickly. She had to calm down. She needed to concentrate.

Across the table, Soren sat next to his father. He had been given new clothes, and his hair was damp and combed from a shower, but she noticed the slump in his wide shoulders, the weariness in his face. He'd been cleaned up, but he seemed more tired than ever.

When he caught her eye, he gave a little shrug of apology.

What did that mean? Had he betrayed her and allied himself with Hess?

Her gaze moved to Hess, and repulsion coiled in her veins. His chiseled features seemed more severe than she remembered, his eyes smaller and hollower. Then again, for the past months she'd only seen him in the Realms through her Smarteye.

During their meetings, he'd favored casual dress. Fine suits. On occasion informal military attire. Now he wore full military regalia—an impressive uniform decorated with ribbons at the collars and cuffs.

Four Guardians came through the door, armed with rifles, pistols, the stun baton they'd used on Perry and Roar.

The sight of so much weaponry sent a bolt of fear through her.

"Is Perry in there?" she said, raising her voice. "Why are we here?"

Then Sable stepped into the room, and her vocal cords clamped shut.

Hess wouldn't acknowledge her presence, but Sable did. He smiled and said, "Hello, Aria. It's good to see you again. Yes, Cinder and Peregrine are both in there. You'll see them soon."

She wanted to look back to the wall of glass, but Sable's gaze kept her riveted. Her mind replayed those last seconds on the balcony in Rim: Liv falling backward and landing on the stones, the bolt from Sable's crossbow embedded in her heart.

"We're all here, I believe," Sable said. "Shall we get started?" Kirra slid into the seat beside him, sending Aria a mocking wave.

Roar's eyes locked on Sable. His hands, tied in front of him, clenched into fists.

"We should start with the Still Blue," Sable said, "since that's why we're all here. It'll help if you all know the challenges we have in reaching it."

"Why should I even believe you know where it is?" Aria asked. "Why should any of us?"

Sable smiled, his pale eyes unblinking. She couldn't tell if he looked pleased or furious at her interruption.

Hess seemed so soft, so tame at his side. In a trim black coat, with a shining Blood Lord chain at his neck, Sable looked electrified and in control.

"Then I'll start with how I discovered it and let you decide whether you believe me or not. Three years ago, one of my trading ships, the *Colossus*, fell into the grip of a storm and was swept out to sea. The crew suffered a tragic loss of life. Only two young deckhands survived. Inexperienced sailors, coincidentally both Seers, they were adrift for weeks when they came to something quite unbelievable.

"We've all seen the funnels of Aether, but what these men described was very different. A wall of Aether. Or, I should say, a *waterfall* of Aether. A barrier that flowed from the sky, extending endlessly upward, and across the horizon as far as they could see. An astonishing sight, but no comparison to what lay beyond. On the other side, through small gaps in the Aether flows, these young men glimpsed clear skies. Still skies. No Aether."

"Where are these men?" she asked.

"No longer available." Sable opened his hands, the gesture matter-of-fact. "I had to secure the knowledge."

He was ruthless. Admitting he'd killed these sailors so frankly and with no remorse. Aria looked around the table. No one seemed surprised.

"You believe this story without proof?" she asked Hess.

"It corroborates our theories."

"What theories?" she demanded. Answers were coming at last. She wanted to know everything.

Sable nodded at Hess, who answered. "It was an early theory that linked the disruption of Earth's magnetism with the arrival of the Aether. Magnetic north and south shifted, a clash that we're still in the midst of. But it was theorized that pockets of magnetism would form . . . cohering the way water droplets do. We think the Still Blue is one of these pockets. A magnetic field that's keeping the Aether at bay. What those two men saw was the boundary—Aether pushing as far up to this field as possible and pooling there to create a wall."

"Why didn't we know this before?" Aria demanded.

"Those who needed to know did," Hess said. "And the knowledge led nowhere. We conducted extensive searches, but nothing was ever found. The idea was abandoned."

It was so much to take in. Aria's entire body felt numb. "And the plan to get through the barrier?"

Hess glanced to the glass wall. "We've had little success controlling the Aether through technological means. Other approaches, biological ones, may still work. The CGB—the research group your mother was part of—had the primary focus of sculpting genetics to make life in the Pods sustainable. But they also ran a few experimental programs. Some of these, like the immunoboost, looked at bringing us back outside the Pods. Another focused on evolutional acceleration."

Aria's mother had been a geneticist. She already knew where this was heading. Hess continued, explaining for the benefit of the others.

"By creating people with a high degree of genetic plasticity—DNA that's extremely malleable—they hoped to create humans who could rapidly adapt to whatever environment they encountered: chameleons who could change on a cellular level, molding to an alien atmosphere, to whatever conditions they met."

As Hess spoke, Sable gave a signal to one of his men at the door. Horn soldiers came in from the corridor, standing along the wall. Hess's Guardians entered as well. Both groups seemed uneasy to be there.

"The CGB had already seen Outsiders who exhibited this type of rapid evolution by assuming enhanced sensory capabilities." Hess glanced at Roar. "But what the program accomplished went further than anyone anticipated. Not only did the test subjects adapt to the Aether; the Aether adapted to *them*."

He paused, just a beat of silence. In that beat, Aria began to count Guardians. Horn soldiers. Weapons.

"It wasn't long before the project was deemed a failure," Hess continued. "There were instabilities that weren't accounted for. As with anything, in solving one problem there's always a possibility of creating secondary, consequential problems. While the scientists had figured out how to create a human with dynamic genetics, they couldn't figure out how to turn those dynamics off. The test subjects expired within years of creation. They were nonviable. They . . . self-destructed."

Hess looked to the glass wall again and said, "All except one."

20

PEREGRINE

Speakers in the ceiling had piped in every word.

"I'm . . . I'm an *alien*?" Cinder said. The scent of his fear flooded the chamber.

"No. That's not what he said." Perry pulled against his restraints, though he knew it was useless. He wanted to shatter the glass between the chambers and reach Aria.

Reach *Sable*.

They'd seen everything too, but Perry knew it wasn't the same from the other side. Whenever Aria or Roar looked over, their gazes scanned, never settling on him or Cinder.

Cinder's eyebrows drew together, his expression desperate. "But I heard that man. He said the word *alien*."

"He also said the word *chameleon*, but you're not one of those, are you?"

151

"No. But they created me as an experiment—that part is true."

"You've made yourself into who you are—not them."

"He said I was going to self-destruct. He said I was going to die. He said—"

Cinder fell silent as Sable's voice came through the speakers.

"We need Cinder to get us through that wall of Aether. He's the only one who can do it."

Aria shook her head. "No. It would kill him. And he won't do it for you."

Sable and Hess exchanged a look, but Sable answered. "I think I speak for us both when I say we're only concerned with your second point, which is why your arrival here couldn't have come at a better time."

He rose from the table and came to the windows. "Hess, make this transparent, please."

The glass lost a faint smokiness that Perry hadn't noticed until then. In the other room two dozen people turned in unison.

Aria shot up from her chair. Fear flashed in her eyes; he hated seeing it. "Hess!" she yelled. "What did you do?"

"It was a necessary measure." Hess rose from his seat and joined Sable. "They're on sedatives to keep them submissive. We couldn't control the boy without them."

"That's going to change," said Sable. He moved along the glass wall until he stood in front of Cinder. "You can hear us, correct?"

"Yes," Perry growled, answering for Cinder. "We can hear you."

Sable smiled, like Perry's reaction pleased him. "Good. Cinder, as you've just heard, you're the key to our survival. You are the only one who can unlock the door to the Still Blue. We need you. But in order for you to help us, you have to be taken off the suppressants so you can regain your strength and access the full power of your gift. What we can't have, Cinder, is you using your ability to harm us."

He turned his attention to Perry. "That's where you can help. From what Kirra tells me, Cinder has already risked his life for you. He looks up to you. He'll listen to you."

Perry's gaze went to Kirra. Two weeks ago, Cinder had driven away the Aether so the Tides could reach the cave in safety. She'd been there and must have told Sable.

"Cinder needs to do for us what he did for you," Sable continued. "That will require your help. Keep the boy in line as he's weaned off the suppressants. Encourage him to cooperate. He has the opportunity to save lives. He can become a savior, Peregrine. A martyr."

"A martyr?" Cinder whispered beside him, terror making his voice shake.

"He's just a *kid*!" The words flew out of Perry's mouth before he could stop them.

"He's thirteen," Kirra scoffed. "That's hardly a *kid*."

"You have no leverage," Hess said. "We have it all."

They did. They had Roar and Aria—they could pressure him to comply—but he still couldn't agree.

153

Cinder began to cry beside him. "I can't!" He looked at Perry. "You know what will happen to me."

Perry knew. The last time Cinder had called the Aether, it had almost killed him. The magnitude of what Sable described would make that certain.

As Blood Lord, he'd needed to put people he cared about in danger to help the tribe, but this . . . a *sacrifice*? He couldn't ask that of Cinder.

"He's not doing anything for either of you," Perry said, looking from Hess to Sable. "And neither am I."

Sable's voice came through the speakers again. He sounded a little smug as he said to Hess, "We'll have to take my approach." Then he lifted his hand in the air. "Cinder, I want you to think of these four words: *Is it worth it?*" he said, counting them off.

"If you attempt to escape or use your abilities against us, that's the question you should ask yourself. Then you should think of Peregrine—of Perry there—and consider how much he means to you. Think about how you'd feel if he suffered because of you. That *will* happen if you don't do exactly as I say, and it won't stop there.

"Aria. Roar. Even the girl at the Tides Kirra tells me you're so fond of. They're all within my grasp. And I don't think you want their pain—or their blood—on your conscience. On the other hand, if you help us, then your friends will stay safe. I'll bring them all on the journey to the Still Blue, where they'll live under my protection. Rather clear-cut, in my opinion. Is all of this making sense to you?"

Cinder groaned. "Yes."

"Excellent." Sable's eyes glinted with intensity. "Then I'll ask once again: As you regain your strength, will you do *exactly* as I tell you? Can I trust you to obey me, Cinder? Will you submit your power to me?"

21

ARIA

No!"

Cinder's answer was a battle cry. A sound of raw defiance.

The echo of his voice hung in the air as his veins lit with Aether, which covered his face and arms and spread over his bare scalp.

The lights in the room shuddered. Gasps rose up from the Guardians and Horn soldiers. Guns flew from their holsters, all of them pointing at Cinder.

"Stop!" Hess yelled. "Put away your weapons! He can't harm you!"

Aria turned to Roar, whose face flashed with the strobing lights, thinking *now.*

Roar pushed back from the table. He grabbed his chair between his bound hands, hurling it at the wall of windows.

It struck with a crack, bouncing off. The glass splintered,

spiderwebs splaying across its surface, but it didn't shatter.

Aria dropped and rolled beneath the table.

She came up on her knees by the door leading to Perry and Cinder's chamber. Behind her she heard yells, footsteps scattering in panic. She jabbed at the security panel. A red flashing message told her what she'd already known. Only a special access code would get her inside.

"Soren!" she yelled, having no idea if he'd help or if he was in league with Hess now.

The rattle of gunfire exploded around her. She covered her ears, tucking into a ball. Gunshots pocked the door in front of her, and the smell of hot metal seeped into her nose. She braced for the same slap she'd felt in her arm when she'd been shot in Reverie. It didn't come.

"Stop! Don't hurt the boy! He cannot be harmed!" Hess shouted over the noise. Aria peered behind her to see him shove a Guardian, who dropped the pistol in his hand. One of the Horns had Roar by the arms, and Soren was belly crawling toward her from the opposite side of the room.

She didn't see Sable.

"Out! Everyone out!" Hess yelled.

Abruptly, the gunfire ceased and men rushed for the door. Guardians and Horns jammed at the exit, pushing, shoving in their hurry to flee. In the kick and trample, the fallen pistol skittered across the polished floor, stopping a few feet from Aria.

She snatched it up, aiming at the man who was dragging Roar outside. "Let him go!"

The Horn soldier released Roar without a fight, plunging into the corridor. The door slid closed behind him.

Sable and Hess. Guardians and Horns. Everyone had cleared out.

Roar rushed to her side, Soren a second after. A high-pitched alarm exploded through the room's speakers.

"We have to get out of here," Soren yelled. "They're going to gas the chamber."

Aria looked up, tuning her ears, listening between the siren's blares. A faint hiss came through the air vents. It was already happening.

"Find something to cut me loose, Soren," Roar said.

Aria faced the glassed room. The only thought in her mind was reaching Perry. She adjusted her grip, finding the trigger with her left index finger, and fired at the glass at an angle. The weapon bucked in her hand five, six times, before the window peeled apart and fell in a heavy sheet.

She vaulted through the window frame into the room, rushing to Perry's side. She set the gun down and began unbuckling the heavy straps. She felt slow and clumsy with her bad hand, but she forced calm into her movements. Panicking wouldn't help.

She glanced at Perry's face and found his green eyes fixed on her. "Are you hurt?" she asked.

He looked tired, his skin washed of color. Cinder was almost unconscious. The brief use of his power had bled him dry.

Perry gave her a small, strained smile. "Too angry to feel pain."

Roar unfastened Cinder's bindings. Soren came over and undid the ones on Perry's feet. Aria saw Soren's hands pause for a moment as he swayed, balance unsteady. The gas was affecting him.

She felt it too. The alarm sounded further away and deeper in tone, like it was disappearing into a dark tunnel.

As soon as she'd freed Perry's hands, she shot to the door and found it locked.

"Aria . . . ," Soren said behind her. "It's too late. I don't have time to hack it. . . . The gas isss . . . ," he slurred.

"It's *not* too late!" She backed away from the door and aimed at the locking mechanism. Her head was spinning. The room was spinning. She couldn't keep her aim steady. A bitter taste like rancid limes slid over her tongue, and her eyes began to burn.

Roar's hand closed over hers. He took the pistol. She noticed he was breathing raggedly. "It'll ricochet. . . . Soren's right."

Disappointment washed over her. Crushing her with the feeling that they'd just made their situation worse.

Aria turned. Perry leaned against the bed, his wide shoulders hunched. "Aria," he said simply.

Soren sat heavily against the wall. Then he slumped onto his side, eyes fluttering closed. The lime taste seared down Aria's throat and the walls flapped, undulating like sails in the wind. She couldn't move.

Perry's head tipped to the side, heavy and resigned. Not the playful tilt she knew. "Come here."

His voice drew her forward. She went to him, walking across the tilting floor. Her face smacked into Perry's chest. He caught her by the arms. She'd only vaguely registered that her bicep didn't hurt at all when she found herself on the floor, with no memory of sitting down.

Perry pulled her against his side, putting his arm around her. Soren had passed out. Cinder lay still on his bed. Roar sat against the door, glaring into space.

He seemed so far. The room seemed to stretch out and go on forever.

"S'good at least that—" Perry turned to face her, and his knee knocked into her thigh. "Sorry."

"Didn't feel it," she managed to say through a numb mouth. "What's good at least?"

"We're together." She saw the flash of a grin just before his eyes slammed shut. He fell forward, his forehead thudding onto her collarbone.

Aria wrapped her arms around his neck and held on as they drifted away.

22

PEREGRINE

That's good. Come on back. There you are," Sable said.

Perry opened his eyes, blinking at the brightness. His first thought was of Aria. Then Roar and Cinder.

He was going to demand to see them. To know how they were—*where* they were. But then he saw the table next to his bed.

A set of tools rested on a tray. A wrench and a hammer. A mallet with a black rubber head. Clamps and knives of all sizes. Finer tools with needle-thin points. Dweller tools that shone like icicles.

He had no doubt in his mind what was about to happen to him. But he was prepared for this. He'd known the instant he'd met Sable that this was possible.

The dark-haired man with the silver horns stood by the door. Kirra and a few Guardians as well.

Hess stood closer, next to Sable, his weight shifting from side to side.

"Do I have to stay?" Kirra asked. Her head was bowed, her red hair shielding part of her face.

"Yes, Kirra," Sable said. "Until I say you can leave."

Sable fixed his blue eyes on Perry, blinking a few times, staring quietly. Scenting Perry's temper. "You know why we're here, don't you? I warned Cinder. I told him what I wanted. He refused me. Unfortunately, the price of that transgression falls on your shoulders."

Perry looked to the ceiling, keeping his breath steady. He wanted, more than anything, to endure what would come next without begging. Even when his father beat him as a boy, he'd never begged. He wasn't going to start now.

"I can't hurt Cinder physically," Sable said. "That would be counterproductive. But I can make him understand that until he concedes, he'll suffer—through you."

He turned his attention to the table; his hand hovered over pliers before he picked up the mallet. He tested the weight of the tool in his hand.

Perry could tell it was substantial.

"I'm thinking bruises. They're showy. Not very messy, and—"

"Get on with it," Perry snapped.

Sable slammed the mallet down on his arm. It struck Perry's bicep, over his Markings. Bursts of red exploded before his eyes. A sound slipped out of him, like he was lifting a huge weight. He held on, waiting as the pain began to fade.

162

"There has to be an alternative to this," Hess said.

"He's our leverage, Hess, as you said. Our only means of breaking down the boy. And the alternative is that we die. How does that sound to you?"

Hess glanced at the door behind him and fell silent.

"Relax," said Sable. "I hit him harder than I intended." He looked back at Perry. "You know I'm being merciful, don't you? I could find the girl he likes—what's her name?" he asked Kirra.

"Willow."

"I could have Willow on this table instead. You wouldn't choose that, would you?"

Perry shook his head. His throat had gone dry, and his arm had its own heartbeat. "There is one thing you should know," he said.

Sable's eyes narrowed. "And what is that?"

"I don't bruise easily."

It was a stupid thing to say, but it gave him some small feeling of control over the situation. And the look on Sable's face, surprised, incensed, was worth it.

"Let's find out," he said, tightly. And the mallet came down again.

This one was easier to endure than the first strike. Every one that followed became easier still as Perry retreated into his mind. His father had prepared him for this, and he felt a strange sense of gratitude. A euphoric closeness to times past, which had been terrible, but which had included Vale and Liv. They'd made him good at finding quiet, even peacefulness, in the face of pain.

When Sable came to Perry's hands, tears pricked at his eyes. They hurt the worst, maybe because they had been smashed so many times before.

Hess turned green and left first. Kirra followed soon after with the dark-haired guard.

Only the men posted at the door stayed, too afraid of Sable to leave.

23

ARIA

Something terrible was happening to Perry.

Aria *felt* it.

"Sable! Hess!" she yelled again. "Where are you?" She pounded on the heavy steel door, screams ripping through her throat. "I'll kill you!"

"Aria, stop." Roar came up behind her. He wrapped her up, pinning her arms.

"Don't touch me!" She struggled against him. "Let go! You did this!" She didn't want to turn on him, but she couldn't hold back. "You did this, Roar!"

He held on, and he was stronger, and she couldn't push him away. She stopped fighting and stood, trapped against him, her muscles shaking.

"I know," he said, when she was still. "I'm sorry. I know I did this."

She hadn't expected him to say that. Hadn't expected to hear the guilt in his voice. "Just let me go."

Roar released her and she spun, looking from his face to Soren's, seeing their worry and fear, and suddenly tears poured from her eyes.

Her gaze cast around the small room. She needed to get away from them. With no better options, she climbed to the upper bunk and curled as close to the wall as she could, trying to keep back the sobs that tore through her.

Below, Soren said, "Do something, Outsider."

"Are you blind?" Roar replied. "I *tried*."

"Well, keep trying! I can't take this."

She felt the mattress sag. "Aria . . ." Roar's hand rested on her shoulder, but she stiffened and moved away.

She was crying too hard to talk, and if he touched her, he would know that she hated him right now. She hated everyone. Cinder, for having been captured. Her mother, for dying. Her father, for being nothing but a figment of her imagination. Liv, because the thought of her only made Aria ache more.

Why was it so hard to bring together the people she loved and keep them safe? Why couldn't she just wake up and spend a day—*one* day—without running or fighting or losing someone?

Most of all, she hated herself for her weakness.

This would help nothing, but she couldn't stop. Her eyes still ran with tears. Her sleeve was soaked. Her hair. The thin mattress. She kept waiting to dry up, but the tears kept coming.

She didn't know how much time had passed when she heard Soren.

"That almost killed me," he said.

She'd fallen quiet, so he must have thought she was asleep. Roar said nothing in reply.

"Are you going to eat?" Soren asked.

Food must have been delivered. She hadn't even noticed.

"No. I'm not going to eat." Roar's response was icy, every word a jab.

"Me neither," Soren said. "It doesn't look that bad, though."

"Your father runs this whole thing. Shouldn't you have a private room somewhere?"

"Whatever, Outsider."

As the quiet stretched out, Aria closed her swollen eyes. What was the point of all of their sacrifices and struggles? Why bother fighting for the Still Blue if Dwellers and Outsiders were only going to tear at each other's throats?

She thought of the Tides and the Reverie group back in the cave. Was Willow watching Caleb make his sketches? Were Reef and the Six extracting the details of their mission from Jupiter? Or were they snapping and snarling at each other like Soren and Roar?

She didn't want to fight just so there would be more fighting. She wanted to believe—*needed* to believe—that things could get better.

"So . . . that girl, Brooke?" Soren said, interrupting her thoughts. "What's she like?"

"Get her out of your head right now," Roar said.

Soren huffed. "I saw her looking at me when we were changing into our uniforms."

"She was looking at you because you're built like a bull."

Soren's laugh was nervous, clipped. "Is that good?"

"It'd be great if she were a cow."

"What's your problem, Savage?"

Aria held her breath, feeling like the future of everything hinged on Roar's response. *Come on,* she silently pleaded. *Say something, Roar. Say anything to him.*

Roar gave a long sigh of resignation. "Brooke is a Seer, and she's lethal with a bow. She doesn't have the same range as Perry does, but she's as good a shot. Maybe even better— but don't ever tell him I said that. She comes off harsh until you get to know her, and then she's . . . less harsh. She's as competitive as they come and about as loyal. You already know what she looks like, so . . . that's Brooke."

"Thanks," Soren said.

Hearing the smile in his voice, she smiled too.

"Oh, one other thing you should know," Roar said. "She was with Perry for a while."

"Nooooo," Soren groaned. "You just ruined it for me."

Agreed, Aria thought. *Ruined it for me, too.*

"So, he got Brooke *and* her," Soren continued, indignant. "How does that even happen? He barely talks!"

168

Roar answered smoothly, like he'd given this some thought. "He ignores girls, and it drives them mad."

"I can't tell if you're being serious," Soren said.

"Oh, I am. I could put on a show, I could get *everyone* laughing, but the next day I'm the one who gets the questions. 'Why was Perry so quiet? Was he angry about something? Was he sad? What do you think he was thinking, Roar?'"

Aria bit her lip, teetering between laughing and crying. She'd been groomed into a performer, but he was a natural. Listening to him doing women's voices was almost too much.

He went on. "Girls don't understand that he was *being* quiet because he *is* quiet. It makes them crazy. They can't resist trying to draw him out. They want to *fix* his quietness."

"So, you're saying I should ignore Brooke?" Soren asked.

"Look, I don't think you stand a chance no matter what you do, especially now that I know you better, but yes. Ignoring her is your best move."

"Thanks, man," Soren said, his tone earnest. "If I see her again, I'm going to do that."

If.

It seemed like that *if* was always there. The tick after the passing of every second.

If they got out of the Komodo—

If they reached the Still Blue—

If she saw Perry again—

She wanted the conversation to turn back to lighter things, to Roar's stories and Soren's sarcasm, but the moment had passed.

Aria wiped her cheeks, as though it would erase a few hours of crying from her face. She sat up, moving to the edge of her bed.

Soren sat on the lower bunk opposite her, his boxy frame propped over his knees. He was kneading his hands. Roar leaned against the bed frame, his crossed feet wiggling anxiously. Seeing her, they both froze.

She knew she must look like a mess. She felt like she had a sticky, salty film over her skin. Her eyes were almost swollen shut, she'd given herself a crying headache, and her wounded arm, her vestigial appendage, was curled tightly at her side.

It was a stupid time for vanity, considering everything that was happening, but she couldn't remember ever feeling so pathetic.

Roar climbed up and sat beside her. He brushed her damp hair off her forehead and stared down at her with so much concern in his brown eyes that she had to fight back a fresh wave of tears.

"I hope you're still angry with me," he said. "I deserve it."

She smiled. "Sorry to disappoint you."

"Damn," he said.

Aria looked at Soren, eager to focus on getting out of there again. "Did you talk to your father when they took you earlier?"

170

He nodded. "I did. He said his hands are tied. He didn't actually use those words, but it was all this 'Sable and I have a contract' and 'Sable is not one to underestimate others' type of thing."

She locked eyes with Roar and knew they were thinking the same thing: Hess was afraid of Sable. It didn't surprise her. Was there *anyone* who didn't fear Sable?

"My father said he would take me and you back," Soren said to her. "He'll bring us to the Still Blue. But no one else. The Hovers outside are all they have, and they're expecting the crossing to be pure Aethery hell. He said he can't take anyone who'd make it more difficult."

His gaze flicked to Roar, but it wasn't hostile. If anything, it was apologetic.

"You should go with him, Soren," Aria said. "You did everything you could. You should save yourself."

He shook his head. "I finish what I start." He ran a hand over his hair and lifted his shoulders. "And anyway, I'm not going to just leave you two here."

You two.

It was a subtle nod to Roar, who went still at her side, absorbing it. Then he tipped his head at Soren, like they'd come to a silent understanding.

Progress, she thought, feeling a small surge of optimism.

At least here, between these two, walls were coming down.

★ ★ ★

A short while later, the door slid open.

Loran stood at the threshold, his intense gaze settling on her. "Come with me. Quickly."

Aria didn't hesitate; her instincts told her to go. She slipped off the bunk and followed him into the corridor.

He was alone, she noticed. Earlier he had brought two other men to escort her to the meeting, but she'd been with Roar then.

Next she noticed the quiet emptiness of the halls. She tuned her ears, unnerved. The sounds drifting through the corridors were odd: the soft groan of metal, a faint screeching sound that raised the hair along the back of her neck. She knew that sound.

"There's a storm outside," Loran said quietly. He walked behind her, where he could anticipate any move she made. She knew without looking that his hand rested on the gun at his belt. "The Aether's close. Only a mile or so away. The fleet of Hovers needed to be moved to safety, so we're at half capacity."

He was an Aud, she realized. He had noticed her focused hearing. *Recognized* it.

"What about the Komodo?" she asked. "Are we moving?"

"The Komodo isn't fast enough to outrun the storm. Hess says we're better off staying put."

She slowed, coming even with him, surprised he was telling her so much. Loran scowled, but she remembered his good-natured smile when he'd sparred with Liv.

"I saw you in Rim," she said. "Liv liked you."

His eyes softened. "I was lucky to have known her."

The comment was earnest and almost tender. She studied him, her curiosity increasing. His hair was black and long enough to skim the collar of his uniform. A long, pointed nose and high eyebrows gave him a natural air of superiority. He looked older than Sable by a decade.

He pressed his lips into a grim line when he caught her staring. "You're going to run into a wall that way. Turn right up ahead."

"Where are you taking me?"

"Somewhere. Hopefully in this lifetime, but at the pace you're setting, that's uncertain."

They came to a door flanked by Horn soldiers.

"Ten minutes," Loran told them. "*No one* comes in that room."

One of the men by the door nodded. "Yes, sir."

Loran's gaze flicked to Aria, his eyebrows knitting together. She saw dread and anticipation in his expression, and horrible thoughts crashed into her mind.

Until that moment, she hadn't been afraid of him. Now she realized how naive she'd been. Loran had shown unusual interest in her the first time he'd seen her. She'd been aware of *him* because she'd sensed his awareness of *her*. She looked from the door to him, fear turning her to stone and rendering her mute.

Loran cursed at her reaction. "Skies! *No.*" He grabbed her arm, lowering his voice. "Keep your mouth shut and don't utter a word about this to anyone. Not a word, Aria. Understand?"

Then he shoved her into the room.

Where she found Perry.

He lay on a narrow cot on his side, asleep or unconscious. Bare, except for a sheet pulled up to his waist. White towels were piled on the floor by the cot. Even in the dim light, she could tell they were stained with blood.

Her legs wobbled as she moved closer, overcome by numbness as she took in his condition.

His arms had always been sculpted with muscle. Now they were bloated. Swollen with purple and red marks that covered his skin. They spread over his chest and stomach. Over nearly every inch of him.

In all her life, her heart had never hurt like this.

Never.

Loran spoke quietly at her side. "I considered warning you. I couldn't decide if it would have helped or made it more difficult. He's expected to make a full recovery. The doctors have said so."

She turned on him, rage igniting in every cell in her body. "Did you do this?"

"No," he said, reeling back. "I didn't." He moved to the door. "You have ten minutes. Not a second longer."

When he left, Aria knelt by the bed. Her gaze went to

174

Perry's hands, and she had to swallow the bile that crept up her throat.

She'd always loved his hands. The way each knuckle was shaped, solid and strong, like iron held him together instead of bone. Now she saw nothing but swollen flesh. His skin was unnaturally smooth, the contours of his joints gone, the lines that made him distorted beyond recognition.

Strangely, his face had been left untouched. His lips were chapped, and the scruff on his jaw seemed darker against the paleness of his skin, brown instead of blond.

His nose was perfectly, normally, beautifully crooked.

She leaned close, afraid to touch him, but needing to be near. "Perry . . . ," she whispered.

His eyes opened. He blinked at her slowly. "Is it you?"

She swallowed. "Yes . . . it's me."

He looked to the door and back, then began to rise. "How did you—" He froze and made a sound deep in his throat like he was holding back a cough.

"Stay still." Carefully, she lay down beside him. There was just enough room for both of them on the small cot. She ached with the desire to hold him, but this was as close as she'd let herself be.

She stared into his eyes, seeing deep shadows that had never been there before. His eyes drifted shut like he was trying to hide them, almost closing. His eyelashes were dark at the roots and almost white at the tips.

With only his face in sight, she could almost imagine he

wasn't hurt. That they weren't imprisoned here. She could almost put herself back to when they'd traveled to Bliss in search of her mother.

They'd spent their nights this way, close, trading hours of sleep in favor of talking and kissing. Sacrificing the rest they needed for just another minute together.

Her eyes began to blur. She didn't know how to handle this.

Perry spoke first. "I don't want you to see me this way. . . . Can you pull the sheet up?"

She reached for it. Her hand settled on his ribs instead. He tensed beneath her fingers, but it couldn't have been from pain; she was barely touching him.

"I can't," she said.

"You can. I know that's your healthy hand."

"I don't want to."

"This is hurting you. I know it is."

He was right, she was in agony, but she wouldn't let him endure this by himself.

"I can't because I don't want you to hide from me."

He pressed his lips together, the muscles in his jaw flexing.

Shame. That's what she saw in the shadows in his eyes. In the tears that pooled there.

He closed them. "You're so stubborn."

"I know."

He fell quiet. Too quiet, she realized, as the seconds passed. He was holding his breath.

"It wasn't a fair fight," he said. "Otherwise I would have won."

"I know," she said.

"You know a lot."

He was struggling to make light of this. But how could he? She moved her hand over the ridges of his ribs. Beautiful skin, marred by bruises.

"I don't know enough. I don't know how to make this better." Anger swelled inside her, the pressure increasing in her chest. In her heart. It mounted with every bruise she drifted over. "Only a monster could do this."

Perry's eyes fluttered open. "Don't think about him."

"How can I not? How can *you* not?"

"You're here. I only want to think about you right now."

Aria bit back the words she wanted to speak. *Tell me you're furious.* She wanted to hear him rage. She wanted to see a hint of the fire that always seemed to burn inside him. After this—after what he'd been through—would he ever be the same?

"I keep thinking about us," he said. "How we were at Marron's and afterward, when it was just the two of us. It was so good being with you." He licked his lips. "When we get out of this, let's go somewhere again. Me and you."

The tension in her chest loosened, relief washing over her. He'd said *when*. Even in his beaten condition, he believed in *when*s and not *if*s. She never should have doubted his strength.

"Where do you want to go?" she asked.

His smile was faint and lopsided. "Doesn't matter . . . I just want to spend time alone with you."

Aria wanted exactly the same thing. And she ached to see him smile—*really* smile—so she said, "And this isn't good enough for you?"

24

PEREGRINE

Y ou're cruel to make me laugh right now," Perry said, trying to keep as still as possible. Any sharp movement and his ribs felt like they'd crack.

"Sorry," Aria said. She was smiling, her lower lip trapped between her teeth.

"Yeah . . . you look sorry."

He couldn't believe she was here. She had no idea what her scent alone was doing to bring him back. He'd retreated deep into his mind since Sable left. Perry wasn't sure if it was his own doing, or if he'd been slipping into unconsciousness, but it didn't matter. Being alert only meant pain—until she'd appeared.

"You know I'll go anywhere with you, Perry," Aria said. Her attention dropped to his mouth, her scent growing warmer, sweeter.

He knew what she wanted, but he hesitated. Lying there

stock-still was almost more than he could handle, and he knew he looked pitiful, black and blue and swollen.

"I want to kiss you," he said. Forget pride. He wanted her too much. "Can I?"

She nodded. "You don't ever have to ask me that again. I'll always say yes."

Her weight settled lightly onto his ribs as they leaned toward each other. He expected her mouth to match the gentleness of her hands, but her tongue thrust cool and sweet between his lips, demanding as it moved over his.

His heart gave a kick in his chest, his pulse suddenly pounding. He moved without thinking, taking her face in his hands.

Pain blazed through his limbs, and he must have made some kind of sound, because Aria tensed and jerked back.

"Sorry," she whispered. "Should we stop?"

"No," he said hoarsely. "We should not."

Their lips found each other again, every rational thought vanishing from his mind. He couldn't see or feel anything beyond her. He was focused completely, wholly, on *more*.

More of her body. Her mouth. Her taste.

Aria held back, careful not to lean against him, when all he wanted was to feel her against him. He ran his hand down her thigh and pulled her leg over his hip, drawing her closer. Aches flared across his legs and arms, but his desire went much deeper. She was all lean muscles and soft curves beneath his hands, skin as soft as her hair. The snug Guardian flight suit covered her from wrist to neck—a brutally unfair barrier. He slipped his hand beneath her shirt, nearly undone by the way she arched into him.

"Perry," Aria said, her breath warm on his cheek.

He made a sound that he hoped passed for *yes*.

"Something's going on between Hess and Sable."

He froze.

She drew back, concern in her eyes. "Are you all right?"

He let out a breath, struggling to recover the power to think. "Yeah . . . I didn't, um . . . I didn't expect you to say that."

"I wish I didn't have to, but Loran's coming back. He'll be here any moment, and we should talk about this while we can."

"Right . . . we should." He pulled the hem of her shirt down and concentrated on Hess. Sable and Hess. "I noticed the same thing earlier. Hess is scared out of his mind. I scented it. Sable has him by the throat."

Aria bit her bottom lip, her eyes losing their focus. "I thought Hess would have the upper hand, since he has all the resources. All the ships and weapons. Food and medicine, too. It all came from Reverie. It's all his."

"None of that matters anymore, Aria. He's in our territory now. Out here he lives by our rules, and he knows that. Maybe he was different before he came out here—"

"No," she said. "He wasn't. He's always been a coward. When he threw me out of Reverie, he had Guardians do it. He had me spy for him. I was the one who set up his connection with Sable. And when he abandoned Reverie, he just

181

walked out and left all those people. If there's any danger or conflict, he runs as far in the other direction as he can." She looked at Perry's arms. "He never would have done this."

Perry's mind returned to that room, seeing the concentration—the care—with which Sable beat him. Obviously, Sable didn't mind violence, or taking matters into his own hands.

He had fallen silent for a few seconds, remembering. Now he jolted back to the present and found Aria staring into his eyes, her temper filling with rage.

"I'm going to kill him for this," she said.

"No. Stay away from him, Aria. Find a way to get us out of here. Use Hess. If he likes to run from problems, let's give him somewhere to go. Another option. But promise me you'll stay away from Sable."

"Perry, no."

"Aria, *yes*." Didn't she understand? He could endure anything—except losing her.

"What if Roar was right?" she said, her eyebrows drawing together. "What if Sable is a problem until we do something? Until we stop him?"

He wanted to tell her *I will*. He'd handle Sable. But he couldn't say it. Not half-naked, blue and beaten. When he vowed to take Sable's head off, he wanted to be on his feet.

She shot away from him, her feet landing on the floor with a quiet thump. Half a second later, the door opened.

The soldier, Loran, stood at the threshold. "Time's up," he said to Aria.

She moved immediately. Pausing at the door, she glanced back at Perry and put a hand to her heart.

Then she stepped out, and he numbed himself again. Shutting out the pain in his muscles. Ignoring the intense ache he always felt without her.

Loran lingered a second longer, sending Perry a cutting glance before he followed.

Perry stared at the door for long minutes after they'd gone, breathing in the residual scents in the small room. Noticing how strange the soldier's temper was, dense and heavy. A brick wall of protection. Stranger still was the glimmer of warmth behind it.

Carefully, muscles quivering, Perry rolled onto his back, absolutely certain.

Loran was more than a soldier. He wondered if Aria knew.

~ 25 ~

ARIA

"I thought you were going to talk to him," Loran said in hushed tones as he escorted her back through the Komodo's corridors.

"We did talk," she said.

It had taken all her willpower to leave Perry in that room. Even now, she wanted to turn back, but something stopped her. A nagging feeling about the man walking three paces behind her.

"That looked like more than talking."

Aria spun, facing him. "Why do you care?"

Loran stopped short. He frowned, opening his mouth to speak, then seemed to reconsider.

"Why did you take me to see him?" she insisted. "Why did you help me?"

He looked down his slender nose at her, his lips pressed tight, like he was trying to keep himself from speaking. She was desperate to understand why he'd taken a risk for her. Why he seemed so intent whenever he was looking at her. Why his dark gray eyes seemed so achingly familiar.

He had a deep musical baritone—a beautiful voice.

And he was old enough—

He was old enough—

She couldn't even let herself think it.

His head whipped to the side. Aria heard Kirra's voice, her sultry purr grating and unmistakable. Was she always roaming these halls?

Loran grabbed Aria by the arm and pulled her down the corridor. He stopped before a door and pressed at a keypad, yanking her inside as it opened.

Across a small room was another door with a rounded window made of two thick panes. Blue light came through it. Electric light that moved like a living, starving thing.

Aether.

"This way." He stepped around her, opening the door, and suddenly she was stepping outside, onto a platform framed by a metal rail, her hair lifting in the wind.

It was night. She'd had no idea. That meant she'd been in the Komodo almost two days. A sea of metal surrounded her—the roofs of the Komodo's individual units—and funnels of Aether twisted above. She saw the red flares. They had spread so much in just the time she'd been imprisoned. Everywhere she looked—east and west, north and south— the funnels lashed down to the earth, in some areas no more than a mile off. She felt the familiar prickling in the air and heard the shrieking sounds of the funnels—the sound of the Aether charging closer.

They were running out of time.

"We need to talk," Loran said behind her.

Aria turned and faced him. By the shifting light of the sky, she studied his face. His expression was too soft for a soldier. Too pleading for a stranger.

He sighed, rubbing a hand over his face. "I don't know where to start."

Emotion prickled behind her eyes. Her heart was slamming. Pounding to get out of her ribs.

He didn't know where to start, but she did.

"You're an Aud," she said.

"Yes."

"You knew my mother."

"Yes."

She pulled in a breath and dove. "You're my father."

"Yes." He looked at her, full on, the moment expanding between them. "I am."

A cold wave swept over her.

She had guessed right.

Her back thumped against the railing as that single thought ran through her mind: she had guessed right. Finally, she'd found her father and didn't have to wonder anymore. The curiosity she'd carried around her whole life could be put to rest, once and for all.

Her eyes filled, the world blurring, not for this

man—who she knew nothing about—but for her mother, who had known him. Had Lumina loved him? Hated him? Aria's mind suddenly filled with questions again, and here, standing before her, was the only person who could answer them.

She shook her head, confused. This wasn't sinking in the right way. He was her *father*. She should feel something besides curiosity, shouldn't she? Something more than missing her mother?

"How long have you known about me?" she heard herself ask.

"Nineteen years."

"You knew when she was pregnant with me?"

"Yes." He shifted his weight. "Aria, I don't know how to do this. I'm not sure if I can think of myself as a father. I don't even like children."

"Did I ask you to be my father? Do I *look* like a child?"

"You look like her."

That stole the breath from her lungs.

The sound of the storm rose up, filling their silence, and she thought about how much time she'd spent wondering about this man. Wanting to find him. He'd known about her the entire time and he'd done nothing about it.

Aria grabbed the railing behind her, fingers closing around the cool metal. She was spinning. Churning like the sky above.

"You were in Reverie. I know that's how you met my

mother." Lumina had said that much. "Why did you leave her?"

Loran's attention moved to the funnels flashing in the distance. His eyes narrowed, his black hair tossed by the wind.

Black hair *like hers*.

"This was a mistake," he said.

"I was a mistake?"

"No," he snapped. "Telling you was." He glanced at the door. "I need to get you back."

"Good. I want to go back."

Loran winced, which made no sense. How could he be disappointed? He'd just said he regretted telling her.

"You're confusing me," she said.

"That's not what I wanted. I wanted to explain what happened."

"How can you ever *explain*?" Instantly she regretted her outburst. This was an opportunity. She should be trying to convince him to help them escape. To give her information.

She did nothing. Only stood there, breathing in and out. Nauseous and numb and shaking.

Loran turned to the door, his hand hovering over the access panel. "I have one question to ask," he said, speaking with his back to her. "How is she?"

"Dead. My mother is dead."

For a long moment, Loran didn't move. Aria stared at his profile over his shoulder. She took in the way he stood there, shoulders shifting with ragged breaths, and was terrified by how much the news seemed to affect him.

"I'm sorry," he said at last.

"You've been gone for nineteen years. Sorry isn't enough."

He pulled the door open and led her back into the Komodo, where there was no wind, and no sound, and no flash of Aether.

She moved without feeling. Without thought, until raised voices up ahead pulled her out of the fog.

Standing by the door to her chamber, two Guardians were engaged in an argument with someone inside.

"Detainees are under Hess's jurisdiction, not Sable's," said one of the Guardians. "Their transport and relocation can only occur at his orders. She should be here."

Aria couldn't see beyond the Guardians' backs, but she recognized Soren's voice when he answered.

"Look, you can talk to me about protocols all day long. I'm just telling you what happened. She left half an hour ago with one of the Horns."

She glanced at Loran. Her *father*. And was suddenly afraid for him. Sable had proved that no matter who crossed him, he punished ruthlessly. But Loran was stoic, all the emotion she'd just seen on his face moments ago gone.

"Where are you planning to take her?" he asked as they walked up.

As the Guardians whirled, Aria caught a glimpse of Roar and Soren watching worriedly from within the room.

Loran's question surprised the Guardians, putting them on the defensive. They answered immediately, and in unison. "To the infirmary."

"I'll take her," Loran said smoothly.

"No," said the shorter Guardian. "We have orders."

"It's no trouble. I was heading there myself."

"We were given explicit orders from our commander to transport her ourselves."

Loran tipped his head down the corridor behind him. "Then you'd better carry them out."

She was handed off, from Loran to the Guardians. In one swift stroke, he had avoided questions and diverted any suspicion away from himself. Clever, she had to admit. She looked back as she was led away for the second time that night.

Loran was still there, watching her.

Hess was waiting alone in the infirmary.

"Come in, Aria. Have a seat," he said, gesturing to one of the cots.

The narrow room smelled antiseptic and familiar, its rows of cots and metal counters jogging Aria's memory. She pictured Lumina in a doctor's smock, her hair pulled back in a sleek bun, her demeanor simultaneously calm and alert. Lumina had made any garment elegant, and every action— sitting, standing, sneezing—graceful.

Aria didn't see herself that way. That poised. She was

messier. More impatient. More volatile. She had an artistic side, which Lumina hadn't possessed.

Was it Loran? Did these sides of her come from him? A *soldier*?

Aria blinked hard, willing herself not to think about this now.

"Where's our coffee, Hess?" she said as she pulled herself onto the cot and rested her arm on her lap. "Our little table along the Grand Canal?"

Hess crossed his arms and ignored her comment. "Soren said you wanted to see me. And he mentioned that you're injured. I've brought someone to take a look at you. I have a doctor waiting outside."

Between her time with Perry and then Loran, she had almost forgotten about the pain. Now the ache came back, originating at her bicep and rolling up her arm. "I don't want any favors from you."

Aria silently cursed herself. This was no time to be principled. He was crooked and heartless, but she could've used help for her arm. At least the pain seemed to be fading, she noticed.

Hess's eyebrows rose in surprise. "Suit yourself." He went to a rolling chair that sat by the door and pushed it in front of Aria's cot. Then he sat, propping his arms on his legs, and stared up at her from his lower position. Burly like Soren, he seemed to engulf the small chair.

As Aria waited for him to speak, she forced her mind to

clear. He had a motive for bringing her there, but she had her own motives too. He was their best chance of escaping. Since Hess never did any favors, she'd need to convince him that helping her was in his best interest. Pushing Loran as far out of her thoughts as possible, she focused on her goal.

"I've dedicated my life to keeping Reverie and its citizens safe," Hess said. "But I never expected that we would come to this. I never anticipated that I'd have to leave so many people behind. That I'd need to leave *my own son*. But I saw no other way. Soren wouldn't budge, and I had no other recourse. I created a rift between us because of the actions I was forced to take. Perhaps you also suffered as a result of my decisions."

He apologized just like Soren, vaguely, lacking any real admission of wrongdoing—a politician's apology—but his back was rigid, and the muscles in his neck seemed ready to snap. Real regret existed inside him somewhere. Maybe even a heart.

Aria nodded and tried to look touched by what he'd just said. He was moving in the direction she wanted; she couldn't afford to be picky.

"I can bring you on, Aria. I'm sure Soren told you. When Cinder is strong enough, and compliant, you can cross to the Still Blue with us. But I can't accommodate your friend."

"Peregrine?"

Hess shook his head. "No, he is a certainty. He will come. He's essential because of his connection to the boy."

"You mean Roar," she said. "You can't take Roar."

Hess nodded. "He's a danger. He has history with Sable."

She couldn't hold back a laugh. "We *all* have history at this point, Hess—don't you think? And it's not just me and Roar. There are hundreds of innocent people out there. Some of them are the people *you* left behind in Reverie. This is your chance. You can still help them. You can correct your mistake."

Red patches bloomed over his neck and his cheeks. "You are being *naive*. There's no way for me to accommodate any of them. Sable is accounting for *everyone*. There simply isn't enough room. Besides, I cannot ask him for anything else. I can't afford to give him anything more. *He* is not dealing with transitioning his people to a new environment. I *am*. Everything is different out here. Do you know what it's like to feel hunger for the first time? To lose everything you've ever known?"

He spoke in an impassioned rush, as though a floodgate of worries had opened. But he stopped himself abruptly, like he'd said much more than he'd intended.

"Yes," she said softly. "I know what those things are like."

In the pause that followed, Aria's heart thumped heavily in her chest. This was her chance to bring him over to their side. Perry's words echoed in her mind. *Let's give him another option.*

"There's another way to the Still Blue, Hess." She leaned forward. "You have the advantage. You have the ships. You don't need Sable for the coordinates—"

"I have the coordinates. That's not the issue. Control over

the boy is the only thing we lack."

"Cinder is *Peregrine*'s . . . not Sable's."

Hess drew a slow breath. She could almost hear his mind opening to other possibilities, fanning out like a deck of cards.

He wanted to believe her. She could do this. She could convince him.

"Peregrine's tribe is roughly the same number as Sable's. Four hundred. Think about it. Anything you need to know about being out here, about the outside world, Peregrine can help you—and you can trust him. You don't have that with Sable. Think about afterward. When you get to the Still Blue, what do you think will happen? Do you think the two of you will suddenly become friends?"

Hess scoffed. "I don't need friends."

"But you don't need an enemy, either. Don't fool yourself into thinking Sable is anything other than that. As much as I hate you, I won't double-cross you and neither will Peregrine. Sable *will*."

Hess thought for a long moment, his eyes holding steady on her. "Tell me," he said. "How is it that you've come to trust the Outsiders, and they you?"

Aria shrugged. "I started with the right one."

Hess stared at his hands. She knew he was imagining how he could cut Sable out. She needed to convince him, but she had to be careful. Her fear of Sable dug deep into her bones, but Hess couldn't be underestimated.

Hess lifted his head. "I want my son to come with me. I

194

want you to help convince him that he should."

Aria shook her head. "You need to help me this time. Not the other way around. This is your chance to choose right."

"I have." Hess stood and moved to the door, stopping there. "I'm not under any delusions. I know the kind of man Sable is. But I also know he won't cross me. He needs me or he goes nowhere."

"He needs you like he needs *a meal*."

Wrong thing to say; she'd pushed too far.

Hess stiffened, sucking in a breath. Then he turned his back on her and left.

Later, with Soren snoring in the opposite cot, Aria told Roar everything. She started with what had been done to Perry.

Roar sat up and pushed his knuckles into his eyes. Long minutes passed and he didn't say a word.

Watching him, Aria remembered the days after Liv had died.

She had considered not telling Roar. Did he really need to hear that the same man who'd killed Liv had tortured his best friend? But she'd needed to talk to him. She'd needed to release some of her anger or her mind would explode. And they were good at this, she and Roar. They had practice handing their worries back and forth.

She broke the silence herself, telling Roar about Loran, and that brought him back to her. He moved to her side and took her hand. He was careful. Gentle as he curled his fingers into hers.

"How do you feel?" he asked.

She knew he wasn't asking about her injured hand. "Like I finally got what I've always wanted, but it's not what I actually wanted."

Roar nodded, like she'd made sense, and stretched his legs out in front of him. "Perry and I," he said after a while, "neither one of us had the best luck with parents."

Aria peered at him. She found him looking at her from the corner of his eye too.

She knew little about Roar's past, considering how close they were. When he was eight, he'd come to the Tides with his grandmother, hungry and homeless, the soles of his shoes worn through. From the way Roar had always spoken, that was the moment his life began. He had never mentioned anything prior to that day—until now.

"My mother wasn't the most monogamous of women. I don't remember very much about her, other than that. Which makes us very different, considering Liv is the only girl I've ever been with, and she was going to be . . . I wanted her to be . . ." He sucked on his bottom lip, lost in his thoughts for a moment. "I never wanted anyone else."

"I know."

He smiled. "I know you know. . . . I meant to tell you about my father, not about Liv. Here's what I know about him." Roar released her hand and counted on slender fingers. "He was handsome."

"I could have guessed."

"Thank you—and a drunk."

"I could have guessed that too."

"Right. Well then, what am I going to say next?"

Aria sucked on her bottom lip. "That I have the opportunity to know more than two things about my father?"

He nodded. "It seems possible. He sought you out, Aria. He didn't need to help you. Or tell you who he is."

All true. "What if I hate what I learn about him? He's Sable's *right-hand man*. How can I respect him?"

"I was sworn to Vale for ten years and I hated him. An oath is a promise—and a promise can be made regardless of feeling." Roar glanced at the door, and then lowered his voice. "Aria, your father . . . he could help us get out of here."

"Maybe," she said, but she didn't see how. They were on opposite sides.

She let out a slow breath and rested her head on his shoulder. She'd always imagined that finding her father would be such a happy occasion. She didn't know what she felt now, but it leaned closer to terror.

As the minutes passed with Soren snoring in the other bunk, her mind wandered back to Perry. She pictured him walking through the woods, his bow over his shoulder. She imagined him dressed in a Guardian uniform, flashing a smile at her that carried a touch of wry embarrassment. She saw him lying on a cot, so beaten he could barely move.

"I can't stop thinking about him," she said, when she couldn't stand it any longer.

"Neither can I," Roar said, knowing intuitively that *him* was Perry. "Maybe a song will help."

"I'm too tired to sing."

Too sad. Too worried. Too anxious.

"Then I will." Roar was quiet for a moment, thinking of a song, and then he began the Hunter's Song.

Perry's favorite.

∼ 26 ∼

PEREGRINE

P erry woke to the prick of a needle in his arm.

A Dweller in a white smock answered his question before he voiced it.

"Medication for the pain," she said. "They want you mobile and well enough to speak."

Without the fear of aches lancing through his ribs every time he breathed, a feeling of intense relief swept over him. Before the doctor had left the room, he fell into a deep, dreamless sleep, until he heard the door slide open.

Some instinctive part of him knew it wasn't the doctors this time. He slid off the cot, thudding to his feet as Hess and Sable entered together.

They stopped talking as they saw him, surprised to see him up.

"Good morning." Sable's gaze raked over Perry's body in a methodical evaluation. His temper trilled with excitement, bright orange and pungent. The scent of obsession.

Hess only glanced at Perry, then crossed his arms and stared at his own feet.

Perry swayed unsteadily. From the corner of his eye, he could tell the bruises covering his arms and chest had darkened to deep purple.

Guardians stood by the door with guns, stun batons, cuffs, looking ready to pounce at the slightest movement.

He felt his mouth lift in amusement. What did they think he was going to do? Talon could have put up a better fight, but apparently he had a reputation. The Guardians looked—and scented—scared.

"You're on your feet," Sable said. "I'm surprised."

Perry was too. Now that he'd gotten to his feet, the drugs he'd been given weren't sitting well. Warm saliva rushed into his mouth; he was maybe five seconds from vomiting all over the floor.

"Is your arm sore?" he asked, buying himself time. He needed his stomach to settle.

Sable smiled. "Very."

Hess cleared his throat. His posture, his expression, everything about him seemed forgettable. Trivial. "We'll be taking you to Cinder in a moment," he said. "He's been distressed since he woke. He's concerned for you, as are your other friends."

Perry thought of Aria. If he hadn't seen her during the night, that comment would have shaken him.

"You can avoid their suffering—and your own—if you

comply," Hess continued. "Cinder needs to acquiesce. He needs to heal and strengthen. And he needs to agree to get us through that wall. Convince him, Peregrine, or none of us stands a chance."

Sable remained quiet as Hess spoke, his stance relaxed, his eyes half-open. He was humoring Hess. Letting him control this part of the proceedings.

Now Sable's mouth curved into a smile. "Bring him," he said to the men at the door.

Perry was shuttled to the room across the hall, where Cinder huddled in the corner. He looked like a newly hatched bird, folded into himself, his head bare, his eyes wide and scared.

As soon as Perry stepped inside, Cinder scampered to his feet and darted across the room. He flung himself against Perry's chest.

"I'm sorry. I'm sorry. I'm so sorry," he said, through sobs. "I don't know what to do. No matter what I do, you're going to hate me."

"Give us a minute." Perry turned away from Hess and Sable, shielding Cinder with his back. He wasn't sure if he was trying to protect Cinder or hide his own shakiness. Either way, this wasn't for them to see. "We're not going anywhere. Just give us some space."

They stayed.

"It's all right, Cinder," Perry said. "I'm all right." He lowered his voice, but he knew Hess and Sable could hear everything. "Remember when you burned me?" He made a fist with his scarred and battered hand. "That was the worst pain I've ever felt. This doesn't even compare."

"Is that supposed to make me feel better?"

Perry smiled. "I guess not."

Cinder wiped at his eyes and stared at Perry's bruises. "I don't believe you, anyway."

"Heartwarming. Isn't it, Hess?" Sable said. "I wish I could enjoy this further, but we're going to need to keep things moving along."

Perry faced them, Cinder pressing close to his side. Kirra slipped into the room, standing by the Guardians at the door. She wore an expression Perry had never seen on her face. Sympathy.

"I hope you've learned that I don't make idle threats, Cinder," Sable said. "When my rules are broken, I punish. You understand that now, don't you?"

Trembling against Perry, Cinder nodded.

"Good. And you know what Peregrine wants you to do. You know he wants you to help us?"

"I never said that," Perry said.

Time stopped. The look on Hess's and Sable's faces—and even the Guardians behind them—was worth any price Perry would need to pay.

"I like you, Peregrine," Sable said. "You know that. But things can become much worse for you."

"I'm not asking him to give his life for you."

"I can be very persuasive. Let's see. In a room not far from this one, I have your best friend, and the girl you—"

"I'll do it!" Cinder cried out. "I'll do what you say!" He looked up at Perry, his tears flowing again. "I didn't know what to do. I'm sorry."

Perry held him close. Cinder kept saying he was sorry, when he was the one who deserved the apologies. From Perry. From Sable and Hess, and everyone. Perry wanted to tell him that, but his vocal cords felt like they'd been clamped shut.

Sable moved to the door. He stopped there, his lips pulled in a satisfied smile. He had what he wanted. "Get the boy strong, Hess. Start him on the treatments we discussed—all of them. We move to the coast now."

"Not yet," Hess protested. "We can't attempt the crossing until the boy is ready. Even with the accelerated therapy programs, he'll need time to recover his strength, and we can't mobilize the Komodo in this storm. We stay here and wait for it to pass while the boy heals."

"This storm will *never* pass," Sable said. "We'll be in a better position on the coast. Poised to make the crossing once Cinder is ready."

Hess's face turned red. "Moving this unit requires foresight. There are preparations, safety checks, dangers to be considered that surpass your understanding. Your *impatience* is going to ruin our chances of surviving."

Perry sensed the energy in the room refocus, shifting to their altercation. Kirra caught his eye. She saw it too: Hess and Sable would eventually collide. Cinder still trembled next to him.

"We act now, or we die," Sable said.

"This ship is mine, Sable. *I* command it."

Sable was silent for a beat, his pale eyes sparkling. "You're making a mistake," he said, and then stepped outside.

On Hess's orders, Guardians pulled Cinder out of Perry's arms. He struggled weakly, questions pouring out of him. "Where are you taking me? Why can't I stay with Perry?"

Another Guardian grabbed Perry by the arm. Perry reacted instantly, pushing him into the wall. He wrapped his hand around the Guardian's throat, pinning him. Two men drew their guns, but Perry held on, staring into the Dweller's terrified eyes.

"Are you finished yet?" Hess asked.

"No." He was nowhere near finished, but he forced himself to release the man and step back. "It'll be all right," he said to Cinder. "I promise." Then he let the Guardians lead him back to his room across the hall.

"Wait outside," Hess said to his men. Then he followed Perry into the room.

The door closed, leaving them alone.

Hess planted his feet and drew his shoulders back, leveling Perry with a cold stare. "If my men hear any sign of a struggle, they will come in here and shoot you."

Perry slumped against the cot. "I could kill you silently if I wanted to." His body hadn't liked the burst of strength he'd used moments ago. His muscles quivered and chills raced up his back, nausea and fury battling inside him.

"So violent," Hess said, shaking his head. "Don't think

I've forgotten that you broke into my Pod and shattered my son's jaw."

"He attacked Aria. You're lucky that's all I did."

Hess lifted his chin, defiant like Soren, but his temper brought blue flashes to the edges of Perry's vision. Hess feared him. Perry was beaten, unarmed, barefoot, but Hess was still afraid.

"I wouldn't have let Sable hurt Aria," Hess said.

"Then you should have spoken up."

"You shouldn't have made this so difficult! As a leader, you must know that the individual serves the group. The sacrifice of one man for the safety of many cannot be so different to your kind."

"It isn't."

"Then why have you resisted?"

Perry didn't answer at first. He didn't want to have this conversation with a man he didn't respect. But he needed to say what he felt aloud—for himself. It was time to accept what he'd known for weeks.

"I knew there'd be no chance for anyone without his ability. But I had to let him decide his own fate." Perry could have ordered Cinder; the boy would've done anything he asked. But this way, Perry hoped, Cinder would feel like he'd kept some small sense of control over his own life. Cinder had been pressured, but he'd still made the choice in the end.

Hess made a huffing sound. "You're his leader. You should have commanded him."

Perry shrugged. "We see things differently."

"How can you pretend to be so noble? Look at you. Look at what Sable's done to you."

"I don't pretend, and these bruises are nothing compared to what Sable will get in return."

Saying those words, the hunger for revenge opened up inside him, terrifying and powerful. He was no different from Roar. He'd only ignored the urge. But he couldn't anymore.

Hess ran a hand over his face, shaking his head. "Your problem is that you want to challenge Sable forcibly. This is not a test of strength! We are not in the medieval era! It is about *leverage* and *strategy*." He waved a hand, growing more anxious. "Look around you. I have control of everything. The Komodo. The fleet of Hovers outside. All the medicine, food, and weapons. I gave Sable some pistols and stun batons, but they are *toys* compared to what I have kept locked away. Medicines. Food. Communications. They are all under me. We go nowhere and do nothing unless I command it."

"You left people off your list," Perry said.

"Nonsense. They're mine too," Hess spat.

"You're sure?"

"I have been a commander far longer than you've been alive, Outsider. My pilots and Guardians are highly trained. If you think Sable's going to—"

The blare of an alarm exploded into the chamber. Hess's eyes snapped up to the speakers.

Perry's balance faltered as the floor kicked up, a feeling

206

like falling in reverse. He jumped off the cot as the room continued to rise in upward lurches. He found his balance and met Hess's shocked gaze just before Hess fled the room.

The Komodo was on the move.

ARIA

"How long have we been here?" Aria asked. "In the Komodo?"

"Forty-eight hours, give or take," Soren said. "Why?"

"I had forgotten it's mobile," she said.

They had their established places in the room now. Soren on the lower bunk nearest the door. Her on the other. Roar alternated between sitting beside her and pacing the small space between the beds.

The Komodo had been moving for an hour; the constant vibration reminded her of train rides in the Realms but far rougher. Occasionally, the chamber jerked sharply one way or another. For the first ten minutes, she'd grasped the bed frame and braced herself when that happened. After a particularly violent jolt, she'd decided not to let go.

"Does this thing have square wheels?" Roar muttered beside her.

"Wheels are circular by definition," Soren said. "But, no, the wheels aren't square. They're on a continuous track with advanced suspension designed for maneuverability and tactical strength, not for bursts of speed."

Roar glanced at her, a crease appearing between his eyebrows. "Did you get any of that?"

She shook her head. "Not much. Soren, what did you just say?"

Soren sighed, exasperated. "This thing weighs . . . I don't even know how many tons. It weighs *a lot*. Moving it is like moving a small city. To do that efficiently over any kind of terrain, each of its segments sits on a rail system—wheels that roll on a track, sort of like old tanks. The track distributes the weight over a large area and makes us stable, so you shouldn't worry that we'll tip over. We won't. The Komodo can climb over anything. What you *should* worry about is the fact that they're forcing a workhorse to be a racehorse."

"I liked it better when I didn't understand him," Roar said.

"They're trying to outrun the Aether storm," Aria said, but that made no sense. Hadn't Loran told her that running was futile? Hadn't he said that Hess recommended weathering the storm in place?

Soren snorted. "That's not going to happen. The Komodo doesn't run; it *crawls*. My father might be an idiot, but he isn't stupid. He wouldn't have issued the order to move during a storm. The Komodo is more vulnerable when it's mobile, since it makes a bigger target for the funnels."

The answer clicked in Aria's mind. "Sable overpowered the ship. Either that or he's forcing Hess to move."

"Neither one of those is good for us," Soren said.

Aria looked up sharply. The lights in the chamber flickered on and off in an erratic rhythm.

Soren waved his hands in a *there you go* gesture and they fell quiet, listening to the deep rumble of the engine.

"I don't think I ever thanked you," Roar said to her after a little while, "for getting us out of Rim."

She saw his handsome face in snatches between moments of darkness, and knew he was remembering that horrible night. Liv thudding onto the stones of the balcony. Their plummet into the Snake River. "You're welcome."

"Tough fall we had."

"It was," Aria said. "But we landed in one piece."

Roar stared at her intensely. His eyes welled with tears, and he looked like he was concentrating. Like he was trying to determine if he actually was in one piece.

She put a hand on his arm. "We did . . . right?"

Roar blinked. He gave a slight nod. "There are moments I think so."

Aria squeezed his arm, smiling. The possibility of wholeness was all she wanted for him.

Maybe his grief was like her wounded arm. Slowly healing. Gradually becoming less consuming as life delivered other worries and other joys. Other sources of pain and happiness. She wanted that for him. More life. More happiness.

Roar's mouth pulled into a smile—a beautiful smile she hadn't seen in weeks.

"Beautiful, huh?"

She drew her hand away, giving him a small push on the shoulder. "Don't act surprised."

"I'm not. Always nice to be reminded, though."

"I give up," Soren said, shaking his head. "Congratulations. You two are the first code I can't break."

"Just trying to see some good in the bad," Roar said.

"You want good news?" Soren said. "I've got some for you. If the Komodo has a complete breakdown because of this Aether storm and it collapses and cracks open and we don't die first, we might actually have a chance of escaping."

Roar narrowed his eyes thoughtfully. "I'd take those odds."

Aria swept her hair forward, twisting it around her finger. "So would I." She wanted the lights to hold steady. She wanted a shower. Coffee. A thick, soft blanket. And Perry, most of all. "If the Komodo has a complete breakdown, then I might too. Wait . . . I already did that." She smiled at Roar. "My breakdown is out of the way."

He lifted his eyebrows, smiling back. "You're right. That *is* good news."

A sudden bone-jarring jolt sent her flying. Her back smacked into the wall, she cried out in surprise, and Roar's hand clamped down on her wrist as blackness flooded the chamber.

PEREGRINE

As the Komodo shuddered to a halt, Perry sat up on the cot and counted off the seconds in total darkness.

Five.

Ten.

Fifteen.

That was enough sitting around for him.

He rose from the cot, his bare feet settling silently on the cold floor. His eyes needed little light in order to see, but there was none—not a single glowing point. Just an impossible blackness, as thick and heavy as iron.

He found the wall and followed it, feeling his way to the door. He stopped and listened. Muffled sounds came from outside—two men, arguing.

Guardians or Horns, he couldn't tell, but it didn't matter.

He briefly considered trying to find a weapon but abandoned the idea. His chamber contained only a few towels and a cot that was bolted to the floor. He was dressed in loose-fitting pants only; he hadn't even been given shoes or a shirt for fear he'd turn them into weapons. He might have attempted exactly that if he'd had either, but with nothing at his disposal, he'd just have to improvise.

Perry's hands drifted over the control panel set in the wall beside the door. Hess and others had used it to come and go, but with no power, the panel was useless—which meant the locking mechanism might be useless as well.

He familiarized himself with the release bar for a few seconds. Then he unlatched it and pulled. The door slid open.

In the corridor, two Guardians were carrying on a panicked exchange. Perry spotted them easily, as both were using the red sighting lasers on their pistols for illumination. One man stood only steps away, his back to Perry; the other stood farther down the corridor. They broke off sharply at the sound of the opening door.

"What was that?" said the closest Guardian, wheeling around and searching the darkness.

The thin beam of red light from the other man's weapon swept toward Perry.

"Stop! Don't move!" he yelled.

No chance of that. Perry drove his legs the few short steps to the nearest Guardian. As he reached the man, he thought better of delivering a punch with swollen knuckles and fingers. He slammed his elbow across the Guardian's face, pain ripping through his muscles. Then he grabbed the weapon and drove the stock into the man's stomach.

The Guardian fell, smacking to the floor.

Down the hall, the other man opened fire.

A loud metallic *ting* exploded behind Perry. He dropped to his knees, shouldering the gun as he aimed for the Guardian's legs and squeezed the trigger.

Nothing. The safety switch—something he never had to consider with a bow. He flipped it, pressed the trigger again, and didn't miss.

Standing, he flew down the corridor, bursting with the need to take action. To find Cinder, Aria, Roar. With Hess and Sable chin-deep in a crisis, this was their chance of escaping.

Halfway down the corridor, a high-powered flashlight blinded him. He brought a hand up, shielding his aching eyes, blinking until he saw Hess appear at the far end.

Half a dozen Guardians stood with him, guns raised, demanding that Perry surrender his weapon.

Outnumbered and outgunned, Perry let out a curse and tossed the gun to the floor.

Hess came forward, his gaze flicking to the Guardians Perry had overpowered. "You make yourself very hard to like, Outsider." The bright light swung to the end of the corridor. "Get them to the infirmary," Hess commanded the men behind him. Then to Perry, he said, "We have only minutes. Come. Quickly."

Having no other option, Perry followed. Guardians fell in behind him as Hess led the way, hurrying through the tunnels of the Komodo. Perry felt like tearing the walls down with his hands. For a few moments there, he'd felt hope, and a taste of freedom.

Far sooner than he expected, Hess led him into a chamber. He found himself staring at Aria, Roar, and Soren, Hess's flashlight moving from one stunned face to the other.

Neither Roar nor Soren hid their shock when they saw the dark welts over Perry's arms and chest. Shame made his face burn, but Aria moved to his side, weaving her fingers gently through his, her touch bolstering him.

Hess posted his men outside, and waited until the door closed before he spoke. "This will need to be brief, which means you listen unless I ask you to speak." He paused and they drew into a tighter circle, waiting for him to continue. Soren was smiling, failing to hide his pride. Hess acknowledged his son with a nod, and then lowered the beam to their feet, creating a pool of light across the floor.

"If we are to ally ourselves," Hess said, "if I am to carry your tribe to the Still Blue, Peregrine, Sable will need to be expelled. His men will need to be thrust from this ship and my fleet of Hovers. That will require planning and coordination to execute successfully."

Perry felt Aria shift beside him. This was what they'd expected. Sable was taking control. Hess couldn't ignore it any longer. He was changing sides. "How long do you need, Hess?"

"Eight hours. We'll move in the morning."

"No. That's too long."

"You're making demands already, Peregrine?"

"You've already taken a hit. Sable is commanding your men. He'll take them all if you give him the time."

"You think I don't know that? That is precisely why I need to know how deep he has already struck before we proceed. A coup won't work unless I can trust those who enact it. In eight hours, when everything is in place, we'll leave the Komodo behind and take the Hovers."

"Give me a knife," Roar said. "I'll end this in ten minutes."

"Do you think I haven't considered that?" Hess said. "What do you think the Horns would do if Sable were slain? Lay down their weapons and surrender?"

Perry knew they wouldn't. With their survival at stake, they would stand and fight with or without Sable. In order for the Tides to be in, the Horns needed to be out—all of them. "Two hours, Hess."

"Impossible. I need time to coordinate the effort, or he'll know. He watches everything. He is shrewd, manipulative, and organized. He is a nightmare. A demon that wears a smile as he sinks his fangs into you."

"He's human," Perry said. "I'll prove it to you when I cut out his heart."

The comment seemed to get through to Hess. His brow furrowed in concentration; his small eyes honed in on Perry. "Four hours. Not a minute less."

Perry nodded, accepting the compromise. He glanced at Roar and Aria, wanting to get them out of there now, but Sable couldn't suspect anything. That meant they needed to stay put.

"What about this meeting?" Aria asked. "What if he finds out about us?"

"Right now," Hess said, "we are experiencing an unfortunate mechanical malfunction caused by an Aether storm. *Coincidentally*, that has happened while Sable and most of his men happen to be in other units of the Komodo. The few Horns who are in this one are in areas suffering from complete power outages. They're being watched by my men with night-vision eyewear as they fumble about in the dark."

"You staged this entire thing?" Aria asked.

"Sable is deep on the inside. It was the only way." Hess turned the flashlight on Perry. "The only thing I didn't account for was natural night vision among my captives. You could have ruined everything if I hadn't intercepted you."

Perry said nothing. Planning the Komodo's breakdown so they could meet in secret was a smart move. He only hoped Hess could continue to outmaneuver Sable. "You have to stay away from him. Sable will know if you plan to betray him, just as I'd know."

Hess waved a hand dismissively. "I'll take care of it."

"You don't understand. He will *scent* your distrust. Your intention to betray him."

"I *said* I will take care of it," Hess repeated. "Four hours. No one even thinks about leaving until then. And I need an assurance from you, Peregrine. If I do this, you promise me you'll get Cinder to break through that wall. You make sure he does it, or we have no deal."

Perry felt sick, but he held Hess's gaze. "You have my word."

The tension eased from Hess's face. "Good."

Aria inched closer. Perry felt her arm rest against his, but he couldn't look at her. He didn't want to see her disappointment—or her approval. Barely a second had passed and he already wanted to unmake his own promise.

"Is that all?" Hess said.

"No," Perry said. "I'm going to need some clothes." He wanted his own clothes. The reassuring weight and toughness of leather and wool. But he'd settle for anything that would keep the bruises Sable had given him out of sight.

Hess nodded. "Of course."

Emergency lights flickered on, a deep crimson color washing over the small room.

"Hurry!" Hess said. "We're out of time. Back to your chamber!"

Perry pulled Aria to his chest, wrapping his aching arms around her. He caught Roar's eye. "Keep her safe."

Roar nodded. "Of course. With my life."

Perry pressed a kiss to the top of Aria's head; then he plunged back through the corridors until he was imprisoned again.

29

ARIA

"How much time is left, Soren?" Roar asked.

"When you asked me that five minutes ago, I guessed three hours."

"What's your guess now, Soren?"

"Two hours and fifty-five minutes, Roar."

Roar dropped his head, peering at Aria through a fringe of brown hair. "I knew he was going to say that."

She forced a smile, feeling restless too. Three more hours until she was free of this room and back with Perry.

The Komodo was moving again, but at a slower pace. She imagined what the caravan would look like from outside: uncoiled, stretched out like a centipede under a sky full of Aether funnels. Every few minutes, the room shifted without warning and she braced, expecting it to stop, but the Komodo kept grinding along.

"You know what I want to know?" Soren said from the

other bunk. "Why neither one of you is talking about Perry. Is torture normal out here? Is it like, 'Yeah, I was brutalized today. Kind of boring. What about you—what did you do?'"

"I told Roar about it earlier," Aria admitted.

"Did you keep it from me because of my father? Was he part of it?"

"No, Sable did it. I didn't tell you because I didn't think you'd care. You always act like you hate Perry."

Soren nodded. "True. I *do* hate him." He leaned over his legs and shoved his hands into his hair. "What am I *thinking*? What are *any* of us thinking?"

"I'm thinking about getting out of this room," Aria said.

Roar pointed between them. "Our thoughts are in harmony."

"I'm thinking this," Soren said. "Sable killed Perry's sister. Perry killed his own brother. My father and Sable *both* left thousands of their people to die. I'm dependent on drugs to keep me sane. And we're the ones who are trying to start over? How are *we* the best hope for a new world?"

"Because we're the only ones left," Aria said. Then she realized she could do better. "We all have the potential to do terrible things, Soren. But we also have the potential to overcome our mistakes. I *need* to believe that. What point is there otherwise?"

She had to believe Hess was capable of redeeming himself. They were depending on him.

Soren lay back on his cot. He crossed his arms over his head, sighing dramatically. "What point is there indeed."

Roar also lay down, resting his head on Aria's lap. He closed his eyes, a small line of tension forming between his dark eyebrows. That line was new, since Liv's death.

Aria wanted to smooth it with her finger, but she didn't. It wouldn't make him feel any better, and what she gave to Roar could only come up to a point. No matter how much she loved him, that line of tension wasn't hers to fix.

Her thoughts turned to Loran. In hours, she'd be leaving him behind. That didn't feel right, but as Sable's closest adviser, he couldn't know what they planned to do, either. She shook her head at herself. Why did she care? She didn't owe him anything.

"If we get to the Still Blue," Soren said, "we should look at how to make more people like you, Aria."

She laughed. "*Make* more people like me? You mean half-breeds?"

"No. I mean people who are forgiving and optimistic and things like that."

Aria smiled at the irony. Her thoughts about her father hadn't exactly been forgiving or optimistic. "Thank you, Soren. That is the nicest indirect compliment I've ever received."

Roar smiled, his eyes still closed. "I'm going to miss these talks." The line between his eyebrows was almost, almost gone.

He sat up at the sound of voices out in the corridor.

The door opened, revealing a pair of Horn soldiers. "Come," said the shorter man. "We have orders to bring you to Loran."

Aria didn't remember making a decision to follow them. One second she was sitting on the cot next to Roar; the next she was moving through the halls.

The sound of people running drifted to her ears, echoing from somewhere distant. Were Hess and his men organizing the overthrow? Something didn't feel right.

"What does Loran want from me?" she asked.

"He gives us orders. We follow them," said the shorter Horn soldier. A casual answer, but tension laced his voice.

Up ahead, two Guardians came into view. They paused, doing a double take when they saw her.

Aria recognized them as the two men who had come to escort her to Hess—the same men whose suspicion Loran had deftly evaded.

"What are you doing? Where are you taking her?" they asked, voices raised in alarm.

The Horn soldiers drew their guns before Aria knew what was happening. They fired at the Guardians, the sound sending a stab of pain through Aria's ears. The Guardians reacted, diving for cover around the bend in the corridor.

The shorter Horn soldier yelled, "Go! Go! Go!" The two soldiers rushed ahead, pursuing the Guardians.

Aria bolted in the other direction.

"Stop!"

She froze, peering behind her.

The shorter man stood at the end of the corridor, aiming his gun at her. "Stay right here, and don't move!"

As soon as he disappeared, she sprinted away.

When she'd left them far enough behind, she forced herself to slow down and walk calmly. Footsteps thundered closer. Her heart seized as a pair of Guardians came running with drawn guns. Panic blazed through her, but they shot right past, their frantic exchange pricking to her ears.

"What was that? Did Hess order an early move?"

"I don't know. I've got no comm."

"Whose orders are we supposed to be following?"

"I said I don't know!"

She backtracked to her chamber, her pulse hammering. Instinct told her that Sable had moved first—just as Perry had predicted. Why else would the Horns have fired at the Dwellers back there? Sable must have learned about Hess's plan and preempted him.

The corridors bustled with activity the closer she came to her chamber. Horn soldiers jogged past, shaking the Komodo, so focused they barely gave her a passing glance. By contrast, the Guardians who streamed through the halls looked stunned and confused.

Her composure returning, she broke her objectives down. Get Roar and Soren. Find Perry and Cinder. Leave the Komodo as far behind as she could.

She'd almost reached the chamber when Loran appeared at the end of the corridor, rushing her way. His eyes locked sharply with hers, like she'd shouted his name. "I'll meet you outside," he told the men accompanying him.

Aria tried to catch her breath as he walked up. She wanted to run away. Or ask him the millions of questions that swirled in her mind. She didn't do either. Her legs wouldn't move. Her lips wouldn't form a single word.

In the pause that spread between them, she realized the Komodo had stopped. Any doubt that Sable had staged a coup of his own vanished.

"I sent my men for you," Loran said.

"I didn't like them. They were shooting Guardians."

"I was trying to help you," he returned, frustration adding a rough edge to his voice. "The Hovers are leaving. Peregrine and Cinder are already outside. You need to come with me right now."

"What about Roar? What about Soren?"

"My allegiance is to Sable, Aria."

"Yes, I know, *Father.* Mine is not."

Loran shifted his weight, shadows falling over his gray eyes. Aria wished she could read the emotion in them. She wished she hadn't just spat *father* at him, like it was an insult. "Are you going to force me to come with you?" she asked.

"No—I'm not." He glanced down the hall and then shifted closer. "I want a chance to know you, Aria," he said, low and urgent. "I'm trying to prove I deserve it."

"And I'm trying to believe you!" Her voice rose, sounding shrill and unfamiliar to her own ears. She backed down the hall, suddenly desperate to retreat.

Loran didn't stop her.

He watched as she spun and sprinted away.

～ 30 ～

PEREGRINE

M ove, Tider! Hurry up!"

Struck between the shoulders, Perry stumbled forward, crashing into a man rushing the other way. Pain tore
through him, sharpest in his ribs. He recovered his balance
and glanced back.

The man escorting him out of the Komodo was a giant.
Perry's height, but built like a mountain, his eyebrows
pierced with metal studs. "You want to untie my hands? I'd
walk faster with them free."

The giant sneered. "You think I'm an idiot? Shut up and
keep moving."

Slowing his steps as much as he could, Perry scanned every
hall and chamber for Aria and Roar. For Cinder. Sable's men
poured through the narrow halls, but he saw far fewer of
Hess's men.

Perry passed a room with a group of Guardians. They

looked panicked and lost, like the rest of the world shared a secret. He shook his head. His gut feeling had been dead-on. Sable had beaten Hess at his own game. Perry had known as soon as the giant had stepped into his chamber minutes ago.

"Get up, maggot," the Horn soldier had taunted, flinging a bundle of ragged clothes at Perry. "Put those on. It's time to go."

It had been far too soon. Only an hour had passed, not the four Hess said he'd needed.

Now the giant's voice boomed at Perry's back. "Faster! Move your feet, or I'll knock you out and drag you outside!"

Perry didn't see how that would help. He'd be harder to carry; that seemed obvious.

Abruptly, the giant pushed him through a door. Perry stumbled halfway down a ramp before it hit him: after days in the Komodo, he was finally outside.

He pulled the cool air into his lungs as he took a few steps over the loose dirt. The night smelled of smoke from fires that smoldered on the distant hills. His skin prickled with the familiar feel of the Aether. The sky churned red and blue and terrifying—a fearsome sight, but worlds better than being trapped in a small chamber.

Hovers lined the field before him, just as when they'd arrived, but the Komodo looked different from the coiled snake he'd seen before. Now it stretched backward and forward, unspooled, its links running in a straight line.

"Peregrine!"

Sable stood with a cluster of men a short distance away. Perry didn't have to be pushed to walk over to him.

"Ready to see the Still Blue?" Sable smiled and lifted a hand to the swirling sky. "Eager to leave all this behind?"

"Where are they?" Perry asked, anger burning in his blood.

"Cinder is loaded up and waiting for you. You'll see him in a moment. As for the others . . . Roar is an aggravation at best, but only a fool would leave behind such a pretty girl as Aria. She'll be here soon. When this is all behind us, I hope to get to know her better."

"If you touch her, I will rip you to pieces with my hands."

Sable laughed. "If they weren't tied behind your back, that might actually concern me. Take him," he said to the giant, who hauled Perry away.

Across the field, hundreds of people loaded crates onto Hovers. They were a mix of Horns who seemed to know little about preparing Hovers, Guardians who were trying to help, and Guardians who had no idea what was happening. Angry shouts volleyed back and forth. Total chaos.

As the giant pushed him toward a Dragonwing, he noticed armed men along the roofline of the Komodo. Everywhere he looked, he saw firepower. Dwellers and Outsiders taking sniper positions. He couldn't tell whether they were working together or in opposition. It didn't seem clear to them, either.

He climbed into the Hovercraft, taking a final look across the crowds massed along the runway, hoping to see Aria and Roar.

"Keep going, Tider," said the giant. He struck Perry between the shoulder blades, sending him stumbling into the Dragonwing.

Perry moved to the cockpit. Cinder slumped in one of the four seats, looking almost asleep. He'd been given warm clothes, and a gray cap fitted snugly over his head. Off the Dweller drugs, he already looked healthier than hours earlier.

When he saw Perry, Cinder's eyes flared with relief. "They told me you were coming. What took you so long?"

"Damn good question," growled the giant. He pushed Perry into the seat beside Cinder.

A Dweller peered back from the pilot seat, his face beaded with sweat and drawn with fear—no doubt owing to the gun pointed at his head by the man in the adjacent seat.

"If it isn't Peregrine of the Tides." The man with the gun leered, showing a mouthful of brown teeth as he smiled. "You don't look like all that much."

"He isn't," said the giant.

"Heard you got your wings clipped," said Brown Teeth, his pistol never leaving the pilot's head.

As they laughed, Perry took in the situation, noticing the pilot's hands were free. They'd have to be, for him to fly the Hover. Perry drew a breath, hoping to find something in his temper besides fear.

"I'm going to tie your feet," said the giant. "If you try to kick me, I will put a bullet through your foot, and then I'll start hurting you. Understand?"

"I understand," Perry said, though he didn't really.

When the giant knelt, he kicked.

The giant's head whipped back, his teeth snapping. He fell in a massive heap, wedged in the aisle between the seats.

The pilot reacted quickly, shoving away the Horn's pistol. The soldier lunged, and the two men fell on each other, a jumble of gray and black wrestling in the close space in front of the controls.

Perry stood, hunching in the low cabin.

"What are you going to do?" Cinder asked.

"I don't know yet." Perry didn't see a knife or tool he could use to free his hands. His options limited, he turned back to the fight and waited. When he saw his opening, he drove his knee into the Horn soldier's head.

The man slumped, staggered for a long second. Enough time for the pilot to scramble to the floor and grab the fallen pistol.

He swung the weapon from Perry to the Horn soldier. His lip bled freely, dripping onto his gray uniform, and fear iced his temper, sharp and white at the edges of Perry's vision.

"Easy. Easy, Dweller." Perry could almost hear the pilot's struggle. Friend or foe? Enemy or ally?

"You're their leader," he said, through labored breaths.

For a second, Perry thought he was being mistaken for Sable. Then he realized he wasn't. The pilot knew of him.

"That's right. I'm going to help," he said, keeping his voice steady. "But I need my hands. I need you to cut me loose. . . . Can you do that?"

31

ARIA

As Aria sprinted through the narrow corridors, she watched the Komodo unravel. Dwellers and Horns pushed past her in a frenzy, their panicked voices carrying to her ears. No one knew what was happening. Only one thing was clear: the Hovers were leaving, and everyone was desperate to reach them.

Except her.

She ran, darting past people, finally reaching her chamber. The door was open. She shot inside and stared at the empty bunks.

No Soren or Roar.

Aria cursed. Where were they? She dove back into the corridors. Rounding a corner, she almost ran smack into Roar.

He yanked her close, his voice soft but scolding. "Where have you been? I've been looking everywhere for you."

"How did you get out?" she asked.

"Really?" Soren barely slowed to a jog. "You two can't talk about this later?"

Roar reached behind his back and handed her a pistol. "Hess came for us," he said, answering her question. "He's planning something. He's trying to put a stop to Sable."

Soren took them to a heavy door, swinging it open. A cool gust swept over her as she darted outside, free of the Komodo at last.

Crowds milled by the fleet of Hovers. Guardians and Horns postured around each other, occupying the same field but standing separate, groups of gray and black. Their voices were low and warning, snarls before the bite. Funnels of Aether flashed in all directions, scoring bright lines down the night sky, but the Komodo sat under a pocket of less-threatening currents—for now.

"Where's Perry?" she asked as they moved into the throng. She couldn't see over the heads around her.

Roar scanned the field, shaking his head. "I don't see him. He's probably in a Hover already with Cinder. But I know who can tell us."

Sable.

A sudden cry rose from the crowd, and the earth began to tremble, vibrating beneath her feet. She looked up, wondering if she'd misjudged the Aether. Blue and fire-red tempests swirled above, but she didn't see any funnels forming.

"The Komodo!" Soren yelled.

Aria didn't understand. People scattered away, shouting as

they searched for cover. As the crowd around her thinned, she saw the Komodo—saw *segments* of it. The command center had disengaged into individual units. Black and hunched and beetle-like, each huge segment rolled on their tracks, the roar of their engines shaking the air.

Aria's head whipped to the other end of the clearing. The Komodo units were surrounding the runway. On top of each one, she saw gun turrets rising up, their barrels aiming at the Hovers, and snipers now stood in perches along the rooflines.

Hess. He wasn't going to let Sable take them without a fight.

Aria grabbed Soren's arm. "This is your father's *plan*? To *shoot* us?"

He shook his head. "Not us. He has to send a message to Sable."

"We're all together, Soren! Look around you."

"It could work! But he better be prepared to—"

"Sable!" Hess yelled.

At the sound of his father's raised voice, Soren took off running. Aria followed, threading through the crowd, hoping Roar was still behind her.

She broke through the press and arrived at the edge of a circle of people. Hess stood at the center. Alone.

He wore full military dress. He held a gun, and he was also wearing a Smarteye.

"Sable!" he yelled again, searching the people around him. "I know you're here! Pay attention! Watch what happens when you force my hand!"

An explosion sent Aria flying backward. She fell to the dirt, the wind rushing out of her lungs, stunning her for an instant that went on forever. She rolled into a ball and slammed her hands over her ears as she gasped, struggling to recover her breath. The sound of the explosion had blown out her eardrums, and pain lanced into her skull. She couldn't hear herself coughing. She heard nothing but the rush of her own blood, her own heartbeat.

Someone grabbed her arm. She lurched away, then saw that it was Roar. Fire reflected in his dark eyes as he spoke words she couldn't hear. A massive cloud of black smoke rose behind him, blocking out the Aether.

He took her arm and helped her up. A gust of hot air blew a pungent, chemical reek into her face, stinging her eyes. At the far end of the fleet, fire engulfed a Dragonwing—part of the craft already scorched down to its steel ribs.

Roar's grip on her arm tightened. "Stay here. Stay with Soren. I'm going to find Perry. Aria, can you hear me?"

She nodded. His voice was faint, but she heard him. Not only what he said but also what he *meant*.

Roar had to find out if Perry was in the Dragonwing covered in flames.

Roar's eyes moved past her as Hess screamed again.

"Come forward, Sable! Come forward, or I will destroy every one of them! They're my ships! I will not let you have them!"

"Yes," Soren said. "Pressure him."

"Calm yourself, Hess. I'm coming."

The sound of Sable's voice rooted Aria—and everyone—in place.

"Where are you?" Hess searched the ring of people around him. "Come forward, coward!"

Aria spotted Sable as he slipped past a few of his soldiers. "I'm right here." He gestured to the burning Hovercraft as he approached Hess. "I would have come without all of that."

Panic crept over Aria with every step he took. He wore a knife at his belt. But Hess had a gun.

She sensed movement behind her. Horn soldiers closed in, forming a wall around them. Roar caught her eye and shook his head. It was too late.

In seconds, Aria felt a gun press against her spine.

Kirra smiled and said, "Hi."

They were stripped of their weapons. Her, Roar, and Soren. Trapped, all three of them. Again.

"We were going to do this together, Sable," Hess said. "That was the arrangement we made."

Sable measured Hess in that same quiet way Perry had. The way of Scires. The flames from the exploded Dragon-wing roared in the silence, the fire a bright spot against the night.

Perry wasn't in that Hover, she told herself. He couldn't be.

"Together?" Sable said. "Is that why you were planning to betray me?"

"You gave me no choice. We made a deal, and you broke it. Tell your people to stand down. We leave on my orders, like we planned, or no one leaves. I'll level every one of the Hovers to the ground."

Sable took a step toward Hess. "Yes, you've said that."

Hess lifted his gun. "Don't come any closer."

"I always keep my word," Sable said, still advancing in deliberate steps. "I didn't break our deal. You only believe that I was going to."

Aria noticed the crowd loosening. People dropped back, responding to some instinctive signal.

"I *will* shoot you," Hess said.

"Yes, yes, yes, do it!" Soren chanted at her side.

Time slowed, every second lasting an eternity. Aria couldn't move, couldn't utter a sound.

"If you shoot me," said Sable, "then my men will cut you down next. That doesn't sound like a solution, does it? It sounds very similar to what you're proposing . . . all or nothing. Lower your gun, Hess. You got what you wanted. We're at a stalemate, and we both know you won't pull that trigger."

"You're wrong about that," said Hess. "Stand *back*."

"Shoot him!" Soren screamed.

Sable's eyes snapped to Soren. "Bring him here," he said to his guards.

Hess found Soren in the crowd, his face transforming with fear. Then everything happened at once.

Soren yelled, "No!"

Sable shot forward in a flash, drawing his knife and slashing it across Hess's chest. Hess rocked back, his scream shrill as it broke into the air.

The wound was shallow, grazing instead of piercing, but to a man who'd never known real pain, it was debilitating.

Hess gasped, eyes glazing as the agony paralyzed him.

Sable moved in again.

He drove the knife into Hess's stomach and ripped downward.

Hess sank to his knees, his flesh and blood spilling through skin and uniform, pouring onto the earth.

32

PEREGRINE

P erry saw everything.

Taller than everyone in front of him, he had a clear view of Sable as he flayed Hess open.

Time came to a stop as Hess crumpled, his blood darkening the dusty earth. The moment of absolute silence felt familiar, reminding Perry of when he'd slain Vale. Power felt tangible. Its shift unmistakable. Something had just ended, and something had just begun, and every person there sensed it: a change as startling and inevitable as the first drops of rain.

Soren's scream broke the spell, a deeper sound than his father's final cry, low and anguished, springing from his gut. Then gunfire broke out, sudden and everywhere.

Perry shot forward, sprinting toward Aria and Roar. Horns and Dwellers fired at each other as they ran for the

Komodo, for Hovers, for any place to take cover. Bodies fell lifeless to the ground. Ten, then twenty, cut down in seconds.

"Aria!" he yelled, pushing through the stampede. She stood at the center of what was quickly becoming a blood-bath.

In a break in the crowd, he spotted Sable surrounded by a dozen of his men, who protected him in a human shield.

Roar's words rang in Perry's mind. *Cut off the head of the snake.*

Perry could do it. He only needed one clear shot.

Roar's whistle cut sharply through the gun battle.

Perry's head whipped to the sound. Roar stood fifty paces away. A Horn soldier held him by the arm, shuttling him to the Komodo. Perry saw Soren and Aria beyond Roar, both of them also under the gun.

Perry slowed and set his feet. He aimed the pistol, finding his mark, and pulled the trigger.

He hit the Horn soldier who had Roar—a square shot to the chest. The man flew back, falling to the ground, and Roar lunged free.

Perry sprinted again, bullets flinging past him. He'd lost sight of Aria and Soren, but Roar ran ahead of him, charging forward on the same path.

Roar reached Soren first, leaping at his captor. He fell on the Horn soldier, who careened into Soren, and all three went crashing to the ground.

Perry ran past them, seeing Aria. Then seeing *Kirra*.

"Stop, Perry!" Kirra yelled. She yanked Aria around.

Perry skidded to a stop as Kirra pressed a gun under Aria's chin. He was only twenty paces away, but not close enough.

Aria tilted her chin up, her face strained with anger. She was breathing fast, her gaze on Perry but her focus elsewhere.

"Drop the gun, Perry," Kirra said. "I can't let you leave. Sable needs—"

Aria rammed her elbow into Kirra's throat, quick and sudden.

She spun away, grabbing Kirra's arm and twisting it behind her. With a hard shove, she forced Kirra down in an arm lock, sending her face smashing to the dirt. Snatching the pistol from the ground, Aria slammed the butt into the back of Kirra's head.

Kirra went limp, knocked unconscious.

Aria jumped to her feet and ran over. "I hate that girl."

Stunned, impressed, Perry felt his mouth pull into an idiotic grin.

"We have to get out of here," Roar said. Soren swayed behind him, ashen, his eyes unfocused.

"This way," Perry said, leading them to the Dragonwing he'd been in earlier.

As they raced down the runway, he noticed battles waged over Hovers—and the Horns quickly gaining control. Every Dweller seemed to be challenged by three of Sable's men. Some were Guardians, already showing allegiance to their

240

new leader. Bodies lay strewn across the field, most of them dressed in gray.

He reached the Dragonwing and jumped inside, Aria, Soren, and Roar right behind him. Cinder waited in the cockpit, exactly where Perry had left him.

"Go!" Perry yelled.

The Dweller pilot was ready, just as they'd planned. He had the craft off the ground before the hatch closed.

33

ARIA

Aria sat on the floor with Soren in the dark hold behind the cockpit. The Hover had barely taken off before he'd begun to rock, choking on sobs.

She rubbed his broad back, biting her lip to keep from offering him platitudes. *I'm sorry. I'm here for you. You don't deserve this.*

She knew nothing she could say would help.

Her ears still hadn't recovered fully from the explosion, but she picked up snatches of conversation from the cockpit. An Aether storm had settled between the Komodo and the coast, blocking their way to the cave. The pilot—a Dweller who'd been in the craft with Cinder—described the path as *impossible* and *unnavigable* and *suicide*.

Her stomach clenched as she listened to Roar and Perry discuss alternate routes, hoping they'd settle on one worth trying. Finally free of the Komodo, she wanted desperately to get home—even if *home* meant a dismal cave.

She didn't hear Cinder, but he was in the cockpit too. They'd all given Soren space—as much as was possible in the cramped Dragonwing.

Soren sat back, wiping his eyes. "He was terrible. He did awful things. You know what he's really like. *Was* really like. Why do I even care?"

Crying had left his face red and swollen. He looked broken, his heart exposed. Nothing like the cocky boy she knew. "Because he was your father, Soren."

"I'm the one who pushed him away. I stayed in Reverie when he wanted me to leave. He never gave up on me. I'm the one who gave up on him."

"You didn't give up on him. He knew that."

"How can you be sure? How do you know?" Soren didn't wait for her reply. He pressed his fists to his face and began to rock again.

Aria glanced up. Roar and Perry stood in the narrow threshold. Shoulders together. Minds together. Both looking so aware of what Soren was feeling.

Behind them, through the windshield, she saw the sky— Aether blue and now Aether red—and she wondered how she could feel lucky with Soren breaking apart before her eyes and after what she'd just seen. But she did.

Perry and Roar. Cinder and Soren.

They had all made it out alive.

By the time they found a clear route to the coast, Soren had exhausted himself and fallen asleep. Aria sat back against the cool metal wall of the Dragonwing. Dawn had broken, the cockpit brightening by the minute, but the light didn't reach the small hold she shared with Soren. Her left arm ached from when she'd hit Kirra, but she noticed less pain in her right. She tested the movement in her hand and found she could almost close her fingers into a fist now. Stretching out her tired legs, she was struck by a pang of longing for her mother, who could have told her for certain whether the wound was healing properly.

It felt familiar missing Lumina's calm advice and assurances. But the immediate turn Aria's thoughts took to Loran was new.

It hit her then: she'd never see him again.

She'd barely spent minutes with him, knew precious little about who he was. It made no sense that she felt so crushed. But like she'd told Soren about Hess, he was her father. That alone meant something. Regardless of all the years he'd been gone, or what might have happened between him and Lumina, she *did* feel something for him.

I want a chance to know you, Aria, Loran had said.

How could those words seem so lacking *and* so promising? What more could she have hoped for him to say?

Perry glanced back from the cockpit, interrupting her thoughts. When he saw that Soren had settled, he ducked beneath the low door and came over.

He knelt beside her, his eyes shining in the dimness. "How are you doing?"

"Me? I'm doing amazing."

"Really," he said, the corner of his mouth lifting. "Come here." He took her hand and lifted her up. In a heartbeat, she found herself in a dark corner made darker by Perry, who towered over her and around her, blocking out the meager light.

Bending, he rested his forehead against hers and smiled. "I had some things I wanted to talk to you about. I think they were important, but I can't remember now."

"Because I said I'm amazing?"

His smile widened. "Because you *are* amazing." He took her injured hand, running his thumb over her knuckles. "How is this?"

She couldn't believe he wanted to know if *she* was in pain. "Not bad . . . I'm becoming left-handed." The pain was either fading day by day, or she was becoming better at coping with it. Either way, she decided to consider it an improvement. "You?"

"A little sore," he said absently, like he'd forgotten the bruises that covered him. "That move you did on Kirra was champ. It would never work on me, though."

"I could pin you in two seconds flat."

"I don't know about that." His gaze dropped to her mouth. "We'll have to see." He cradled her face with callused hands, and bridged the distance between them.

His lips were gentle and soft as he kissed her, unlike

the flexed muscles in his forearms. He felt solid and real and safe—everything she needed. She took the hem of his shirt and pulled him closer.

His kiss deepened as he leaned into her. His hands slid down her waist and settled on her hips, sending a warm wave of desire flooding through her. She wrapped her arms around his neck, wanting more, but he broke their kiss and made a low hissing sound by her ear. "You know I'm at a steep disadvantage here, right? When you want me, I feel it. It's impossible to keep my hands off you."

"Sounds like an advantage to both of us."

He drew back, giving her a lopsided grin. "It would be if we were alone." His gaze strayed toward the cockpit, a familiar, steady focus returning to his eyes. "We're almost there."

Through the windshield, she saw ocean and Aether—a sky twisting with Aether—but she found herself smiling. She couldn't wait to see Caleb again. She couldn't wait to see Molly and Willow, and even Brooke.

Perry straightened, taking her hand. "The pilot says he has the coordinates to the Still Blue. They were transmitted to the entire fleet."

"So we have that piece," Aria said.

He nodded. "We do. That's not stopping us any longer." Carefully, he wove his fingers through hers. "Aria, we need to be united about something. If Jupiter and Brooke made it safely, we've got the Belswan Hover they brought back, and now this Dragonwing. Between the two, I'm guessing

246

they'd fit a hundred people, maximum."

"It's not enough. That would barely fit a quarter of us. You're not thinking of only sending a hundred people to the Still Blue, are you?"

He shook his head. "No. I wasn't. I'm not ready to give in yet."

Aria realized she'd already known his answer. They felt the same way about this. Hundreds of years ago during the Unity, there'd been a selection to choose those who'd take shelter in the Pods and those who wouldn't. It had divided her ancestors and his, but she couldn't let that happen again. How could she value one person's life more than another? How could she choose Caleb over Talon? Jupiter over Willow?

She couldn't, and neither could Perry. They had brought Dwellers and Outsiders together, and that was how it would stay.

"We have to be prepared, Aria. Not everyone will see it the way we do."

"We'll make them see it. We'll find another solution."

"I have some thoughts on that." He glanced at the cockpit again. Roar stood next to the pilot, directing him over the last stretch toward the cave. "We'll talk later."

She knew they would, but she wanted to tell him something now, while Roar was occupied. "I have a favor to ask."

"Anything."

"Talk to him."

He understood right away. "We're fine." He shifted his

weight, his green eyes darting back to Roar. "He's my brother. . . . We don't need to apologize."

"I didn't mean that you should apologize, Perry." Roar's anger had faded in the Komodo, but he stood no chance of accepting what had happened to Liv unless Perry did. Unless they got through it together.

Perry stared into her eyes like he saw all her thoughts in them. Then he brought her hand up and pressed a kiss to her knuckles.

"I promise," he said.

They arrived at the bluff at midday.

Aria climbed down to the cove and stared at the horizon, trapping her hair against the wind in one hand. Ashes blew past her like swarms of moths, disappearing into the surf. Her eyes burned, and an acrid smoky taste slid over her tongue.

"It's from the fires we avoided to get here," Perry said, coming to her side. He tipped his head to the south. "The storms aren't moving anymore. Just spreading."

The knot of Aether that had been raging when they'd left for the Komodo had expanded. Funnels scored down a vast portion of the horizon, reminding her of the rainwater streaking down the Hover's windshield the day they'd started the Komodo operation.

"I feel like it's going to drown us. Like eventually we won't be able to breathe. Strange, isn't it? You can't drown in fire."

Perry blinked at her, his lips lifting in a tired smile. "No. Not strange at all."

He took her hand as they walked to the cave. Roar and Cinder stepped inside first, the pilot a few steps behind them.

As soon as she and Perry entered, the Tides surrounded them, sweeping Perry away. They swallowed him up with their greetings and laughter. In less than a minute, he held Talon in his arms while the Six slapped his back, jostling him. Not the gentlest welcoming, but they didn't know about Perry's battered condition. And judging by the smile on his face, he didn't seem to mind.

Aria heard Flea's happy barks and spotted him at the edge of the crowd. She caught sight of Willow just as she flew into Cinder, knocking him clean to the ground. Aria smiled. No gentle welcome there, either.

Roar stood with Brooke nearby, waving Aria over, but she couldn't join them yet. She took Soren's hand. He looked so dazed and heartbroken, his gaze hollow and unfocused. She needed to find Jupiter for him, or a place where he could have some quiet. It'd be one or the other; Jupiter and quiet didn't happen together.

As she led Soren away from the crowd, she remembered the pilot. He'd be exhausted, and terrified of this new environment. After she got Soren settled, she'd make sure to check on him, too.

Molly stopped her before she'd gotten far. She cupped Aria's face with papery hands and laughed. "Look at you! You're an absolute fright!"

Aria smiled. "I can imagine. I haven't seen a brush in days."

Molly eased back. Her gaze flicked to Soren before coming back to Aria. "Brooke told me how the mission began. You had me sick with worry."

"Sorry," Aria said, though she loved knowing that Molly had missed her. She let herself enjoy the feeling of being cherished for a moment before turning back to her tasks. "Molly, we flew in with a pilot—"

"I know. We're feeding him. Then we'll take him to the Dweller cavern. He's doing just fine."

Aria smiled at the older woman's efficiency. "Where's Caleb?" she asked. Most likely Jupiter wouldn't be far off.

"Same place. The Dweller cavern. They're all there." Molly's smile faded as she noticed Soren's silence and sensed something was wrong.

"Why are they in there? Are they still sick?" Aria asked.

"Oh, no. They've recovered, every one of them. But they won't come out of there. I'm sorry . . . I've tried."

"They won't *leave?*" Aria said. Stunned, she left Molly and hurried to the Dweller cavern, towing Soren along. As they stepped inside, she and Soren received a much more lukewarm reception than Perry and Cinder had. The Dwellers seemed more leery than relieved to see them, but Caleb came over, smiling warmly. Jupiter came too, favoring one leg, accompanied by Rune, who walked slowly in order to keep pace with him.

"I never thought I'd see *you* again," Rune said, her lips tugging into a smile.

She was Jupiter's girlfriend now, but she'd been Aria's friend first. Seeing her brought a rush of memories of times they'd spent together, with Paisley, Caleb, and Pixie. Aria's heart twisted for the friends she'd never see again.

She lifted her shoulders. "Well, here I am."

Rune's shrewd eyes studied her. "You look like you stepped out of a horror Realm."

Aria laughed, unsurprised by her directness. Rune had been the honesty in their group. A perfect foil to Paisley's unfailing sweetness and Caleb's rambling creativity. "So I've heard."

She embraced Rune, who patted Aria's shoulder and let herself be hugged. An awkward display of affection, but it was better than Aria could have hoped. At least in a small way, Rune was adjusting to life on the outside.

Aria drew back and they all stood, glancing at Soren. Looking at one another and feeling the absence of their lost home and their lost friends.

Eventually they sat, gathering in a circle. Aria kept Soren close to her side, worried about him. Jupiter and Rune held hands, and Aria wished Paisley could be there to see them. She wouldn't have believed it; greater opposites didn't exist.

Aria answered their questions about her mission to the Komodo, doing her best to avoid mentioning Hess out of respect for Soren, who listened in silence. The conversation quickly turned to her Outsider friends. Unsurprisingly, Rune wanted to know about Peregrine in particular.

"Caleb said you're *with* him?" she asked.

Caleb winced, sending Aria a little shrug of apology. She smiled, so he'd know she didn't mind. She saw no better way of helping them accept the Tides than by being open about her relationship with Perry—the exact opposite of the tactic she'd tried the first time, with the Tides.

"Yes. We're together." Saying the words aloud gave her a little shiver of pride.

"Do you love him?" Rune asked.

"Yes."

"You love a Savage? *Love* him?"

"Yes, Rune. I do."

"Have you and he—"

"Yes. We have. Can we move on now?"

"Yes," Caleb and Jupiter answered in unison.

Rune narrowed her eyes. "You and I are talking later," she said.

Then it was Aria's turn to ask questions. "Have you all been here the whole time I was away? Cowering here, in the back?"

"We're not cowering," Rune said. "We're just keeping our distance. It's easier for everyone this way." She glanced at Jupiter, who tapped a rhythm on his shoe. "They don't like us, right, Jup?"

He shrugged. "I don't know. Some of them are all right."

"What do you mean they don't like you?" Aria asked. "What have they done to you?"

"Nothing," Caleb said. "It's the way they look at us."

"You mean the same way you look at them?"

Rune quirked an eyebrow. "Well, they are disgusting."

"That's kind of sharp, Rune," Jupiter said, his hands going still.

Caleb rolled his eyes. "They aren't *disgusting*. They're just . . . *rustic*."

Aria ignored the comment. She was pretty sure she'd become *rustic* too. "How long are you planning to keep yourselves segregated? Forever?"

"Maybe," said Rune. "It's not like forever will be long. We're not going to the Still Blue. All we're doing is waiting out our last days."

The sounds of nearby conversation quieted. Aria felt the attention of others focus on them. Everyone was listening. "Just because we failed once doesn't mean we should stop trying."

"Trying to what, Aria? Make friends with the Savages? No, thanks. I'm not interested. I don't understand why you took us out of Reverie just so we could die here instead."

Soren shook his head. "Unbelievable," he muttered.

Aria had heard enough too. She stood, forcing calm into her voice as she spoke. "You think Soren and I saved your life by getting you out of Reverie? We didn't. We gave you a chance. You have to choose whether you want to live or die, not me. Hiding back here isn't either."

34

PEREGRINE

S o, what happened?" Twig asked. "The Dwellers couldn't hold on against the Horns?"

Perry sat at the edge of the wooden platform at the center of the main cavern. He'd changed into his own clothes soon after arriving. Then he'd spent a little time with Talon, catching up on the past couple of days. Now Perry was surrounded by his people, who gathered along the platform with him and pressed together at nearby tables.

He felt crowded and mildly panicked, as he always did inside the cave, but like he was exactly where he should be: immersed in the Tides.

Marron was there. Old Will. Molly and Bear, and the Six. Wherever he looked, he saw smiles. Their happiness flooded his nose with bright scents, their tempers bringing him the spring the Aether had taken.

Perry hadn't realized how scared they'd been until then. The relief he scented was potent; he wondered how many in the tribe had believed he'd never come back from the Komodo.

Nearby, Talon, Willow, and Brooke's sister, Clara, played a game to see who could jump furthest from the platform. Cinder acted as judge, Flea sitting beside him. Everyone else—everyone over thirteen—waited to hear what happened in the Komodo.

Perry looked at Roar, who was the storyteller between the two of them, but Roar smiled and shook his head.

"This one's yours, Per," he said. He tipped back a bottle of Luster, taking a healthy drink, his temper the mellowest Perry had scented since Liv's death.

Perry started with their breach of the Komodo, and then told the tribe about their imprisonment and escape, leaving out only what Sable had done to him. When he skipped that part, Reef pinned a searing gaze on him. Perry expected questions from him later.

As he talked, bowls of fish soup were passed around, along with huge loaves of bread and thick slices of cheese. A luxury, Perry knew, and he said as much.

"Oh, enjoy it!" Marron offered in a rare show of abandon. "You're home, Peregrine. You've made it back safely, all of you, and we're so happy."

He sat next to Roar, who'd insisted that Marron share his bottle of Luster. Marron's cheeks were flushed, his blue eyes carefree. Seeing him that way made Perry smile.

Reef crossed his arms. "Hess and Sable turned on each other."

Perry nodded, taking a huge bite of bread. His appetite for real food—not the Dwellers' plastic-tasting meals—was enormous. The only thing he wanted more at the moment was a bed.

A bed with Aria in it, he amended.

"We should learn from that," Reef continued. "We should take that as a warning. We're at risk of the very same thing happening here."

Perry swallowed. "What are you saying?"

"The Dwellers," Molly explained. "They're keeping their distance. They're scared of us, Perry. That's all."

Reef crossed his arms. "Fear is dangerous. It sparks violence much faster than anger. Doesn't it, Peregrine?"

"It can, yes."

From the corner of his eye, Perry caught the small shake of Roar's head. It felt so right, Reef's lectures and Roar's annoyance at Reef's lectures. The moment strengthened him more than a bellyful of food.

"The Dwellers are harmless," Molly said. "They'll mix with us now that Aria is back. I'm more concerned about other things. Perry, you said we needed Hovers to reach the Still Blue. . . . We only have two."

Perry acknowledged the problem and stated his position on the matter. Two Hovers wasn't enough, but the Tides—and the Dwellers in the back—would stand together. He and

Aria had agreed; they wouldn't make a selection of people to go.

"I support that stance," said Marron. "I'm behind you."

"I'm behind you," said Reef, "but I don't support that stance. Why should we all perish?"

"Hold on," Twig said. "Isn't there another option besides *perishing*?"

"We could try to locate more Hovers," said Marron, slurring a little.

"From another Pod?" Reef shook his head. "We don't have time for that. We don't know if other Pods even exist anymore."

They wanted to take action, which Perry understood. It was always his impulse too. But this time, their best course was simply to wait.

Sable needed Cinder. He would come to them—soon. Perry had no doubt in his mind. But that knowledge would only put the tribe in a panic, so he held his tongue. The Tides would know soon enough.

As the debate continued, Perry's gaze drifted to the children again. They took turns running up and smacking Straggler on the head, trying to get him to chase them. Cinder had moved off. He sat with Bear, looking especially small and frail next to the huge farmer whose life he'd saved.

Cinder's favorite black cap had found its way back to his head. Molly's doing, Perry was sure. She'd have had it waiting for him.

Cinder saw Perry watching him and forced a smile, though his eyes were almost closed.

"He's tired," Molly said. "I'll find him a quiet place to sleep soon, but let's give him a few more minutes. This is doing wonders for his heart." She smiled, and added, "And mine." She studied Perry, her brown eyes knowing. "They wanted him for his ability."

Perry nodded. "He's the only way to get through the barrier of Aether that surrounds the Still Blue."

Molly pressed her lips together, falling silent for a moment. "You saw what it cost him to channel the Aether in the compound, Perry. He's barely recovered at all since then. You know what it would mean for him to use his ability in his condition?"

"I do." It was all he wanted to say about it now. He shut away his worries about Cinder behind thick walls, with his memories of Liv.

Liv.

His heart began to pound. He looked at Roar, who had the bottle of Luster halfway to his mouth. Roar stopped and made a face, his eyes narrowing in question.

"Walk with me?" Perry said.

Roar's mouth broke into a grin. "Finish that," he said, pushing the bottle of Luster at Marron. Then he hopped to his feet and said, "Lead the way, Per."

Perry walked to the cove outside and kept going, climbing the bluff and then following the trail back to the Tide compound. He hadn't set out to return home; his feet just carried him there out of habit.

Illuminated by thick Aether flows, the night was as bright as twilight, as all nights were now. Ashes flittered through the air; soft as feathers underfoot. His pulse beat too fast for the easy pace he and Roar made.

They arrived at the compound and walked to the center of the clearing. Perry felt raw, like every step brought him closer to the edge of a cliff. His gaze swept across the homes, hollow and eerily quiet. Bear and Molly's house stood out, looking like a rotten tooth with its listing walls blackened and leaning at odd angles. He remembered the night Bear had been trapped under those walls.

Perry's house still stood, though. It didn't look the same, but it didn't look different, either. He stared at it for a long time, trying to figure out what had changed. Debating whether he wanted to go inside.

"Remember when I tripped you during the summer festival," Roar said, "and you fell into Vale's mug and chipped a tooth?"

Used to his spontaneous stories, Perry answered smoothly. "I remember Vale chasing me down and beating me for spilling Luster all over his lap."

"Well, you shouldn't have fallen *on* him."

"Right. That was stupid of me."

"It was. You've always been terrible at falling."

Despite their joking, Perry felt sure now that Roar was seeing all the same memories he was. All the times they'd torn through the compound as kids, barefoot, noisy, safe, no thought in their minds that this place would ever change. That people they loved would vanish.

Or be murdered.

He cleared his throat. It was time. "I'm supposed to talk to you about things. About what's been going on."

"Really? Why start now?"

"Aria. I promised her."

Roar's smile was faint. He crossed his arms and stared at Perry's house. The house that had also been Liv's.

Perry caught a sob in the back of his throat and drew a quick breath. The ache he felt for Liv was a monstrous thing, clawing at his chest. He began before he lost his nerve.

"Liv is alive in my peripheral vision. When I'm not thinking about her . . . when she's just past the point where I can see her, it feels like she's still there. Thinking of ways to embarrass me. Telling me all the stupid things you said, like I don't already know. Like I wasn't there to hear them myself. But when I look right at her, I remember she's gone and I—" He stared at the sky for a few moments, forcing himself to draw a few breaths before he continued. "I couldn't let myself feel that kind of anger. That lost. Not with the Tides needing me to be Blood Lord."

"Why don't you just tell me the truth, Perry? Why can't you ever say what you're really thinking?"

Perry glanced at him, surprised. Roar was still staring at Perry's house, his jaw clenched. "Why don't you tell me

260

what you think I'm thinking?"

Roar wheeled and faced him directly. "You *blame* me! I was there and I couldn't protect her—"

"No."

"I told you I'd bring her home and I didn't. I lost her. I—"

"No, Roar," he said again. "No one on this earth would have fought harder for her than you—and that includes me. You think I haven't thought about what I could've done to get her back? To have stopped it from happening?"

Roar's eyes blazed with intensity, but he said nothing.

"I don't blame you," Perry said. "Stop acting like I do, because I don't."

"When I showed up at the cave, you couldn't even stand to look at me."

"That's in your head."

"It's not. You're hardly subtle." Roar waved a hand. "About anything."

"You vain bastard. I wasn't *avoiding* you. You just sulk whenever you're not the center of attention."

Roar lifted his shoulders. "Maybe that's true, but you were acting like Liv never existed. I was on my own."

"Which was a disaster. You're miserable on your own. And stupid. Turning back in the Komodo was the dumbest thing you've ever done. Without question."

Roar smiled. "You're making this so easy, Perry." A laugh burbled out of him, but it didn't taper off. What started as a chuckle gained momentum, growing in volume.

Roar's laugh was wicked and high-pitched, resembling the cackle of a wild turkey. It was one of the funniest sounds Perry had ever heard; he was powerless against it. Soon they were both howling, standing in the middle of a place that was, and wasn't, home.

By the time they settled down and took the trail back to the cave, Perry's ribs ached.

"Why were we laughing?"

Roar gestured to the south, where Aether funnels scored down to the earth. "Because of that. Because the world is ending."

"That shouldn't be funny."

Apparently it was, because it got them started again.

Perry had no idea if he'd expressed half of what he'd intended. He knew he'd been selfish, leaving Roar to deal with Liv's death alone. He hadn't let himself accept that she was gone, so he'd failed his friend, and himself, but he meant to change that. He was terrible at falling—Roar was right about that—but nothing ever kept him down.

As they walked back to the cave, a piece of him that had been broken felt whole again. Nothing looked the same or smelled the same, and maybe the world was ending, but he and Roar would walk to that end side by side.

When they arrived, they found the main cavern empty, everyone already gone to sleep. Perry left Roar and headed for his tent, half-asleep himself.

Reef and Marron intercepted him on the way.

"A few words?" Reef said.

"Sure," Perry said. "A few." He was so tired; every time he blinked he felt like he dreamed.

"Did you and Roar talk?" Marron asked.

Perry nodded. "Just did."

Marron smiled. "Good."

"He's selfish and arrogant," said Reef.

"But he's good for Perry, Reef," Marron said.

Reef grunted—as enthusiastic as he'd ever sounded about Roar.

Marron reached into a satchel. "I forgot to give this back to you earlier." He removed the Blood Lord chain, handing it over.

"Thank you," Perry said, pulling it on. The weight of the metal around his neck was more familiar than comfortable. He wondered if it would ever be both.

Marron and Reef exchanged a look, and then Reef drew a noisy breath, pushing back his braids. "You brought us both into the Tides, Perry. Neither one of us would be here if you hadn't let us into your tribe."

"That's right," Marron said. "You offered us shelter when we needed it most. When you couldn't afford to, you helped us."

Perry had never felt like he'd done either of them a favor. It had always felt the other way around.

"Between my group from Delphi and Reef's Six, we're

fifty-three people," said Marron. "Fifty-three who'll willingly stay behind. We won't take the place of your tribe on those Hovers."

Reef nodded. "There's no way forward that isn't through pain and hardship, Peregrine. You must see that. It's your task as Blood Lord to do what's best for the whole—for as many of your tribe as you can help—not what's easiest."

"We'd like you to just consider what we're saying," Marron said. "That's all we ask."

Perry pretended to think for a few seconds. "It's a noble offer. . . . Did either of you think I'd accept it?"

Reef and Marron went still, neither one replying, but the answer was plain on their faces.

Perry grinned. "Well, you were right." Clapping them on the shoulders, he bid them good night.

In his tent, Perry found Cinder asleep next to Talon. Flea was rolled into a ball under Cinder's arm.

Perry knelt and scratched his coarse fur. The dog angled his head up, his tail padding against the blankets. He loved to be scratched in the soft slope between his wide-set eyes.

Perry's gaze moved to Talon and Cinder. The boys had fallen in together like they'd known each other since birth. He owed that to Willow.

"And you too, fleabag," he said.

Cinder's eyes blinked open. Perry smiled, too happy to see him there to feel sorry for waking him. "How'd you get him away from Willow?" he asked, nodding to Flea.

Lying on his side, Cinder gave a one-shouldered shrug. "I didn't do anything. He just came back with me."

"Willow was fine with that?"

The corner of Cinder's mouth pulled up. "Sorta. She told Flea he could stay with me this one time only, since I just got back."

"Generous of her, actually."

"Yeah," Cinder said. "I know." His smile widened. "She's still cursing. You thought she'd stop when I got here, but she hasn't."

"We already knew that Willow is unstoppable."

"I know," Cinder said again. "She is."

As the moment settled between them, Perry looked from Cinder to Talon, and his vision began to blur. These boys—only one of them his blood relative, but both of them family—replenished him. They gave him confidence and purpose. Wearing the chain made sense when he looked at them, when he thought of them with Willow and Clara, whooping as they leaped from a platform into the darkness. They were the future, and they were so good.

Perry pushed a bit of small talk past his lips, buying a moment to compose himself. "So, how are you doing?"

"I'm tired."

Perry waited, knowing there was more.

"And I'm scared," Cinder said. "Are we going to the Still Blue?"

"I don't know . . . maybe."

"If we do, I'll have to get us through."

Reef's words echoed in Perry's mind. *There is no way forward that isn't through pain.* He shook his head, pushing them away.

"Whatever happens, Cinder, I swear to you, I won't leave your side."

Cinder didn't say anything, but Perry scented the easing of anxiety from his temper. That seemed to be all he needed to surrender to sleep. In seconds, Cinder's eyes fluttered closed.

Perry stayed a moment longer, soaking in the quiet. Flea began to whimper, his legs twitching as he dreamed about chasing something. Perry wondered if it was the Still Blue.

He stood, moving to the trunks containing the remnants of his family's belongings. Talon's falcon carvings. Vale's ledger. One of Mila's painted bowls, which he and Liv had cracked while wrestling and then fixed unsuccessfully. These things might never go anywhere, he realized now.

He stepped out of his boots and was unbuckling his belt when Aria slipped into the tent. "Hey," he said, going still.

"Hi." She glanced at Cinder and Talon, smiling when she saw Flea, but her temper brimmed with anxiousness. He felt it coil inside his chest, stealing away the peaceful, tired feeling he'd felt a second ago.

He didn't know what to do next. He didn't know whether to pull off his belt. It seemed like a bigger decision than it should have been. Belt off was normal for him at the end of the day, but he didn't want her to think he assumed something would happen between them.

Even though he wanted it to. Badly.

He was being an idiot. She trusted him. He knew that. He'd only make this more awkward by dressing again.

He pulled off his belt and placed it on the trunk. "I went out with Roar," he said to fill the silence.

"How was it?"

"Really good. Thank you."

"I'm glad."

Her smile was genuine, but faint. Something was on her mind. Her gaze flicked to the empty bed and then to the tent flap.

He spoke quickly, worried that she might leave. "It's a little crowded, but I'm glad you're here. If you decide you want to stay. I'm glad you're here even if you don't want to stay. Either is fine. Anything you want is perfect."

He scratched his chin, shutting himself up. *Perfect?* He'd never used that word until she'd appeared in his life. "How are your friends? Caleb and Jupiter?"

"I saw them earlier," Aria said quietly. "I yelled at them."

"You . . . *yelled* at them?"

She nodded. "Maybe it wasn't yelling. But I raised my voice."

He finally understood her temper. Her anxiousness wasn't because of him; she was worried about her friends. "Did they deserve it?"

"Yes. No. In a way. They've been keeping themselves separate. Did you know that?"

"Molly mentioned it."

"I couldn't stay with them, so I left. I spent the afternoon in the Battle Room trying to figure out why they're back there." She sucked on her bottom lip, the smooth skin between her dark eyebrows wrinkling with worry. "I just expected them to be further along, and I don't know how to change the way they think. I want to help, but I don't see how I can."

A hundred thoughts flooded his mind, but they all came down to one: being a leader wasn't easy. Trust and respect had to be earned, and that only happened over time. He'd spent the winter and spring learning that with the Tides. Aria was just beginning to learn it now.

"You know I'm here," he said. "I'll do whatever I can."

"Will you come see them with me tomorrow? Maybe if we talk to them together it'll help."

"Done."

Aria smiled, then her gaze traveled to his waist. "Perry, did you know your pants are falling down?"

"Yeah." He didn't have to look; he could feel them sliding down his hips. "I, uh . . . I took my belt off to make you feel comfortable."

"You took your belt off to make *me* feel comfortable?"

He nodded, trying to hold back a laugh. "I worked it out in my head that this would be more natural."

"Your pants falling down is natural?"

He grinned. "Yeah. If they fall any further, it's going to be very natural."

She laughed, her gray eyes shining as she shook her head. "So nice of you to think of me."

"Always do."

A blush crept over her cheeks as they stared at each other, one second giving to another. Her temper filled the small space, beckoning him closer.

"In the Komodo you said you wanted us to have some time alone," she said.

He snatched his belt off the trunk and took her hand, darting out of the tent before she'd finished speaking.

ARIA

"Perry, I can't see where I'm going."

Aria jogged to keep up with him as he pulled her through the cave. He was barefoot, buckling his belt with one hand and holding on to her with the other, but she was still lagging behind. She didn't have his eyes, and at this late hour, with only a few scattered lamps still burning, the cave was nothing but blackness ahead of her, below her, everywhere. Every step she took, she felt as though her foot might never touch the ground.

He tightened his grip on her hand. "It's even footing and I won't let you fall," he said, but she noticed he slowed down.

It was a relief when they left the dark hollowness of the cave. A relief to hear the roar of the waves and to have the Aether lighting the way. The reddish glow at the edges of the funnels seemed more vibrant now than just hours ago.

"Are we swimming?" she said as he took her down to the water's edge. "Because the last time I did that wasn't very enjoyable."

She'd been in the ice-cold waters of the Snake River with Roar, fighting desperately to stay alive.

Perry gave her a crooked smile. "Same," he said, and she remembered how he'd almost drowned trying to save Willow and her grandfather. He put his arm around her shoulders, guiding her closer to the waves. "But it's the only way, and it's not far."

"Only way to what? Not far to where?"

He stopped and pointed down the beach. "There's a cove on the other side of that point."

She didn't see a cove. What she saw were waves pounding against rocks that jutted out of the ocean. "Aren't we standing in a cove right now?"

"Yes, but the one around that point is magic."

She laughed, surprised by his choice of words.

He glanced down at her, his eyes narrowing. "Are you telling me you don't believe in magic?"

"Oh, I do. But the way to the magic cove looks cold. And dangerous . . . and cold."

Perry's hand slid to her injured arm. "You can do it," he said, homing in on the real source of her apprehension.

Aria stared at the point. It was shrouded in darkness, and the tide looked rough, and she had no idea if she had the strength to swim all the way there.

"I'll be right beside you if you need me, but you won't.

And I can't do anything about the cold until we get there, but it'll be worth it. There are no problems in the magic cove. Everything over there is . . ." He paused, smiling almost to himself. "It's perfect."

Aria shook her head. How could she say no to that?

They waded out past the waves together. She started shivering when the water reached her shins. Her teeth chattered when it reached her thighs. By the time it rose up over her waist, she decided this was the best idea he'd ever had.

Every wave that crashed past them was exhilarating, sending bolts of adrenaline through her. Her mind cleared and her senses opened to the salt water she tasted. To the sound of Perry's laugh mixing with hers, and his grip tightening when the water pushed them back. She hadn't even seen it yet, but the magic cove was already perfect.

"We have to go under the next wave," Perry said, letting go of her hand. "Dive and then swim out as far as you can before you come up. Ready?"

She didn't have a chance to answer. The wave came, towering and dark and capped in white. She dove and kicked, pushing until her lungs burned for oxygen.

When she came up, Perry was smiling. "All good?" he said.

She nodded, her teeth already chattering. "Race you," she said.

They swam past the breakers toward smoother water. Cutting through the waves pushed her beyond thought, turning

272

her into pure action. It took strength and yet it demanded surrender as well. It was both, folded into one. Aria only caught glimpses of Perry when she came up for air, but she knew he was right there.

When they finally waded out onto the beach, she was in desperate need of warmth, but she felt better than she had in weeks. The cold had numbed her arm, allowing her to move freely without guarding herself against pain.

Perry pulled her to his side. "What did you think?" he asked, smiling.

"I think you should look more tired." He'd moved through the water with the same power and effortlessness with which he did everything.

"Not with you to look forward to. Let's get a fire going."

Shivering, Aria hurried to gather driftwood. Nearby, Perry hoisted a large piece over his shoulder. He seemed unbothered by the bruises that still covered his arms and legs. Shaking a strand of seaweed from a branch, she remembered a story Roar had told her.

"Did you really sneak into the compound once wearing only seaweed?" she asked.

"Had to." He dropped the wood onto a growing pile. "Liv swiped my clothes. It was either seaweed or nothing, and I wasn't keen on the idea of strutting into the compound completely bare." He smiled. "For days afterward I woke up to seaweed hanging on my front door."

Aria laughed. "The Tides wanted an encore?"

Perry knelt and began stacking the wood. "Never found

out. . . . It was probably Liv again. She was like that. She could never let something go."

Aria couldn't see his face, but she knew from the tone in his voice that he wasn't smiling anymore. While it hurt to see him suffer, it felt better than seeing him retreat behind walls. Liv was gone, but he was letting her back into his life in a new way.

"I wish I'd known her better, Perry," she said, adding her wood to the pile.

"If you spent an hour with her, then you knew Liv. My sister was . . . she was . . ."

He trailed off, so she finished for him. "Like you."

"I was going to say willful and hardheaded." He smiled. "So, yeah . . . like me." He took a piece of flint and a dagger from the sheath at his belt. "How's your arm?"

"Surprisingly good," she said, sitting on the sand.

"I knew you'd be fine. What'll really be surprising is if I can get this lit." He turned his back to the wind, bending over his hands. He had sparks flinging into the tinder within seconds. She watched him blow the flames to life, consumed by him. He was as wild as the fire. As vital as the ocean. His own element.

He peered up as the fire took and smiled. "Impressed?"

She wanted to say something quick-witted, but she said the simple truth. "Yes."

"Me too," he said, putting the blade away.

They sat, growing quiet as they let the fire warm them. Since they'd reached the magic cove, they hadn't spoken

274

about Hovers, or about Sable or the Still Blue. It was almost like being free. She realized the last time she'd been this relaxed, this happy, had also been with him.

Perry shifted beside her, sitting forward and draping his arms over his knees. The bruises on his forearms were fading, and his hair was drying in spirals.

She'd only meant to glance at him, but the lines that made him—the muscles along his arms and shoulders, the angle of his jaw, and the crook in his nose—were lines that mesmerized her.

He glanced over. Then he moved to her side and put his arm around her. "Are you trying to kill me with that look?" he whispered by her ear.

"I was trying to get you over here—and it worked."

He brushed a kiss over her lips and then took her hand. "You know how Roar calls you Halfy and Ladybug?"

She nodded. Roar was always coming up with pet names for her.

"I want to call you something too. Something special. I've been thinking about it for a while."

As he spoke, Perry absently pressed his hands around hers, wrapping them in a cocoon of warmth. He ran so hot. The chill melted out of her fingers in seconds.

This was *them*. Everything that passed between them felt easy and right.

"You have?" She'd always loved that he called her Aria. She had plenty of nicknames. Her mother had called her Songbird. Roar called her just about everything else. Perry—after the initial period of *Mole* and *Dweller* when they'd first come together—had taken to calling her, simply, Aria.

It wasn't simple, though. Spoken in his unhurried, golden voice, the sound of her name became something beautiful. It became what it was. A song. But a nickname was what he wanted, so she said, "What have you come up with?"

"None of the usual things are good enough for you. So I started thinking about what you mean to me. How even the smallest things remind me of you. Last week, Talon was showing me his bait collection. He keeps this jar of night crawlers, and I wondered what you'd think of it. If you'd find them disgusting, or if you wouldn't mind them."

She smiled, seeing an opportunity she couldn't resist. "Night crawlers, as in earthworms? You want to call me Earthworm?"

His laugh was a burst of surprise. *"No."*

"I could get used to . . . Earth . . . worm."

He shook his head at the sky. "I never say the right things to you, do I?"

"I don't know. I think I might like Night Crawler even better. It almost sounds dangerous—"

He moved suddenly. In an instant she was on her back on the sand, pinned beneath him. She was reminded of his strength—and just how careful he usually was with her.

"Now you're making me desperate," he said, his eyes moving over her face slowly.

He didn't look desperate. He looked focused. Like he knew exactly what he wanted. Her hands were splayed on his chest. Was he trembling or was she?

"Tell me what to say. What can I say to make you want me the way I want you?"

The words sent a thrill up her spine, making her shiver. She smiled. "That worked." She pulled him down and kissed him, needing his warmth. Needing his mouth and his skin and his taste. Her fingers found the hem of his shirt. She pulled it over his head and found him smiling, his hair ruffled.

He leaned down, bracing his arms on either side of her, his lips soft as they kissed a trail from her mouth to her ear. "What I was trying to say," he whispered, "is that I see you in everything. There isn't a word for you that means enough, because you're everything to me."

"Perfect words," she said, her smile wobbling with emotion. "Magical."

He looked into her eyes, flashing a proud grin. "Yeah?"

She nodded. "Yes."

His mouth found hers again, his kisses hungry, his weight settling onto her. She wove her fingers into his damp curls, and she was gone. Swept away. Nothing else existed beyond his body and hers, moving like strength and surrender, folded into one.

Cinder and Talon still slept soundly when they returned to Perry's tent, but Flea was gone.

"Willow," she said.

Perry nodded. "He stayed longer than I thought he would."

After they changed into dry clothes, Aria curled against him, comfortable and warm.

She listened to his heartbeat grow steadier and slower, but she couldn't fall asleep. They had escaped their problems for a few hours, but now reality settled over her again, burying her with worries of this shelter, with its dwindling supplies and combustible politics. The world outside, with its fires and storms. No matter how much she tried to push them away, the problems wouldn't leave her alone.

"I think you might like this piece of metal more than I do," Perry said.

"Sorry." She realized she'd been toying with the Blood Lord chain at his neck. "I didn't mean to keep you awake."

"You didn't. I can't sleep either. We should try talking. . . . We're getting so good at it."

She gave his ribs a gentle nudge for his sarcasm, but accepted the suggestion. "We need to figure out our next move, Perry. We're stuck here. The only way that's going to change is if . . ."

"Is if . . . ?"

"We go back to Sable. He has the Hovers we need." She instantly wanted to take the words back. The thought of going back to Sable couldn't have repelled her more, but what other choice was there? If they didn't try something, they were no better than Caleb and Rune, resigned to waiting out their last days.

"You're right about the Hovers," Perry said. "I've been thinking the same thing. But we won't have to chase Sable.

He'll come to us. I was going to tell you that earlier."

A chill rippled down her back. "Why do you think so?"

"Cinder." After a pause, he added, "And it's what I'd do."

"Don't say that, Perry. You're nothing like him."

"He told me I was, in the Komodo."

"You're *not*."

He didn't say anything for a long moment. Then he kissed the top of her head. "Try to sleep. Tomorrow's coming, whether we worry about it or not."

She dreamed of a fleet of Hovers, perched along the bluff and crowded along the cove's beach, their iridescent exteriors catching the light of the Aether. And of Sable, a dark figure against the pale sand and the foaming waves, only the jewels at his neck sparkling.

In the morning, that was exactly what she saw.

36

PEREGRINE

He wants to talk to you alone, Peregrine," Reef said. "No weapons. No one else. He said he'd clear the cove or meet you on neutral footing of your choice. There's one other thing. He wanted me to tell you that he gave his people orders to storm the cave if you kill him."

Perry rubbed the back of his neck and found it damp with sweat. The Tides stood around him in the central cavern, murmurs of agitation rising from them.

Perry had expected Sable to come, but he wasn't sure if he was capable of negotiating with the Horns' Blood Lord. The last time they'd been together, he had sworn to rip Sable apart with his bare hands. He wanted that more than ever, but he was cornered. He had no other options.

"I'll go," he said.

Everyone spoke at once.

The Six, cursing loudly and protesting.

Cinder, yelling, "You can't go!"

Roar, stepping forward. "Let me go with you."

Perry's eyes went to Aria, quiet amid the chaos. Marron stood beside her. They watched him with worry in their eyes. They understood. Talking with Sable was his only move.

Less than ten minutes later, he walked outside, weaponless as requested.

Sable stood by the water, his stance relaxed as he waited. His territory was in the mountains—jagged peaks, topped year-round with snow—but he looked comfortable with his shoes sinking into wet sand.

As Perry neared, Sable lifted his eyebrows, amusement flashing over his face. "You know, I did say alone."

Perry followed his gaze. Flea padded silently over the sand a few steps behind him. Perry shook his head, but it actually heartened him to see the dog.

Sable smiled. "You're looking well. Almost healed. Wearing your chain proudly in spite of everything."

Every one of his words carried a darker meaning. A hidden jab. It reminded Perry of his brother. Vale had spoken this way too.

"What's going through your mind right now, Peregrine? Is it the way you'd like to beat me as I did you?"

"It would be a start."

"We should have taken a different path, you and I. If you'd come to Rim with Olivia, as Vale and I had planned, it could have changed everything between us."

The look on Sable's face was so rapt, so absorbed, it made Perry's stomach turn. "Get on with it, Sable. You're here to offer us passage?"

Sable crossed his arms, turning to the water. "It had occurred to me." Beneath the vibrant red and blue of the sky, the water looked gray, the waves like hammered steel. "Striking a deal would be easier than me having to force my way into that den of yours to get what I need. I hope we can find a way to compromise. The only way we survive is together, which you realize or you wouldn't be here."

"I have over four hundred people," Perry said. "If you can't accommodate all of them, then I have nothing more to say to you."

"I can. I have room for all of them on the fleet."

Perry knew why Sable had space on the Hovers—but he couldn't stop himself from asking. "What happened to the Dwellers from the Komodo?"

"You were there," Sable answered without looking away from the ocean.

"I want to hear you say it."

Sable's temper heated at Perry's tone, and a low growl rumbled from Flea.

"Quite a few were lost during the insurrection. Hess's fault, not mine. I was trying to avoid bloodshed. Of those who survived, I kept the useful ones. Pilots. Doctors. A few engineers."

He had kept them and killed the rest. Fury washed over Perry, though he wasn't surprised.

"How many weren't useful?" he asked. He didn't know why he needed a number. Maybe it was the only way to grasp the loss. To connect with people who'd died senselessly. Maybe he wanted to quantify Sable's ruthlessness. Futile, Perry knew. He could drop a stone into the black well of Sable's heart and never hear it hit the bottom.

"I don't see how it makes any difference, Perry. They were just Dwellers. Ahh . . . wait. I see now. Aria. She's made you sympathetic to the Moles, hasn't she? Of course she has. Amazing. Three hundred years of segregation undone by a single girl. She must be as incredible as she looks."

"So that we're clear," Perry said, "I don't care if it means everyone on this earth loses any chance of surviving. If you mention her to me again, I will take your head off and watch your blood pool at my feet."

Sable's eyes narrowed, his mouth turning up in a faint smile. "I've made many enemies in my life, but I do think you're my finest achievement." He turned back to the water. Across the southern horizon, only a mile away at points, funnels lashed down. "I did what I had to do in the Komodo. You know what happened in the Unity. I had no interest in being discarded by the Moles. In being shut out by them like some mangy dog left in the rain. No offense to your friend here. I have Dweller numbers that I can control now. That was my only intention."

Perry wasn't interested in Sable's justification for what had been a slaughter. He needed to get them back on target. On the task of leaving to the Still Blue. If he focused on his hatred, the conversation would lead in a clear and violent direction.

"You said your offer is for everyone."

"Yes," Sable said. "There is a place for every one of them. Dweller or Outsider. That is what I'm here to offer. But you have to bring the boy."

Perry looked down at Flea, suddenly feeling weightless. Like he had lifted out of his body and was floating upward. He saw the shape of the Tides' coast in his mind. He saw himself there on the beach with Sable, discussing Cinder's life like it was a bargaining tool, when it was actually a blood sacrifice.

He forced himself to finish what had begun. "When we reach the Still Blue, we separate. As soon as the journey is done, the Tides and Horns part ways."

"We could make some kind of arrangement when we get there, I'm sure."

"No," Perry said. "We make an arrangement now. You walk away from my tribe."

"Parting ways might not be the most beneficial decision. We have no idea what we'll—"

"Swear to it or we're done."

Sable stared at him, his ice-blue eyes calculating. Perry concentrated on keeping his breathing even. On controlling the furious beating of his heart. His thoughts were already shifting to Cinder and the conversation he'd need to have.

Finally, Sable nodded, accepting Perry's demand. "After we cross, the Tides will remain yours alone." He was quiet for a moment, a smile spreading over his lips. "So, Peregrine," he said. "I can uphold my side of our bargain. . . . Can you uphold yours?"

37

ARIA

Perry's eyes flashed like daggers as he came back into the cave.

He strode up to Aria, his expression intent and feral, barely pausing as he leaned in to her. "I have to talk to Cinder," he said, his voice breaking with emotion. "I'll be back as soon as I can."

He asked for Cinder and Marron and then he was off, making a direct path to the Battle Room.

Aria watched him go, her heart beating hard in her chest. What had just happened? What had Sable said? She looked around, seeing dazed looks on the faces of everyone around her.

"Did I miss something?" Straggler asked.

"I think we all did," said Brooke.

They had expected a decision, news of some arrangement with Sable, but the waiting wasn't over yet. Slowly, one by one, the crowd dissipated.

Roar stood in a small circle with the Six, exchanging ideas about what might have happened. Aria tried to follow their conversation, but she couldn't concentrate.

"Aria," Brooke said, walking up. "Do you have some time?"

Aria nodded. She moved away from Roar and the others and sat heavily on the wooden platform.

"I didn't see you last night," Brooke said, sitting next to her. "I mean I saw you, but we didn't have a chance to talk."

She was making an effort to be friendly, finally, but Aria felt numb. Her mind was on Perry, and she couldn't think of anything to say in return.

Brooke looked away; her eyes scanned the darkness before coming back to Aria.

"When you first came to the Tides, I had lost Liv. And . . . Perry, too, in a way. You even took Roar, which I didn't realize I'd care about as much as I do—"

"I didn't *take* anyone."

"I know," Brooke said. "That's what I'm trying to say. I know you didn't, but it felt that way. When you came, everything that was mine suddenly became yours . . . except for Clara. You brought my sister back. You got her out of that Pod, and she matters more to me than everything else. Anyway, I wanted to thank you. And . . . sorry it took me a while to say it," she added. Brooke stood and walked away.

Aria watched her go. She hadn't forgotten how badly Brooke had behaved, but on top of those memories were better ones. Newer ones. Brooke's bravery during the mission. Her loyalty to both Perry and Roar. Her quick wit with Soren.

That gave her an idea. Aria jumped up and caught up with her.

Brooke stopped, suddenly guarded. "What?"

"I could use your help with something," Aria said. "If you're willing."

Brooke shrugged. "Sure."

Aria took her to the Dweller cavern, explaining on the way. Inside, they found Jupiter, Rune, Caleb, and Soren sitting in a circle, playing a game with tattered cards.

She and Brooke sat down without waiting for an invitation.

Brooke nodded to Jupiter in greeting. Then she raised her hands and wiggled her fingers in the air. "Hi, Soren," she said.

Soren smiled for the first time since his father had died. It was a tired smile, a little sad, too, but it was a smile. He lifted his hands, wiggling back as he said, "Hi, Laurel."

They were teasing each other, but for a second Aria thought she saw something gentle pass between them.

Then Brooke looked at Rune and said, "How do you play this game?"

"*You* want to *play*?" Rune challenged. Her eyes flicked to Aria. It was clear she knew this was Aria's idea.

Brooke shook her head. "I don't want to play; I want to win. But if you give me the rules, I'll take it from there."

288

Her confidence stunned Rune, whose mouth went slack.

Soren sat up, scooting closer into their circle. "I need to see this."

A grin spread over Jupiter's face. He dropped an arm around Rune's shoulders. "Go on, Ru. Teach her."

Caleb glanced at Aria, smiling in giddy anticipation. She could almost read his thoughts. Rune and Brooke were either going to attack each other, or become fast friends before this was over.

Aria already knew the outcome.

She watched them play, trying her best to keep her thoughts here instead of on Perry and Cinder.

Some time later, Talon and Willow came running. "Aria! He's out!"

She shot to her feet and hurried back to the main cave. Her friends followed her. Other Dwellers came too.

The Tides were somber and tense as they crowded around the stage. Aria searched every face standing around the stage twice but she didn't see Perry.

Marron climbed up to the platform, smoothing the front of his shirt as he waited for people to give him their attention. His blue eyes found Aria. The look he sent her—sorry, worried—made her knees soften.

"Peregrine is with Cinder," Marron said. "He'll be along soon, but since time is of the essence, he asked me to make this announcement on his behalf."

He addressed the Tides calmly, without changing the tone

or volume of his voice. Drawing a breath, he continued. "An agreement has been reached with the Horns. We're leaving. We're joining them on the journey to the Still Blue."

The crowd thrummed with surprise and cries of celebration. Amid the happy sounds were others, angry voices and harsh words.

"That can't be right," Roar said. "Perry would never join up with Sable."

"Not unless he's lost his mind," said Soren.

Reef's and Twig's reactions were less coherent. A stream of curses poured from their mouths.

Marron waited for quiet to return before he spoke again. "He did indeed reach an agreement with Sable. There is passage to the Still Blue for anyone who desires it. Certainly, though, none of you are forced to come. Let there be no mistake: the journey there will be far from safe, and the destination itself is something of a question. What we know is this: Here, your life is certain to be over shortly. Our food stores are down to days. We have no wood to warm this cave beyond the end of the week. . . . We have exhausted everything. Whether you decide to take a chance on something else, be it better or worse than this, is up to you."

A murmur moved through the crowd. Jokes about who was mad enough to stay. Aria heard them through a haze.

Marron continued to speak. He gave instructions on the preparations that were needed. Aria watched Bear and Molly and the Six leave to coordinate the groups. The logistics of their exodus.

Exodus.

The word fixed in her mind, grave-sounding. Unbelievable, despite how many months she'd anticipated this moment.

They were *leaving*.

The crowd thinned once again as people rushed off to gather their belongings.

Aria didn't move. Roar and Soren had stayed behind with her. They were both watching her like they expected her to say something, so she did.

"Why is he still in there, Roar?"

"Because he knows what this means, and he doesn't want to do it."

"Which *he*?" she asked. "Cinder or Perry?"

"My guess?" Roar said. "Both."

Within minutes, the cave bustled with activity as the Tides began packing and organizing their supplies for the journey. Food and blankets. Medicines and weapons. Everything was culled down to the most essential items and loaded in storage crates.

Sable sent two dozen of his own soldiers to assist them. Unsurprisingly, they were led by her father.

Loran barely glanced at Aria as he entered the cave. She, on the other hand, couldn't stop watching him.

She was relieved to see him. Thrilled and terrified. For nineteen years they hadn't seen each other, but now fate had brought them together several times.

Right away he and the Horns set a tone of dominance. Their assistance took the shape of tersely issued commands and berating comments. The Tides quickly grew tight-lipped and anxious. Only a few pushed back, refusing to be ordered. Reef and the Six held their ground, as did Bear and Molly. When Twig got into a shoving match with one of the Horns that nearly turned bloody, Aria had seen enough.

She pulled Loran aside. Her heart was racing. "Your men are too harsh. You don't have to treat them this way."

Loran crossed his arms, covering the horn emblem on his chest. He was shorter than Perry, narrower in the shoulders. Fit for a man his age.

Aria scowled at him. "What, now you've got nothing to say?"

His dark eyebrows lifted. "Actually, I'm interested in hearing your idea of how I should treat people."

She reeled back, stung, though he hadn't spoken harshly. If anything, he'd sounded amused.

Loran looked away from her, surveying the activity around the cave.

Aria waited for him to leave. *She* should leave after a comment like that, but she couldn't. Something kept her feet planted.

Her gaze fell to the horns on his uniform. She wanted him to be someone different. Someone who would see the scene around her the same way. Someone who never would have left her, or her mother.

Loran's gray eyes came back to hers, his expression both

frustrated and hopeful. It occurred to her that she might be looking at him the same way.

"The Hovers don't have endless supplies of fuel," he said. "The Horns are out there—exposed—and the storm in the south is not *south* anymore. It is bearing down on us. East and north are no better. West is all that's left. The only way we can go is toward water, but that won't be an option for much longer.

"My men and I aren't interested in *almost* surviving, Aria. We want to live. Perhaps that desire looks like harshness to you, but I would rather be alive and cruel than dead and kind."

"Did you mean what you said about wanting a chance to know me?"

The question passed through her lips before she knew it. Loran blinked at her, as surprised as she was.

"Yes," he said.

"Even if you learn that there's a part of me that hates you?"

He nodded, a smile lighting in his eyes. "I think I've glimpsed that part already."

He was teasing her, letting warmth come through. If she wanted to know him, she'd have to return that warmth. She couldn't, and she didn't know why, because she *wanted* to.

As the seconds passed, the lines around Loran's eyes deepened with disappointment.

One of his men called to him, drawing his attention away. Loran turned to leave, but then he paused, looking back at her. "You're assigned to Sable's Hover—his orders. Nothing

I can change, but I tried to put all your friends on the same craft as well."

Aria watched him walk away, waiting until he was out of hearing range before she let herself say, "Thank you."

Two hours later, Aria pulled her satchel over one shoulder and Perry's over the other.

Talon had helped her sort through the trunks in Perry's tent, though he had warned her repeatedly that his uncle Perry didn't really care very much about those old things. She'd known that too. Perry cared about his bow and his knife. He cared about his land and about hunting, and most of all about people. But books? Shirts and socks? Not important to him.

She'd packed a few of her favorite items anyway, taking special care with the collection of falcon figures he'd carved with Talon. Perry's belongings were more than what she had—which was nothing. If he didn't want them, she'd claim them herself. His things already felt like they were hers, and his shirts were more than mere shirts. Maybe she was losing her mind, but they meant something to her just because they were his.

Now she carried her leather satchel and his, along with his bow and quiver, the weight of his belongings a poor substitute for him. For the arm she wished were resting across her shoulders instead.

Aria stopped just before leaving the cave. Most everyone was outside already, and only a few people were gathered at the stage. Perry wasn't one of them.

She was beginning to think he was avoiding her.

She shifted the satchels higher on her shoulders, taking one final look. "Good-bye, cave. I never want to see you again."

She stepped outside onto the sand and made her way up the switchback trail that climbed the bluff. Roar and Talon walked ahead of her with Willow and Flea. Behind her were Soren and Caleb. All she heard was the wind and their steps, and the crash of the waves growing more faint.

She felt like her head wasn't attached to the rest of her body. Like she wasn't attached to the earth or even to the air around her.

They were leaving. It was what she'd wanted. What was necessary. But it felt too sudden. Too wrong, with Sable. And too empty, without Perry.

As she crested the bluff, she saw the Hovers, spread in lines over the rough terrain. Giants perched on the edge of the earth. The fleet was a sight that had amazed her once. Now her eyes moved right past the massive craft, scanning the people milling around in search of a tall figure with blond hair.

Aria spotted him at the same moment he saw her. Perry stood with Cinder and Marron, the three of them huddled close. Roar, Soren, and the others flowed past her, but she couldn't move.

Perry came to her.

He walked over, and stood before her with swollen, red

eyes. He'd been crying. She hated that he had hurt so much and she hadn't been there.

"You've been gone," she said stupidly.

"I couldn't leave Cinder." He looked down, his gaze falling to the falcon carving in her hand. It was the one she'd taken all the way to Rim and back. She didn't realize she'd been holding it. She didn't even know when she'd taken it out of his pack.

Perry took it carefully from her hand. "You kept this."

"Of course I did," she said. "You gave it to me."

Perry ran his thumb over it. A faint smile came to his lips. "I should've given you one of my arrows. I make better arrows than falcons."

Aria bit her lip, dread snaking in her stomach. He was making small talk. Stalling. Almost everyone had loaded up. Only a few people were left, making their way into the Hovers.

He lifted his head, and the look in his eyes made her breath catch. "I didn't know how to say this, Aria."

"You're scaring me. Just tell me what it is."

She saw tears in his eyes, and she knew what he'd say before he uttered a word.

"I have to go with Cinder. I can't let him go alone."

38

PEREGRINE

Perry saw the exact moment that Aria understood. Her eyes flew open and her temper washed over him, pure ice. He kept talking, trying to explain.

"Cinder is going in his own Hover. . . . He'll have to pull ahead of the fleet at the barrier of Aether, and I'm going with him." His throat felt like it was closing up, but he pressed ahead. "What's out there sounds bigger than anything any of us has ever seen. And you know the way he is afterward. If it doesn't kill him, he'll be close to dying. Maybe . . . maybe he won't come out of it."

Perry stared at the tufts of sea grass by his foot, unable to look at her anymore. He watched the fine blades blowing in the wind, and drew a few trembling breaths before he continued.

"I'm the only person he trusts. The *only* one. How can I ask him to go out there for us, if I won't fight for him—for *his* life? And he's terrified, Aria. If I'm not with him, I don't know if he'll go through with it. We'd all lose if that happened."

Perry had talked it over with Marron and Cinder earlier in the Battle Room. He and Marron had even planned for the possible outcomes, and who would lead the Tides should he not make it back. Then Marron had left to speak to the Tides and, after, to arrange everything with Sable.

Now Perry looked up. Tears brimmed in Aria's eyes. Discussing the consequences of his death had been easier than telling her that he had to leave her.

"I'll go with you," she said.

"*No.* Aria, you can't."

"Why not? Why is it all right for you to go?"

"Because I need you to watch Talon." He let out a breath, frustrated with himself. That hadn't come out right. "What I meant is that if I don't come back, Molly will take him, but I want him to grow up knowing you and Roar. We don't have any family left, but you—" His voice snagged. He swallowed. Couldn't believe the things coming from his mouth. "You and Roar are that to me. And I want Talon to have you both. For anything he needs."

"Perry, how can I say no to that?" she said desperately.

He knew she couldn't.

"So are we saying *good-bye*?"

"Only for a while."

Movement further along the bluff drew his attention. The Six were approaching, their strides long and faces grim.

Others, too. Proof that word had spread despite his hope it wouldn't. He didn't want to say four hundred good-byes. He couldn't bear it. This one with Aria had already broken him open.

Quickly, he pulled Aria close. "Do you hate me?"

"You know I don't."

"You should."

"I don't," she said again. "How could I ever?"

He kissed her head and then spoke with his lips on her skin, like he might make what he said more permanent. More true. "I promise you," he whispered. "We'll both get there, and I'll find you."

He would do it. If he survived.

39

ARIA

A ria watched Perry as he spoke with each of the Six. Gren and Twig first. Then Hyde, Hayden, and Straggler. He went to Reef last, and then moved on, speaking with Molly and Bear.

She didn't hear anything they said. Their words were lost to her. Their clasped hands and fierce embraces seemed unreal. Brooke came over, linking arms with her. Aria felt surprise and gratitude, faint and quickly fading away.

Some time later she found herself in front of a Dragonwing. It was like someone had flipped a switch to shut her off, carried her there, and powered her back on.

Cinder, Willow, and Talon sat on the edge of the Hover, legs swinging as they took turns tossing a ball to Flea. Aria blinked, recognition filtering through her dulled mind. It was a tennis ball, the lime green bright as a shout in the gray dawn. She stared at it, marveling over the artifact, this thing that had been absent. Preserved for hundreds of years. Had the owner decided it wasn't worth bringing on the journey to the Still Blue? Had it been carefully guarded for lifetimes only to end up in Flea's mouth?

She heard Roar's voice behind her, and turned.

"I never should have introduced you to Cinder," he said to Perry.

"You didn't," Perry replied.

They stood alone, some twenty paces off. The crowds had thinned; most everyone had loaded into the Hovers already. Aether clawed down across the sky, the sound of the funnels loud in her ears. They were leaving just in time. The funnels were almost on top of them.

"But you met him because of me," Roar said.

"Yeah." Perry crossed his arms. "I did."

They both looked over, noticing her. Neither of them looked away. They watched her, their faces grave and worried, like they thought she might blow right off the edge of the bluff. Nearby, one of the Hover engines buzzed to life. Then another and another, until her ears filled with the sound, and she didn't hear the Aether shrieking anymore.

Her attention moved to a group coming toward them.

Horn guards. Her father. And Sable.

It was almost time to leave.

As Roar spoke again to Perry, Aria found herself shutting out the sounds of the Hovers, the wind and the surf below, and the storms, focusing solely on them.

"I don't like this idea, Perry."

"I knew you wouldn't."

Roar nodded. "Right." He rubbed the back of his neck. "We'll be waiting for you."

Perry had told Aria that he'd return, but he made no such promise to Roar now. As the pause stretched out between them, she wondered if Perry had only said what she'd wanted to hear.

"All right then, brother," Roar said at last.

They embraced—quickly, firmly—something Aria realized she'd never seen before and never wanted to see again. It made them look scared and breakable, and they weren't. They were magnificent, both of them.

Perry moved closer and called to Talon, who jumped down and met his uncle. Kneeling, Perry took Talon's face in his hands, and then Talon was crying and she had to look away.

Her father and Sable were almost there. Wind pushed Loran's black hair into his eyes, but Sable's was just a shadow over his skull.

As she watched them approach, her conversation with Perry played over in her mind. He *had* told her that he would come back. Hadn't he? What had she said to him? Had she been rude or ungrateful, like the last time she'd seen her mother?

The *last* time.

This couldn't be.

Was it?

She could have lived every minute she'd had with him better. She should have always spoken the best words she could to him.

Sable arrived, his face flushed, his eyes full of energy. He stood talking with Loran, but Aria knew he was watching everything.

Perry hugged Talon and then sent him with Roar to board a Hovercraft. Then he came to her side and she took his hand, her weak hand somehow clinging to his scarred one. She wanted to firm her grip, to create an unbreakable grasp that would keep him close forever, but he'd chosen a path. And though she ached to stop him, she wouldn't.

They watched Roar pick Talon up like he was a child of four instead of eight. Tears streamed down Talon's face as he wrapped his arms around Roar's throat. He was shouting, but Aria couldn't hear a word he was saying. Willow ran ahead with Flea. Without seeing her face, Aria knew that she was crying too.

"Ready, Cinder?" Sable's voice was like a hook pulling her back to reality.

Cinder tugged his black hat lower and drew his legs up into the Hover. He glanced at Sable, and then away, to Roar and Willow and Talon, who were boarding another Hover farther down the bluff.

Cinder appeared grown to Aria then, more a man than a boy. At some point in the course of his being kidnapped and held prisoner, the bones in his jaw and cheeks had widened, taking on more heft. He had a handsome face, an appealing mix of broodiness and confidence that sat just right on his features.

When she'd met Cinder, he'd lashed at her and Perry and Roar while trailing after them like a lost child. That time in the woods seemed so long ago. He *fit* now. He had achieved the same thing she wanted herself. Cinder had found Perry. He'd found Willow and Flea and Molly. He had a place. A family.

Aria understood why Perry was going with him. And she hated that she understood.

"Thank you for what you're doing," Sable said.

Aria glanced at Loran. Did he hear Sable's falseness? He was an Aud; surely he had to.

"I'm not doing anything for *you*," Cinder snapped. He stood and disappeared into the craft.

"So long as he does it," Sable said, with a small shrug. He turned to Perry. "We went through a good deal of trouble getting here, didn't we? Suffered a few bruises along the way, but the important thing is that we made it. Everything is prepared. The Dragonwing will be controlled remotely by one of the pilots on my craft. We'll get you close, Peregrine. All you and Cinder have to do is the rest."

He had the nerve to make it seem as if he were doing the difficult part. She could hear Perry's breath beside her, fast and irregular. As hard as this was for her, it was so much worse for him.

Sable inclined his head. "Good luck."

Aria didn't even see Perry's face before he hugged her. "I'll be thinking about you," he said, lifting her off the ground. "I love you."

She said it back, and that was it.

All that mattered. Everything there was to say.

At. didn't even see Perry's face before he hugged her. "I'll be thinking about you," he said, lifting her off the ground.

"I love you."

She said it back, and that was it.

All that mattered. Everything he'd wanted to say.

~ 40 ~

PEREGRINE

The hatch closed the moment Perry boarded the Hover, controlled by some unseen Dweller under Sable's command.

He fell into the pilot seat, concentrating on breathing. Just breathing in and out, and not thinking about what had just happened. In the chair beside him, Cinder gripped the armrests as he stared through the windshield.

"There you are, Peregrine." Sable's voice filled the small cockpit. "I can see both of you, but I'm told you can only hear me."

Perry rubbed a hand over his face and sat up, forcing himself to gather his wits. "I hear you," he said. He wondered if Roar or Aria was also there, watching and listening. He doubted it.

Their Hover was docked on the edge of the bluff. Outside, past fifty yards of dirt and sea grass, there was only sky. Only Aether. Perry had to stop himself from imagining shooting off the bluff and dropping to the coastline below.

Faintly, through the speakers, Perry heard pilots moving through flight commands. And then one by one, the other Hovers in the fleet rose off the ground. When their craft lifted with a jolt, Cinder gasped, his eyes flying wide open.

Perry swallowed through a dry mouth. "Buckle yourself in," he said.

Not the most soothing words he'd ever spoken, but it was the best he could do at the moment.

Cinder looked over, scowling. "What about you?"

Perry glanced down, muffling a curse as he snapped his own harness on.

The Hovers didn't shoot over the bluff like he'd pictured. They turned south and hugged the edge of the coast, following the trail to the compound that he and Roar had walked just yesterday.

As the fleet formed up like a flock, his Hover fell to the rear. Perry's gaze moved to the Belswan at the lead.

Talon. Aria. Roar. Marron. Reef and the rest of the Six.

He couldn't stop listing their names. They were all in there. Sable had handpicked the people closest to Perry and brought them on his Hover. It made Perry's stomach churn to think they were in Sable's control now.

In minutes, the Tide compound came into view, sitting up on a small rise. It was still his land, despite the flash of Aether and the trails of fire along the hills. He still felt it calling to him—but in a voice he no longer recognized.

"Did I ever tell you that my home in Rim was bigger than the whole of your compound?" Sable asked.

A jab, but Perry couldn't have cared less. His house had always offered enough space. Even when the Six had slept wall to wall across the floor, there had always been enough room for everyone.

"You want to compare sizes, Sable? I bet I win."

Perry didn't know why he said that. He'd never been one for bragging—that was more Roar's manner—but the remark made Cinder look over and smile, so it was worth it.

"Take one last look at your land," Sable said, changing the subject.

Perry did. As the Hovers soared past the abandoned compound, he took in as much as he could, aching and nostalgic. Amazed at this new, shocking perspective of the place he'd lived in since birth.

After passing the compound, the fleet turned west and sped up, covering the half-hour walk over the dunes to the ocean in a heartbeat.

The beach where he'd learned how to walk and how to fish and how to kiss was a blur of beige and white. Gone in an instant, and then there was only water. Only waves that stretched out as far as he could see.

This journey was nothing like what he had imagined. For years, he'd pictured himself crossing over hills or deserts with the Tides in search of the Still Blue. He had expected a land voyage, not the steel blue of the ocean below and the glaring currents of the Aether above.

"I don't know why you came with me," Cinder said, pulling him from his thoughts.

Perry looked at him. "Yes, you do."

He'd explained his conversation with Sable to Cinder in the Battle Room, though Cinder had already known. Cinder had already decided to help the Tides, he'd told Perry. From the moment he'd acquiesced to Sable in the Komodo, he'd said he felt ready.

But now his eyes filled with tears. "Remember when I burned your hand? How you said that was the worst pain you've ever felt?"

Perry looked down at his scars, flexing his hand. "I remember."

Cinder said nothing more. He turned forward, but Perry knew what he was thinking. His ability was a wild, untamed thing. He tried to control it, but didn't always succeed.

Perry didn't know whether either of them would live through the next hours. He had been around Cinder a few times when he channeled the Aether. This time would be very different—it was the only thing he was sure about.

"I want to be here, Cinder. We're getting through this, all right?"

Cinder nodded, his bottom lip quivering.

They fell quiet again, listening to the tremble of the Dragonwing and the hum of the engine. The ocean seemed endless, hypnotic. As they put mile after mile behind them, Perry imagined hunting alone. Tickling Talon until he broke into big, hiccupping belly laughs. Sharing a bottle of Luster with Roar. Kissing Aria and feeling her breathing, sighing, shivering under his hands.

He was deep in his thoughts until he saw a thin line of brilliant light on the horizon.

He sat up. It was the barrier, he had no doubt.

"Do you see it?" Cinder said, looking at him.

"I see it."

With every minute that passed, the line became larger, broader, until Perry wondered how it had ever looked like a line. He squinted, eyes straining at the brightness. The barrier seemed endless. Great twisting columns of Aether rained from above, but they ran upward as well, circling. The flows formed a curtain that was larger than anything he'd ever seen, reaching up infinitely—like the ocean had been lifted up to the sky.

Cinder let out a whimpering sound as the Hover slowed.

Sixty feet below, the ocean currents churned in whirl-pools, stirred by the Aether. Crossing in boats would have been suicide. Without the Hovers, they'd have been doomed.

Perry could see very little beyond the curtain of Aether—it was like looking through flames or rippling water—but in the small glimpses he did catch, he saw that the color of the ocean was different there.

The waves shimmered with unfiltered sunlight.

The Still Blue was golden.

41

ARIA

Aria's mind flitted from one thing to another. Falcon Markings that reached shoulder to shoulder. Sandals made of book covers. Opera songs and earthworms and a voice as warm as the afternoon sun. They had one thing in common.

Perry. Every thought came back to him.

She sat in the cargo hold of the Belswan Hover with Talon on one side and Roar on the other, her eyes on the window on the opposite side of the hold. She had been staring at it since leaving the bluff, watching the Aether outside and wondering if she should move closer. If she should look outside, where she might see Perry's Hover.

She'd passed hours this way, she was almost sure, but time didn't feel right.

Nothing did.

When the Hover slowed, her stomach leaped into her throat. She jumped up, Roar right beside her.

"What's going on?" Talon asked.

The question was suddenly on everyone's lips.

"We're here," Sable said over the speaker, silencing them. "Or I should say, *almost* here. Before we make the crossing, why don't we hear some words from your Blood Lord? Go ahead, Peregrine."

Aria heard Perry clear his throat. Her eyes filled with tears, and he hadn't even said anything yet.

"I've, uh . . . I've never been one for speeches," he began. "Wish that weren't the case right now." His voice was even and unhurried, like he had all the time in the world. Like he always sounded. "I want you to know that I did my best to look after you. I didn't always succeed, but you're not an easy group. I think that's fair to say. You fought me sometimes. You argued with me. You expected me to be more than a simple hunter. And because of you, I became more than that. So I want to thank each of you for letting me lead you. And for the honor I've had of serving you."

That was it.

Sable came back on. "I thought that was well said, actually. Very capable, your young lord. You'll see him again soon, when we reach the Still Blue."

He kept speaking, but Aria didn't hear the rest.

Her gaze moved to the window again, and she went to

it. People made way for her, clearing a path. Even Sable's soldiers stepped aside for her. Roar, Talon, and Brooke came with her, lining up beside her at the thick glass.

"There," Brooke said, pointing. "Do you see them?"

i. People made way for her, clearing a path. Even Sable soldiers stepped aside for her. Roar, Talon, and Brooke came with her, lining up beside her at the thick glass.

"There," Brooke said, pointing. "Are you sure them—"

42

PEREGRINE

The Dragonwing surged forward again, pushing Perry against the seat and making Cinder gasp.

They passed the other Hovers in the fleet, one after another, and then there was no one left. Nothing in front of them but Aether in every direction.

"You'll need to tell us how close you want to be," Sable said.

Perry looked at Cinder, who bugged his eyes and shrugged.

It was such an honest reaction that Perry found himself smiling. None of them had been in this situation before; how close they should be was anyone's guess.

Strangely, Perry felt better, his focus returning by the second. He'd said what he'd needed to say to the Tides. Now it was time for action—always where he felt surest.

The craft gave another sudden lurch that threw him against his restraints; then it began to shudder. The instrument panel came alive, flashing with red warning messages, and the blare of an alarm filled the cockpit with an urgent pulse.

Cinder blurted, "That's good! We're close enough!"

The craft slowed and then bobbed unsteadily in place. Here the ocean was even rougher, rising in huge swells. Perry estimated a distance of one hundred and fifty yards between them and the barrier. He'd have liked to fire an arrow at it. A dozen arrows. He'd have liked to be the one to pierce it and tear it down.

"Time to do what you've promised us, Cinder," Sable said. "Do this, and we'll get both of you home. Willow is waiting for you."

Cinder's eyes had glazed over. Silent tears spilled down his cheeks.

Perry tugged his seat restraints off and stood, knowing this was the hardest thing he'd ever have to do. He sank into his legs to keep his balance in the pitching craft and unbuckled Cinder's restraints.

"I'm right here," he said, holding his hand down. "It's all right. I'm going to help you." Cinder's arm shook violently as Perry helped him to his feet.

They moved into the small hold behind the cockpit together, Perry half carrying him.

The bay doors opened. Wind and spray swept inside in a violent rush. The air was cool and tasted of salt, as familiar to Perry as anything, except for the sting it carried, like bites all along his skin and over his eyes.

The wall of Aether churned and roiled ahead of him;

Sable's pilots had turned the craft parallel to it. For long moments he stared in awe, unable to look away, until he caught movement from the corner of his eyes.

Cinder was bent into a corner of the craft, his back convulsing as he retched.

"What's happening?" Sable's voice moved through the speakers. "I can't see what's happening."

"We need a minute," Perry snapped.

"We don't have a minute! Get Aria up here right now," Sable ordered.

"No! Just hold on!"

Cinder recovered and climbed to his feet. "Sorry . . . it's so bumpy."

Perry let out his breath, realizing Cinder was only seasick, not sick with fear. "That's all right. I'm surprised I haven't done it myself."

Cinder smiled weakly. "Thanks," he said. "For being here with me."

Perry nodded, accepting his thanks. "Do you want me to stand next to you?"

Cinder shook his head. "I can do it."

He moved to the bay doors, bracing a hand against the opening. Then he closed his eyes, the fear easing from his face. Webs of Aether spread beneath his skin, moving up his neck to his jaw, then higher over his scalp.

He looked relaxed. The world raged around him, but it didn't feel that way to Perry. Standing behind him, watching him, Perry felt like the world was raging *for* Cinder.

Seconds passed. Perry began to wonder if Cinder had changed his mind.

"Peregrine," came Sable's voice, "make him—"

A blast of air pushed Perry backward. He slammed against the rear wall of the Hover, staggered.

Cinder hadn't moved. He stayed planted by the doors.

Beyond him, in the distance, a gap formed in the barrier of Aether—a hollowed area that the currents flowed around, like river water past a rock.

The opening seemed almost insignificant in size. Twenty or thirty feet. Not big enough to fit even the smaller Dragonwings, to say nothing of the larger Hovers.

But through it, Perry could see what lay beyond the wall clearly: ocean, sitting beneath sunlight. That golden color that he'd glimpsed through the sheets of Aether was even warmer. And he saw sky. Endless, clear blue sky.

"What's he waiting for? That's not enough!" Sable yelled.

There was no point in talking to Cinder now. Perry had seen him like this. He was in another place. Lost to his surroundings.

"Peregrine!" Sable yelled.

As the seconds passed, relief moved through Perry. Maybe they wouldn't make the crossing, but Cinder would live.

Horror followed quickly. What would they do now? Forge ahead through the barrier, and hope they made it through? The alternative, turning back to the cave, sounded worse. They couldn't go back.

Cinder turned, fixing a blazing stare on him, and Perry understood.

What Cinder had just done was only the beginning. A test, to see what this would cost him. Looking into his eyes, Perry knew the answer.

Cinder turned back to the Aether.

Perry saw white, and then he saw nothing.

43

ARIA

"Do you see them?" Brooke said. "They're right there."

Aria nodded. Perry and Cinder's Dragonwing was just a small point in front of the barrier of Aether, but she saw it.

An explosion of light blinded her.

Shouts erupted as the Hover dipped sharply. Aria flew into the person behind her. Blinking, fighting for her vision, she righted herself and lunged back to the window.

The barrier now had a rift. A wide seam, like parted curtains. Through the barrier, the glittering ocean stretched out, as promising as anything she'd ever seen. Aria wanted to stare at it forever, but she tore her eyes away and searched for the Dragonwing.

"Where did they go?" she asked. Perry's Hover had disappeared.

"I'm looking," Brooke said.

Roar was there too, searching. Grabbing her arm and steadying her when their Hover surged forward. Cursing softly when Sable's voice came through the speakers again, announcing that they were going ahead with the crossing.

"Where are they?" Aria asked, her panic rising.

Brooke's face paled, her quiet concentration changing suddenly to wide-eyed shock. "Water," she said.

Aria's gaze dropped to the ocean below—where Perry's Hover tossed in ferocious white-capped waves.

44

PEREGRINE

When Perry opened his eyes, he was on his back, the concave ceiling of the cockpit above him. He couldn't move, and it took him a moment to realize that he wasn't paralyzed, only pinned in the small space between the wall and the back of the pilot seat.

His right shoulder throbbed, the pain as intense as when he'd dislocated it weeks ago—and his left shin stung sharply. There were other aches, less intense. Good signs. Pain meant he was still alive.

He pulled himself up, clutching the back of the seat for balance. The Hover was tilting wildly. Waves pounded the windshield, covering them completely, each torrent of water so thick that it plunged the cockpit into darkness.

Perry lumbered back into the hold, unsteady, nauseous. He swiped at his stinging eyes and came away with blood on his hand.

Through the open doors, he saw the sea. Thirty-foot swells of white and silver and Aether blue. The craft pitched, and water rushed up to his ankles.

The Hover had become a boat—with a missing side. Miraculously it was still afloat, but that was changing with every wave that surged inside.

"Cinder!" he yelled. "Cinder!"

He could barely hear his own voice over the waves. Yelling was useless, anyway. His eyes swept across the small hold. There was nowhere for Cinder to hide. To have gotten lost. Perry staggered to the door, almost pitching forward into the ocean as the Hover hurtled down the face of a wave.

"Cinder!"

He fell against the cabin wall as the Hover rocked again and stayed there, pressed against the wall, the air rushing out of his lungs. Out and out and out. He didn't think it would stop, the expansion of emptiness inside him.

"You survived, Peregrine," crackled through speakers. "But not Cinder, from the sounds of it. I'm very sorry."

Perry shot back into the cockpit. The nose of the Hover dipped suddenly, sending him flying against the windshield. The water in the craft surged forward, soaking him completely.

"Get me out of here!" Perry yelled.

The doors began to close as soon as the words left him. Across the cockpit, the dashboard controls flickered on.

Sable said, "What are you doing?"

A terrified voice answered, "Bringing the ship back up—"

"I issued no such order," said Sable.

"Sir, if we don't act now—"

"Shut it down."

A beat of silence.

"I said shut it down."

Perry cursed, turning in time to see the bay doors pause for an instant, and then open again to the raging sea. In the cockpit, the controls fell dark.

"This pains me, Peregrine. I like you very much and this isn't what I wanted. But I can't take any chances."

Then Perry didn't hear Sable any longer, only the waves pounding against the Hover.

45

ARIA

Do something!" Aria yelled. "They're still out there!"

Loran stood at the door of the cockpit, blocking her way inside. It was the first she'd seen of him in the Hover. "I can't let you in there," he said.

"You have to! You have to help them! Help *me*!"

Loran stared into her eyes. He said nothing, but she could tell he was battling with himself.

Sable's voice came through the speakers again. "We've had no contact from either Cinder or Peregrine. There's no sign from either. We've lost control of their ship, and I'm afraid it's too dangerous to attempt a rescue."

Roar pushed forward, standing almost nose to nose with Loran. "We can't give up on them. We have to get down there!"

Reef exploded next. "Sable could be lying! How can we know he's speaking the truth?"

A great ringing sound swelled in Aria's ears, and she was jostled, shoved between huge bodies that pushed and yelled. Through the noise and confusion, she still heard Sable.

"No one knows how long that barrier will remain open. Our priority needs to be making the crossing while we can."

He kept speaking, his voice soothing, rational, as he explained why they had to leave Perry behind and how sorry he was for the Tides. Aria didn't hear the rest. She couldn't hear anything over the shrill sound in her ears.

Somehow she made it back to the window.

They were almost upon the barrier of Aether. Outside, the wind was brutally strong, whisking up ocean spray. Water obscured everything, but she spotted Perry's Hover by the white ring of waves that broke around it.

It was listing to the side and half swallowed by the sea.

As she watched, they flew right past it, into the Still Blue.

"Aria, look," Brooke said, nudging her.

Aria was still at the window. She'd been there since they'd crossed the barrier and left the Aether behind. The ringing had left her ears, but now something was wrong with her eyes. She had lost the ability to focus. She'd been staring out the window without seeing anything.

Roar stood at her side, his arm around her. Twig held a sleeping Talon in his arms on Roar's other side. The spot where Talon had cried against Aria's stomach was damp.

"Land," Brooke said, and pointed. "There."

Aria saw a break in the perfect line of the horizon. From a

distance it looked like a black bump, but it broadened as they neared, gained color and depth. Becoming verdant slopes, covered in lush foliage.

These hills were folded and rolling, and they couldn't have been more different from the rocky bluffs they'd left behind. The colors she saw were crisp, unlike the dullness caused by the smoke that had clung to the Tides' territory. Here the land was vibrant green, the water turquoise, both almost garishly so.

A buzz of excitement swirled inside the Hover as word spread. Land had been spotted.

Aria hated them for their happiness. She hated herself for hating them. Why shouldn't they enjoy this moment? This was a new beginning, but it didn't feel that way to her.

She wanted to turn back—how could she possibly want to go *back*? But she did. Perry was the rugged cliffs and the crashing surf. He was the Tide compound and the hunting trails and everything else she'd left behind.

Talon shifted in Twig's arms. Sleepily, he raised his head and moved from Twig's arms to Roar's. Aria looked from one to the other and back.

They had to be enough. Maybe someday she'd feel like they were.

Voices carried from the cockpit. The pilots and engineers, assessing the terrain. For an hour—and then two—all she heard was the careful trading of coordinates. The running of tests that evaluated freshwater sources, elevations, and soil quality. The cataloging of every feature from the air as carefully as a spider creeping over its web, with technology so sensitive, so advanced, that it seemed like magic. Once, this kind of magic had built worlds for her in the Realms. Now it was discovering a new world, taking its temperature. Mapping the best place to establish a settlement.

What they were really looking for, she knew—*everyone* knew—was people. Such a discovery would bring a host of issues to consider. Would they be welcome? Would they be enslaved? Turned away? No one knew.

Until Sable emerged from the cockpit. "It's ours. It's uninhabited," he said, sounding a little breathless.

"Good fortune at last," Hyde said softly. He stood behind her, tall enough to see over her head to the window. All of the Six were there, crowded around her. They had been since they'd crossed the barrier.

She didn't know what to make of that. She didn't know whether it was supposed to mean something, all of them standing around her like a wall.

"About time," Hayden said. "I've got no fight left."

Twig let out his breath. Reef met Aria's eyes, and she wondered if he'd been hoping, irrationally, for the same thing as her. That the instrumentation would find one human. A young man of almost twenty, with green eyes and blond hair and a crooked smile that he used infrequently, but to powerful effect. A young man with the purest heart imaginable. Who believed in honor and who never, not for a moment, placed himself over others. But of course such a person hadn't been found. Magic wasn't real.

Marron stepped between Hyde and Twig, joining them. "I wouldn't call it good fortune. Millions of people lived here once. Now there isn't a soul left. That seems far from good fortune. And we might have benefited from some compassion and some help. We are so few."

Aria bit her lip to stop herself from snapping at him. She didn't know why she was suddenly so angry. It was those words: *We are so few.* Why had he needed to say that? They weren't few. They were *lacking.* They were missing Perry.

The Hovers regrouped, and she felt their velocity slow. There was a sudden descent, which made people gasp and reach for one another. Then the Hovers put down on a beach, one after another, a flock of iridescent birds alighting.

When their craft landed, Twig said, "We're here. I can't believe we're here."

Aria wasn't. She didn't feel there at all.

Reef motioned Roar closer. Talon was still sleeping in Roar's arms.

"I want the three of you to stay together," Reef said, looking from her to Roar. "Hyde and Hayden will be watching you, starting now."

Watching them? She didn't understand. Roar pursed his lips and nodded, resigned, and it began to make sense. He had been after Sable since Liv's death. That was no secret to anyone, least of all Sable. And Talon was Perry's nephew. Eight years of age, but a successor nonetheless. Aria wasn't sure why Reef thought she needed to be protected, but then her mind wasn't working right.

Reef disappeared and Aria was suddenly looking up at ·
the brothers, at Hyde and Hayden, and then looking away,
because they had bows over their shoulders. Because they
were the same height and blond-haired, though not the right
shade of blond. Was she going to move through the rest of
her life seeing failures and deficiencies everywhere? Wishing
everyone was more like Perry? Wishing everyone was *him*?

Sable was the first to leave the Hover, with a group of his
soldiers. She only heard him leave. Everyone in the large
hold had come to their feet, and with Hyde and Hayden in
front of her, all she saw were their backs, and arrows poking
from quivers. She listened to the soft hum of the ramp being
lowered, a familiar sound now. Daylight flooded the Hover,
and then a warm, gentle breeze floated in, carrying birdsong
and the rustle of swaying leaves.

The crowd thinned around her as people began to disem-
bark.

A new land.

A new beginning.

She put her arm around Roar, telling herself that she could
do this. She could take a few steps.

As the crowd thinned, she could see further ahead. Marron was exiting the ramp, accompanied by some of Sable's
men. She was about to search for Loran when she caught a
flash of Reef's braids. He was leaving the Hover with Gren
and Twig at his sides.

Fear shot down her back, sudden and unexplainable,
yanking her from her daze.

Sable always moved first. He never waited. Never hesitated to put down a threat before it ever fully materialized.

"Reef!" she screamed.

An instant later, gunshots.

One. Two. Three. Four.

Precise sounds. Premeditated. The gunshots kept going as screams filled the air.

The crowd surged, retreating into the Hover. Hyde's back rammed into Aria's face, smashing her nose. She reeled back, her vision going black for an instant.

"What's happening?" Talon cried, jarred awake.

"Roar, get back!" Aria yelled, pulling him deeper inside the Hover. From the corner of her eyes, she saw Hyde and Hayden loosing arrows. She caught a glimpse of Twig on the exit ramp, lying on his side. Bleeding. Then silence came, as sudden and loud as the first gunshots.

"Weapons down, all of you," Sable said coolly.

She heard the clatter of wood and metal as guns, bows, knives dropped.

Sable walked past them. Past Twig, who was clutching his leg and weeping. Further down the ramp, Aria saw Reef and Gren. Deadly still, both.

Slowly, Sable's gaze swept across the Hover and found Aria. He stared at her for a long moment, his eyes sparkling and energized. Then his gaze moved to Roar.

"No!" Aria yelled. *"No!"*

Sable put his hands up. "It's over," he said. "I want no more bloodshed." He looked pointedly at Marron, who stood just a few feet away from him, flanked by Horn soldiers. "But if any of you are interested in taking Peregrine's position as Lord of the Tides, be advised that that position no longer exists. Any attempt to claim it will receive lethal consideration, as you've just seen.

"If you still think you can challenge me, I want you to remember one thing: I know everything. I know your desires and fears before they have even made themselves known to you. Yield to me. It's your only option." His ice-blue gaze drifted over the crowd, eliciting a silent wave of tense, held breaths. "Have I made myself clear?"

No one dared speak.

"Good," Sable said. "This is a new beginning for all of us, but it's not a time to throw away our past. Our traditions have worked for centuries. If we respect them—our ways, the old ways—then we will flourish here."

Silence. Nothing but the sound of Twig's agonized cries.

"All right, then," Sable said. "Let's get started. Leave all your belongings in the Hover, step outside, and form into lines."

46

ARIA

A ria watched as Sable and his men sorted her friends into lines along the beach.

Roar went first, far away from her. Then Caleb and Soren and Rune. Brooke and Molly and Willow. She tried to identify Sable's strategy in creating the groupings, but it seemed unorderly. He was mixing old and young. Dwellers and Outsiders. Men and women. Then she understood: That was the point. He was creating lines of people who would be least likely to band together in rebellion.

She felt no anger or fear as the sorting continued, and as the sun began its descent behind the lush hills. She felt nothing, until she saw that Talon was placed in Molly's group. Molly would watch over him. Like Perry, she watched over everyone.

Preoccupied, Aria only then realized she stood alone.

The Hovers were empty. Everyone stood in lines along the beach—except her.

Sable stood nearby; she felt his gaze on her, but she wouldn't look at him.

"Take her back to the Hover," he said.

Horn soldiers escorted her back to the window in the hold, which looked over calm water that was greener than blue, and so clear she could see the sand beneath. She stayed there, under guard, watching the daylight fade through the window. Even though the ramp to the beach was open, she couldn't look toward land. Hours passed. Her eyes wouldn't turn away from the water.

This had to change. She needed to acccpt what had happened, find a way to move forward somehow. She tried to come up with a plan to get to Talon and Roar, but she couldn't concentrate for more than seconds. And just to save Talon and Roar? How would that help? Sable held every one of them in his grip.

Somehow, he'd come away with control over *everything*.

"Oh, don't be so glum."

She turned, seeing him stride up the ramp into the Hover.

He dismissed the two soldiers who'd been guarding her. Then he leaned against the inner wall of the Hover and smiled at her.

Outside, darkness had fallen—a soft darkness, unlike in the cave at the Tides. This darkness held warm shadows and the sound of rustling trees. Reef's and Gren's blood had been washed from the ramp, she noticed.

"Your friends are all well." Sable crossed his arms, the movement making the jewels of his chain sparkle in the dim hold. "A few fresh blisters but nothing terrible. I put them to work, which can't surprise you. There's much to be done. We have a camp to set up."

Aria stared at the chain and imagined strangling him with it.

"You're not the first to want to do that," he said after a moment. "The first was many years ago. A landowner in Rim—one of the wealthiest men pledged to me. I'd only worn the chain for a few months when he accused me of overtaxing him—which I did not. I am fair, Aria. I have always been fair. But I punished him for making the accusation. A hefty fine, which I thought was both lenient and fitting. In answer, he tried to choke me in the middle of a feast one night in front of hundreds of people. If he'd survived, I imagine he would have regretted that decision.

"I may not tromp around with a weapon like Peregrine or Roar, but I can defend myself. Quite well, in fact. You'd be wise to put an end to that line of thinking."

"I'll find a way to do it," she said.

His eyes flared for an instant, but he didn't reply.

"Are you going to have me killed now for saying that? You should. I won't stop until you're dead."

"You're angry that I've established my rule here. I've been assertive—perhaps to a fault. I understand. But let me tell you something. People *need* to be commanded. They cannot be in doubt over who leads them. Do you want to see another situation like in the Komodo? Do you want that kind of chaos to happen again? Here, when we have the opportunity to start over?"

"What happened in the Komodo was your doing. You betrayed Hess."

Sable pursed his lips in disappointment. "Aria, you're smarter than that. Did you really think Dwellers and Outsiders were going to hold hands and forget three hundred years of separation and hostility? Name one civilization led by two people—a pair. It doesn't happen. Do you know what the fastest path is to creating enemies? Forge a partnership. I'm a better Blood Lord for the Tides than Reef would have been. Or Marron, though he seems able enough. I'm best suited for the responsibility."

She couldn't look at him anymore. She couldn't argue with him. She didn't have the strength.

The scent of smoke drifted in from outside. It smelled different from what she'd grown used to. Not the burning of forestland, or the stale smell of the fires in the cave. This was the scent of campfire, clean and alive, like the one she and Perry had built together only a night ago. The memory of him coaxing the flames to life between his hands filled her mind—all she saw until she realized Sable was staring at her.

With every second, his irritation became more evident. He wanted her to understand him. He wanted her approval. She didn't want to ask herself *why*.

"You're actually making me miss Hess," she said.

Sable laughed—not what she'd expected. She remembered

the sound from her time in Rim. She'd thought it appealing then. Now it sent a chill through her.

"I've ruled thousands," he said. "I was ruling at your age. That should comfort you. I know what I'm doing."

"Where are those thousands now?"

"The ones I need are where I want them. And all the people out there—Horns and Tides—are mine now. They won't draw a breath unless I allow it. That means there will be no disruption as we rebuild. Because of me, we'll survive here. Because of me, we'll thrive. I'm simply giving us all the best chances possible. I don't see how that's wrong."

"Killing Reef and Gren wasn't wrong?"

"Reef would have challenged me. He was a threat, and now he isn't. Gren was in the way."

"Reef was only trying to protect the Tides."

"Which I also want, now that they're mine."

"Why are you here, Sable? Why are you trying to convince me that you've done the right thing? I'll never believe you."

"You respected Peregrine. That means you're capable of good judgment."

"What are you saying? You want me to *respect* you?"

He stood very still for long moments. She saw the answer in his piercing gaze. "Given enough time, you will."

Again, she could think of nothing to say in reply. If he believed that, then he was well and truly insane.

★ ★ ★

An hour later, Sable began his campaign to win her over with an invitation to supper. He had set up an area outside, up the beach, with a fire for himself and his most trusted circle. He asked her to join him.

"Fish soup," he said. "The Tides' specialty, I'm told. Nothing to rave about, in all honesty, but it is fresh, unlike the horror of the Dwellers' prepackaged meals. And the stars, Aria . . . I cannot begin to describe them to you. It's as though the heavens themselves—the very roof of the universe—have been scattered with embers. An incredible sight. I want to show it to you, but if you choose not to come, I understand."

He was an expert manipulator, offering her the heavens. The stars! How could she refuse?

She remembered how he'd manipulated Liv, too. Sable had told Liv, his purchased bride, that he would grant her freedom if she wanted it. He could be kind, when kindness lured a person to take a sip of poison. He could be charming and considerate. He could fool a person into believing he had a heart.

Did Scires only come in two kinds? As forthright as Liv and Perry, or as dishonest as Sable?

She shook her head. She didn't want to eat. She didn't want to see stars. She wanted to see Roar and Talon. But Sable wasn't offering her that.

"I don't want to see the universe," she said. "I don't want to see you one second longer than I have to."

Sable inclined his head. "Another time, then."

Instead of disappointment, Aria saw determination in his eyes.

After he left, she tried to make herself comfortable as the night deepened. When the wind blew the right way, and when the waves were gentle enough, she heard Sable's voice drift into the Hover, mingling with the campfire smoke.

He spoke with his soldiers about plans for the coming weeks. Priorities.

Shelter. Food and water. Control of the Tides.

She tried to focus. She might learn something helpful. But the words blew right through her mind; she couldn't hold on to anything.

Soon she grew cold and began to shiver. More likely, she realized, shock was what shook her uncontrollably. The temperature had hardly dropped since sunset, and she only felt cool when a breeze carried inside. She curled up on her side, but that didn't help. Eventually, her captors noticed.

"I'll get her a blanket," one of the men said. She watched him reach into the storage lockers. She watched him return.

"Is Sable going to cut your throat open for giving me this?" she asked as he stood over her.

The man startled, surprised to hear her speak. Then he dropped the blanket on her. "You're welcome," he said gruffly, but she saw fear flicker in his eyes. Sable's own men were terrified of him.

As he left, returning to his post by the ramp, the strangest sensation swept over her, like she wasn't just missing Perry, aching for him, bleeding for him. She was grieving for the loss of herself. This was changing her. She would never be the same.

At some point, her father arrived.

Loran came carrying a bowl of soup. He moved with effortless grace, smooth and swift and without spilling. He had excellent balance, like all Auds. Like her. Whether she admitted it to herself or not, a connection existed between them.

Aria met his eyes, and saw that connection in his gaze. The openness and understanding in his eyes rocked her. She suddenly found herself blinking back tears.

She would *not* cry. If she did, then it would be real, and none of this could be real. Not Perry's death, or Sable's control of everything, or her solitary imprisonment here in a Hover.

Loran set the bowl down, sending the men who'd been guarding her away. He listened for a while, staring outside, no doubt ensuring they had privacy before he spoke. Or maybe giving her time to regain her composure. She had to fight for it, drawing a few breaths against the ache in her chest, and focusing on the sounds of the night until the raw feeling in her throat receded.

It had grown quiet and still. No trace of Sable or his advisers anymore. Not even a breeze. Time felt as though it had stopped, until Loran turned to her and spoke.

"He divides people to break morale, as you've probably guessed, and it's working. The Tides are confused and angry, but they're unharmed—except your friend."

"Roar?"

Loran nodded. "He attacked one of my men earlier. Hess's son was involved as well. They were trying to get to you. I tried to inform them that you weren't being harmed, but they wouldn't believe me.

"They're alive for now, but when Sable hears of it, which he soon will, they won't be. He will snuff out any spark he sees—you saw that earlier. He will put down any threat at once, especially now. This is the most critical time for him. He's firming up his rule before the Tides can organize or react."

Aria let out a slow breath. It was too much to take in. Perry and Reef were gone, and now suddenly Roar and Soren were in danger too?

"What should we do?" she asked.

"Not *we*," Loran said sharply. "I brought you soup. While I did so, I gave you information about your friends, but I did *not* help you. He'd know if I did. As it is, it won't be long before he becomes suspicious. He'll know through our tempers that there's something more between us."

Aria considered the words *something more*. She could accept that description of them. It was vague enough. It left her room to decide exactly what kind of *more* simmered between them.

"If he learned about us, would he come after you?"

"If he believes there's any chance I'd come between you and him, yes. Without a doubt."

340

"There is no *me* and *him*."

"You're here, Aria. Alone, while everyone else is out there."

"Why?" she said, her voice rising in pitch. "What does he want with me? Am I just another one of his tools, like Cinder and Perry? Why did you tell me about Roar if you won't help me?"

"I told you where my allegiance lies, Aria. I'm sworn to him."

"Why?" she cried again. "How do you serve a man like that? He's insane. He's a monster!"

Loran leaned close. "Lower your voice," he hissed.

Was he trying to intimidate her with his size?

She leaned in as well, matching him. "You make me sick! You're pathetic and weak and I hate you." Rage lit inside her as she spoke, cutting through the numbness and shock. Her thoughts kept tumbling out. "I hate that you left my mother. I hate what you did to me. I hate that I'm made of half of you."

"I don't think much of you, either. I thought you had a backbone, but all you seem capable of doing is staring out of windows. I'd never have guessed a child of mine could wallow so much."

"Take your stupid soup!" She threw the bowl at him.

Cursing, Loran jerked back, gaping at the soup that dripped over the horn emblem on his black coat.

She kicked him while his eyes were down, slamming her boot into his temple.

He should have flinched. Loran was Sable's highest-ranking soldier. He should have made a move to protect himself, but he took the kick squarely and fell back with a thud.

For an instant, Aria was stunned. Then she shot to her feet and tore down the ramp.

She'd just reached the sand when she heard two words uttered softly behind her.

"Good girl," said her father.

47

ARIA

S he ran.

She sprinted over the hard sand along the water's edge. A trail of high-powered lights illuminated a path from the Hovers, up the wide beach, to the tree line. There, through a web of branches, she saw a brighter concentration of light. The campsite.

She ran away from it, leaving behind people and Hovers, with no notion of where she was going except toward darkness.

When the lights were well behind her, she snatched a piece of driftwood in case she came across anyone and headed toward the trees.

Her thighs burned as she raced over softer sand. Halfway to the tree line, she noticed something looked different. Something besides the shape of the beach, or the delicate tropical trees.

Then she realized *everything* looked different.

Aria's breath caught, and she stopped in her tracks. She hadn't looked at the sky yet. She'd been so lost, so numbed, that she hadn't even looked *up*.

She sank to her knees and lifted her head. She had become so accustomed to the rippling blue tides closing her in, pressing down on her, but this sky was open . . . this *night* was infinite.

She felt like she might fall upward forever, drifting into space. Floating across the stars. Sable had spoken of embers scattered across the roof of the universe. It was a good description.

Aria shook her head, not wanting his voice in her mind. She didn't care what Sable thought of the Still Blue.

It was the worst time to think of Perry then, but she couldn't help it. She imagined him there, grinning, his hand closed over hers.

A sob slipped through her lips. She shot to her feet and broke into a sprint. She reached the tree line at the top of the beach and plunged into the woods, where she slowed down, her breath coming in gasps. The night air smelled loamy and green, and she wondered what Perry would have thought—

No. No. No.

Not now. She pushed him out of her mind. Concentrating on her hearing, she took her time as she wove through the lush woods, creeping back to Sable's camp. The sound of voices drifted to her ears. She followed them, growing steadier and more focused with each step. She had to find Roar and Soren.

The voices led her to a wide clearing. Aria crouched, her heart pounding.

Dozens of people slept in blankets under the open sky.

The men she'd heard were guards, two of them, who spoke softly to each other. They had positioned themselves on a large overturned tree on the opposite side of the clearing, which gave them an elevated lookout over the camp.

She scanned the people nearby, unsure what to do next. There had to be nearly a hundred people in this group alone. Since they were under guard, she knew they had to be Dwellers or her friends from the Tides, but in the darkness, wrapped in blankets, every one of them looked the same.

How was she going to find Roar and Soren?

She pulled herself up and utilized all the power of her Sense to move with absolute silence as she rounded the clearing. Twenty yards of open land stretched between the sleeping people and the tree line where she hid, but near the guards that distance was much smaller. If she drew closer to them, she'd have a better chance of spotting the people she hoped to find.

As she crept toward the guards, her eyes went to one of the larger sleeping figures, drawn by the shine of blond hair. Hyde. But she didn't see Hayden or Straggler. It was the first time she'd seen Hyde without one his brothers. Not far off, she also spotted Molly with Talon curled between her and Bear.

Should she try to free them all? Where would they go? Roar and Soren had a chance of disappearing. They could run into the woods and hide, but could Molly, whose joints bothered her doing the simplest things? And what about Talon? Sable had all the soldiers and weapons. He'd hunt them down and punish them for escaping.

She *couldn't* help everyone, but only Roar and Soren were in imminent danger. Quietly, Aria stole closer to the guards. Soren and Roar had caused problems for the Horns already. Most likely they'd be directly under watch.

She drew nearer—as close as she could without risking exposure—but she still couldn't distinguish between the sleeping lumps. Too many of the huddled forms were turned away, or had blankets pulled over their faces, or it was just too dark to make them out.

The guards' conversation drew her attention.

"How much longer, do you think?" said one.

"Of this? Who knows. I don't see how the Tides will ever come around."

"He'll sway them. Sable always finds a way."

"Yeah . . . he does."

There it was again. The fear the Horns had of Sable, their own leader. Aria heard it in their voices.

Panic clawed at her stomach as she stared at the final stretch between her and the men. Half an hour had passed since she'd escaped from the Hover, she guessed. How much longer until Sable's people started searching for her? Were they already?

An image of Liv lying on the balcony in Rim flashed before her eyes, pushing her into action. She hurried, almost to the guards when she stepped on a twig and heard it snap. The sole of her boot muffled the sound, but she froze, silently cursing herself. Haste had made her careless. There was little cover where she stood, and any Aud within fifty feet would've heard her—the guards were less than half that. She waited, adrenaline coursing through her, making her feel weightless.

The two men didn't look her way. They didn't even pause in their conversation. But amid the sleeping people in front of them, a dark head lifted, turning slowly toward her before lying back down.

She couldn't see Roar's features in the darkness, but she knew it was him. She knew his shape and the way he moved.

Aria sank to the ground, setting the heavy piece of driftwood down. She picked up the twig under her foot. Her right hand was weak, but she could still do this.

Please work, she prayed. This was either a perfect test, or suicide.

She snapped the branch again.

Neither of the guards turned. Not Auds, then. Unlike Roar, who responded to the sound by raising both arms up high, his fingers interlaced like he was stretching.

She shook her head. A little obvious, but Roar did everything with a bit of flash.

Time to move. She was as sure as she could be. The guards weren't Auds. Roar knew she was there. She picked up the driftwood and moved again, drawing as close as she dared. Then she stopped and firmed her grip, licking her lips.

"In five seconds, cough loudly," she whispered, knowing Roar would hear her.

She counted off the seconds. When Roar coughed, she sprinted the last steps to the Horns.

The men looked at Roar, oblivious to her as she charged them from behind.

She swung the driftwood at the closest man's head, putting all her weight behind the strike. She did it with so much force that she felt the muscles in her back pull. The sound of the impact was horrid and made her gasp despite herself.

He toppled over the log, falling limply behind it.

She turned, searching for the second man. Roar had him on the ground already, trapped in a headlock. She heard the guard's feet buck and scrape on the dirt. A soft gurgle, and then nothing.

Roar sprang up. He held his hands in front of him oddly. Then she saw why.

"Your hands are *tied*?" she whispered.

"Yes. I *showed* you."

"Just get Soren."

Roar bent by one the sleeping figures. A second later, Soren popped up.

Their noise had woken Twig—another Aud. Aria saw him assess the situation and come to the same conclusion she had. If they all tried to leave, they'd wake Sable's guards elsewhere—who would be armed and likely wouldn't hesitate to shoot.

348

"Later," she said to him. Later, she'd figure out how to help the rest of them.

Twig nodded. "Get them out of here."

Aria melted back into the woods. She caught up with Roar and Soren—who sounded like a rhinoceros crashing through the undergrowth, but she could do nothing to help that.

They ran for half an hour until Roar stopped them.

"We're good," he said. "There's no one behind us."

Sweat ran down Aria's back, and her legs trembled. Waves broke gently in the distance, and the trees rustled with a breeze.

She looked at Roar, noticing the dark shadow pooled under his left eye. A black eye. From fighting Sable's men, she realized.

"What's wrong with you, Roar?" she yelled, unleashing the fury and fear she'd been holding back. "You *attacked* Sable's guards?"

He jerked back in surprise. "Yes! You were alone in that Hover and I thought . . . I was worried, all right?" Roar looked at Soren, who put his hands up.

"I wasn't worried," Soren said. "I just felt like hitting somebody when he did."

Aria shook her head, still furious, but she couldn't waste any more time. "You have to go. Both of you. Go somewhere. I need to get back."

Roar scowled. "*What?* Aria, you're coming with us."

"I can't, Roar! I promised Perry I'd watch Talon. I have to go back."

"I made him the same promise."

"But you can't keep it anymore, can you? You should have *thought* before you made yourself a target."

"I was already a target!"

"Well, you made it worse!" she yelled, her eyes filling.

"He *killed* Liv and *beat* Perry. I had to try to get you!" Roar tugged at his hair in anger, then dropped his hands. "How is what I did different from this—from what you just did?"

"It's different because my plan *worked*."

He pointed. "You going back there—to *Sable*—is a plan that worked?"

"I just saved your life, Roar!"

He let out a vicious curse and stalked away. She wanted to scream at him for walking away from her, which made no sense. Wasn't she trying to walk away from him?

Soren was leaning against a tree, pretending not to pay attention. It occurred to her how strange this was. Her and Roar fighting while Soren stood by, calm and quiet.

Roar returned. He appeared in front of her, his eyes gentle and pleading. She looked into them and couldn't bear it.

"Aria, if I lose you too—"

"Don't say another word, Roar. Don't make me doubt. Don't make me want to leave with you."

He stepped closer, his voice dropping to a desperate whisper. "Then just say *yes*. Come with me. Don't go back there."

She pushed her sleeves at her blurry eyes, hating how easily she felt like crying now. It was a reflex. Any small thing that reminded her of Perry brought the urge. She couldn't let the tears go, but she felt them. She carried them with her everywhere she went. She imagined holding them there for the rest of her life. An ocean of tears, existing inside her.

"Aria . . . ," Roar said.

She shook her head and backed away. "I can't." She had promised Perry. She had to look after Talon. No matter the cost. "I have to go," she said.

Then she raced back to Sable's camp.

48

PEREGRINE

I s he breathing, Roar? Is he alive?"

"Shut up. I'm trying to listen to his heart."

Perry forced his eyes open. Through a bleary film, he saw Roar leaning over his chest. "Off. Get off me, Roar."

Perry's throat was so dry that the words were no more than rasps. All he could think about was water. He ached for it. Every fiber of his body demanded it. His head pounded. It hurt so badly he was afraid to move.

Roar's head popped up and his eyes flew wide. "Ha!" he yelled. *"Ha!"* He shook Perry by the shoulders. "I knew it!" He leaped to his feet and shouted that he knew it, over and over, until he finally sprawled on the sand. "That was horrible. That was so horrible," he said between pants.

Soren, who'd been watching Roar in silence, appeared over Perry. "Want some water?"

★ ★ ★

They gathered by a fire as the sun set, surrounded by foreign scents and sounds. Every breath was like hearing a new language—a process of recognizing soil and plant and animal scents, but also learning them as new. This land was green and young, and even as spent as he felt, his heart thudded with the desire to explore it.

After drinking enough water to make his stomach cramp, Perry learned that Roar and Soren had escaped from Sable's camp two days ago. They'd been familiarizing themselves with the terrain, finding freshwater and food, while trying to devise a plan for taking Sable out. Then it was Perry's turn to talk. He told them what had happened with Cinder on the Hover.

"That was the last time you saw him?" Roar said. "Before you blacked out?"

Perry considered that, remembering those final moments. Saying he blacked out didn't feel right. He'd seen only white. But he nodded and said, "That was it. I didn't see him after that."

Roar rubbed his jaw, giving a small shrug. "Maybe that's how it should have been. I doubt you could have helped him."

"But I would have tried," Perry said. "I'd have done all I could."

Soren poked at the fire with a stick. "From where I'm sitting, you did."

It was a decent thing to say. Perry nodded in thanks.

He leaned his back on the raft—the raft that had saved his life—and wove his fingers together on his stomach. He wanted to rush to Aria but he was too weak. He had to replenish the water his body desperately needed. Hour by hour, his muscle cramps and his headache faded and he felt more like himself.

He saw the scars on his hand, scars Cinder had given him, and his throat tightened. The feeling he had of incompletion—of wishing he could have done more, or differently, or better—wasn't new. But he was tired of bashing his head against the past. He tried to do right—in every situation. Sometimes that wasn't enough, but it was all he could do. The only thing he truly had power over. He was learning to accept that.

He watched the ashes from the fire flicker upward into the darkness. To the stars. The lid had come off the sky, and now they were connected, earth with everything. Him to Cinder. To Liv and his brother and his father.

He was so close to feeling peace. Only one thing stood in his way now.

"Per, how did you know that thing was on the Hover?" Roar asked, tipping his chin to the raft.

Perry's eyes moved to Soren, remembering the Dweller's comment when they'd been preparing to go after Cinder in the Komodo.

That's an inflatable boat, Outsider. And if that's what you're wearing, I'm out of this operation.

Soren grinned. "Go on, admit it. I saved your life."

His tone was friendly. He had changed in the past week, Perry thought. The way he looked and the way he spoke.

"You helped," Perry said. When Sable had left him for dead, Perry had shot right to the storage lockers, Soren's wisecrack loud in his mind. He had hoped the Dragonwing, a smaller craft than the Belswan, also carried the raft. Luck had been on his side. He'd immediately located the inflatable boat, which had assembled with just the press of a button. He could say one thing about the Dwellers: they built good ships.

Perry had escaped the Dragonwing with only seconds to spare. He'd watched the Hover sink behind him and then he'd come through the barrier of Aether, the last of the Hovers in the fleet soaring above him.

They'd pulled ahead quickly then. The fleet had probably made the journey there in hours, where he had spent a day battling rough seas, and then two more in calmer water.

Three days alone, but they hadn't been difficult. He preferred hunting, but he was a fisherman by birth. He'd been fine with the ocean ahead of him, a new sky above. His only real problem had been the lack of water.

Dehydration, he'd realized quickly, was worse than burns or the pound of a mallet. By the time he'd dragged himself and the raft up the beach, into the cover of the trees where Roar and Soren found him, reality had lost its sharpness.

He'd thought that maybe he was only imagining that he'd reached land when Roar and Soren showed up.

"It would have been easier on me if you'd taught me how to fly the Hover," Perry said to Soren now. "Could have saved me a few days."

Soren grinned. "You keep saying you want to learn, Outsider. I'm ready. I'll teach you anytime."

"I'm proud of both of you," Roar said. "I just have to say that."

He was joking, but there was a seed of honesty there. Perry was sharing a jug of water with Soren. They were talking easily. Perry had never thought it possible.

He sat up and asked the question that had been on his mind all day. "How is she, Roar?"

Roar met his eyes directly. "How would you be if you thought she was dead?"

Perry couldn't even stand to imagine it. He found himself biting down into his teeth. "What has Sable done?" he said instead.

Silence.

"Tell him, Roar," Soren said.

Perry leaned back and shut his eyes. He already knew. "Reef."

"Yes," Roar said. "Gren, too. The moment we got here. Twig was shot, but he was holding on when we left."

Reef. Perry sucked in a breath and held it there, pushing back on the pressure. In half a year, he'd become so much to Perry. Brother. Father. Friend. Adviser. Perry's eyes blurred, another gap opening inside him.

"I'm sorry, Per," Roar said.

Perry nodded, bracing himself. "Marron?"

"He's fine. At least he was when we left."

It made sense. Marron was brilliant and respected, but he wasn't ambitious or aggressive. He'd never challenge Sable for power—he'd reason for it. Reef had represented the only real threat to Sable. He would have picked up the Tides as his own. He'd have done it for Perry.

"Sable has control of everything," Soren said. "You could feel it even before he set down on the beach. As soon as you left with Cinder, he took control. He's a madman. Completely psychotic."

"He'll be completely dead soon," Perry said.

For the next hours, he talked with Roar and Soren about the camp Sable had set up. They discussed the basic layout of the settlement, the surrounding geography, and the advantages Sable had—which were many.

When it was late, Roar said, "What are you thinking, Per?"

Perry rolled his shoulders back, his muscles finally loosening and feeling stronger. "We go after him. But we have to do it the right way. If I show up and the Tides see me, it could turn into an uprising. It could escalate and become us against the Horns. That can't happen. They have all the weapons. . . . It'd be a bloodbath. Worse than the Komodo."

Roar crossed his arms. "Then we hit him fast."

"Right. And while he's not expecting it. We'll come up

on him tomorrow night in the darkness. We get close, and we take him down when he's not looking." He looked at Roar and Soren. "It means you have to trust me, and do exactly what I say this time. No mistakes."

49

ARIA

S able was planning a party.

"What we need is a celebration of our triumph. An event to celebrate a new beginning," he said, his bold voice filling the quiet afternoon, though he spoke only to her. He turned in profile, waving out beyond the Hover door to the sandy beach outside. "Darkness and ruin are behind us. We left that poisoned land and we made it here. Most of us. The good lot of us. And this land shows every sign of being more hospitable. More robust. We'll flourish here. Our lives will be so much better, and that deserves a feast."

They were in the Belswan's cargo hold. Aria hadn't stepped outside since she'd freed Roar and Soren two days ago. She had come back to the camp just before dawn, and found her father pacing by the Hover. "It took you long enough," Loran had said as she slipped inside. Right back to here, her prison cell.

She'd had no company other than the two mute guards who kept watch over her, and Sable, who visited her in the mornings and afternoons. Each time, he'd talked at length about his search for the best location to establish a city, carrying on a one-sided conversation about *progress* and *the future*, his words airy, floating right past her.

But now it seemed his search had ended.

Sable turned back to her, the look in his eyes restless, manic. "I had a field cleared this morning. It's beautiful, Aria. It sits right beside a small river that flows down from the mountains. You remember my home in Rim? Proximity to water is essential to any prosperous civilization. I'm going to build a similar city, but I'll improve upon it." He smiled. "I'm getting ahead of myself. A city will come soon enough. First, we'll dance on the very ground that will become the streets of Cape Rim. Then tomorrow we set about the work of establishing a new civilization."

Finally, he turned his full focus on her and frowned. He seemed surprised that she wasn't swept up with him.

"Aria," he said, moving closer to where she slouched against the inner wall of the Hover, beneath the window where she'd last seen Perry's ship.

Sable knelt, studying her. "Will you come with me tonight as my guest? I'd prefer not to force you."

She smiled. "And I'd prefer you dead."

Sable's pupils flared with surprise at hearing her speak. He recovered quickly. "That will change. One day it will be better between us."

"No, it won't. I will always hate you."

"Will you be the only one, then?" he asked, eagerness tingeing his voice. "The only one I can't bend to my liking?"

Aria couldn't answer that question. If she told him yes, she would only feed his sick obsession.

Outside, Kirra approached with Marron. Sable must have heard them, but he didn't turn to look. He kept his gaze on Aria, as if by the force of his intensity alone he could bend her to his wishes.

Kirra stepped inside, her red hair losing its brilliance as she moved into the shadow of the Hover. She still had a nasty bruise over her jaw, where Aria had hit her.

Marron was disheveled and sunburned. He brought a trembling hand up, covering his mouth when he saw Aria. Did she look as dead as she felt?

Kirra's lips curled into a cruel smile. "He's here, Sable," she said.

"Wait outside with him," Sable replied. "I'll be along soon."

It was unnerving, the way he spoke with Kirra behind him while staring at Aria.

"She's going to betray you like Olivia did," Kirra said, anger seeping into her voice.

"Thank you, Kirra. Outside, please."

Kirra shook her head at Aria and dragged Marron outside.

"Are you going to hurt him?" Aria asked when they were gone.

"Marron? No. I need him. I've called him here to get a status report. Nothing more."

For a long moment, Aria just breathed as relief swept over her.

Kirra had stopped to speak with someone outside, her voice drifting into the Hover.

"How can you stand her?" Aria asked.

Sable smiled. "She's served me for many years. I like her well enough, particularly when there is no one better around. Before you say anything, remember that she's a Scire. Kirra knows where she stands with me and she accepts it."

That word, *Scire*, took Aria right to Perry. She looked down at her hands, unable to hold Sable's gaze.

"I'm tired, Aria. I want peace."

"You want peace now that you have taken everything."

"Not quite everything."

She looked up. The desire in his expression nauseated her. At least he knew that. Her temper would tell him so without her having to say a word.

"We could accomplish great things together," he said. "The Dwellers look to you as a leader, and you have the respect of the Tides. We can rebuild here. We can bring them together. Can't you see it? Can't you picture what we could be?"

"I can picture all the ways I want to end your life."

Sable sat back on his heels, letting out a sigh. "You need some time. I understand. I'm in no hurry. You've suffered quite a lot." He stood, pausing, his lips turning up. "I'll send your father for you later."

She froze, her heart squeezing in her chest. How long had he known about Loran?

Sable's smile widened. "No need to worry. He's a trusted warrior. A man of great character. That should make you very proud. He is very valuable to me. Almost indispensable," he added with a smile. He moved to the ramp, turning back for one last comment. "Oh, and I've been meaning to tell you. Your friends who mysteriously disappeared? Roar and Soren? Not to worry. I'll find them for you. My people are looking for them."

Loran arrived to fetch her at dusk.

"He knows," Aria said as he walked up the ramp.

Loran crouched in front of her. "Yes."

"You're in danger because of me."

"I want to be."

"You *want* to be in danger because he knows you're my father?"

"I'd prefer that he didn't know, but he does. It was bound to happen. He was bound to scent how I feel. He is like all Scires . . . a master at using leverage to get what he wants. An expert manipulator."

"Not all Scires are that way," she said.

"No . . . you're right. Not all." With a sigh, Loran sat. "Sable applies pressure on the psyche," he said, his voice unhurried and soft. "He's very pleased to have learned that we're connected. I have the respect of his soldiers, and he is

363

wise enough to know that he needs me to keep order. And now he's confident that I won't step out of line. He has found a very big weakness of mine."

"Would you have stepped out of line?"

"Never before," he answered quickly. "But recently . . . recently someone I met has me asking questions about integrity and what it's worth."

"What is it worth?"

"A great deal."

"So now you're questioning him, but he has a means of controlling you . . . and that's me?"

Loran shook his head. "You misunderstood. I'm not questioning *him*. I've always known who he is. What I'm questioning, thanks to a girl with a tooth-rattling kick, is who *I* am."

She hugged her knees, unsure what to say. She'd hoped that finding her father would lead to her knowing herself better. She'd never considered it might also happen the other way around. "So . . . who are you?"

His gaze fell to his boots. "I don't know where to start, Aria. This is new to me. I want to tell you so much, but I don't want to burden you with more than you want to know."

"I want to know everything."

He lifted his eyes, and Aria saw a change in them. She thought it was surprise at first. Then she realized it was tenderness.

"My family," he began, "and yours, has been in the service

364

of the Horn Blood Lords for generations. We are soldiers and advisers who hold the highest military positions. It's the life I was born to, the one I knew I'd lead eventually, but twenty years ago, when I was close to your age, I wanted nothing to do with it. When I asked my father for a few years to be on my own, he granted me one. It was more than I had expected."

Loran had music in his voice. It was beautiful.

"I'd only been traveling a month when a Hover chased me down on the edge of the Shield Valley. I found myself inside a Dweller Pod, a place I'd only ever heard about in rumors."

Loran glanced behind him, out to the beach. "There is no forgiveness in the north. We do things a certain way, as you know by now. So when I was taken captive, I expected something along the lines of what happened to Peregrine. Your mother was the first person I saw when I came to. She did *not* look frightening." He smiled to himself then, lost in an image of Lumina that Aria wished she could share. "She promised I wouldn't be mistreated. She told me I would go home one day. I heard sincerity in her voice. I heard kindness. I believed her."

As he spoke, Aria felt like she was wearing a Smarteye. Part of her listening to Loran. Part of her in a Realm in which Lumina was a young researcher, fascinated by an Outsider.

"From that moment on, I didn't worry. I had left Rim to see what was different from what I knew." He lifted his shoulders. "I couldn't have landed in a better place.

"Her studies dealt with adaptations to stress. Dwellers, she

365

explained, had less resilience to it than we do. Sometimes she'd put me into simulations in the Realms, but most of the time she asked me questions about the Outside. Eventually, she was answering *my* questions." He ran a hand over his jaw. "I don't know the exact moment that I fell in love with her, but I will never forget the moment she told me she was with child.

"As much as I cared for her, Aria, and I did, very deeply, I realized I would never be accepted into her world. Her people would never be mine. She couldn't come to the outside with me, either. I knew that, but I still asked her a thousand times. But she wanted our child to grow up in safety. In the end, we both agreed the Pod would be the best place for you."

Aria bit her lip until it stung. *Our child.* For a few seconds, the words flapped around her mind like bats. "So you left?"

Loran nodded. "I had to. When I returned to Rim, I'd been gone exactly a year. Leaving her was the hardest thing I've ever done."

A sense of unreality seeped through her as she stared at him. Her eyes filled, and her lungs felt like they were going to explode.

"What is it, Aria?"

"I lost my mother, and I lost Perry. If I started to care . . ."

Her tears came like a torrent. They came so violently, with such an eruption, that she could only yield to them, letting the pain shake her, unravel her piece by piece.

After a long while, her grief shaped into something different.

Surprise.

Loran's arms wrapped around her, holding her. When she looked up, she saw concern on his face—*intense* concern—and a flicker of something else.

"I'm sorry you're hurting," he said, answering her unspoken question, "but this is my first act as your father. At least it feels that way to me. And it's . . . very fulfilling."

She brushed her fingers over her eyes. "I want to try. I want to give us a chance too."

They weren't the prettiest words she'd ever spoken, but they were a start. And judging by Loran's smile, they were enough.

They turned toward the open hatch at the same time, following the sound that carried from outside. Drums pounding in the distance.

"We'd better go," Loran said.

Sable's party had begun.

The clearing in the woods was much larger than the one at the heart of the Tides' compound. It was bordered on one side by a river that stepped down the hill as it wove around smooth boulders. Lush foliage decorated the banks, and trees bowed low, trailing their branches in the burbling water. It couldn't have been more unlike the deadly cold and stark alpine shores of the Snake River.

Around the area, torchlight wavered. Night was falling, the deep blue sky pierced by the stars that flickered to life one by one. Aria heard music. Two drums beating a rhythm, and strings as well. A few instruments had survived the crossing, then.

Sable was right. This place *was* beautiful. This land *had* promise. But she couldn't separate the suffering of the people from the beauty of the place.

Across the field, the Tides gathered in subdued groups, standing, sitting in circles. Her eyes moved over them, her stomach twisting with anger. They didn't look like guests at a party or like proud founders of a new settlement. They looked like what they were: captives.

Her gaze landed on Hyde. He was so easy to spot, tall as he was. Hayden and Straggler were scattered elsewhere, one close, the other across the field, near Twig. The remaining members of the Six looked lost without Reef, Gren, and Perry. Without one another.

Aria located Marron with a circle of children around him and saw Molly and Bear there too.

Sable's people stood like watchdogs, strategically placed around the clearing, imposing with their weapons and black uniforms, horns twisting in sinister patterns on their chests.

"Great party," she said.

Beside her, Loran said nothing.

As they walked toward the center of the clearing, where a table sat up on a dais, she spotted Caleb and Rune with a few other Dwellers. Of the thousand or so people in the clearing, the Dwellers made up a fraction. So much for their supposed superiority over Outsiders.

"Aria!"

Talon ran over, Willow on his heels. He wrapped his arms around Aria's waist.

"Hey, Talon." She held him for a second, feeling better than she had since she'd left the cave. And keeping him close meant keeping Perry close in some way too.

Not far off, a few of Sable's men watched them.

"We don't know where Roar is," Willow said. "No one's telling us anything."

Her eyes were puffy and scared. She didn't look like herself. *No one* looked like themselves.

"He's fine," Aria said. "I'm sure he's fine."

"What if he's not?" Several people looked over at Willow's raised voice. "What if they shot him?"

"They didn't."

"How do you know? They shot Reef and Gren. They shoot everybody!"

A low growl drew Aria's attention to Flea.

"I will have that dog shot as well, if you can't control him," Sable said as he walked up. He spoke evenly, like he was stating a fact.

"I hate you!" Willow yelled.

"You can't do that!" Talon yelled. Flea's barks became grittier and louder. Hyde came over, drawing Talon and Willow away. Hayden picked Flea up and carried him off.

Aria couldn't believe that only the children would stand

up to Sable. This place, which should have meant survival and freedom, was a prison.

Sable's gaze fell on her. He smiled and held out his hand. "Join me? I have a special place set up for us."

She took his cold grip, only one thought in her mind.

Sable needed to die.

50

PEREGRINE

From his hidden spot in the darkness, Perry watched Aria take Sable's hand.

"I can't be the only one who feels sick," Soren said.

"You're not," replied Roar.

Perry didn't feel ill. He felt focused. He was on the hunt; this was what he did best.

He settled onto a knee behind a stand of broad-leafed shrubs and considered the situation. Roar and Soren crouched at his sides.

They hadn't expected to find a feast. This would change things.

Tides and Dwellers sat in groups strewn across the clearing, but Sable had erected a platform at the center, where a table decorated with candles and arrangements of lush foliage and colorful flowers had been set up. Sable led Aria there, joining a few of his men and a handful of Guardians.

Perry noticed that his own fighters were scattered. Sable had wisely broken them apart to keep them in check.

"I guess taking him out in secret is no longer an option," Roar said.

Perry shook his head. "He couldn't be in a worse position for me to get to him."

The platform sat at the center of hundreds of people, half of them Horns. Perry knew the second he stepped out into the open, if he wasn't shot on the spot, he'd likely incite an outright revolt. As subdued as the crowd seemed, the tempers wafting his way seethed with rage. The Tides weren't defeated. They were dry kindling, just waiting for a spark.

Talon's position was the only thing he liked about this situation. His nephew sat between Hyde and Molly, Marron and Bear only a few feet away.

Perry knew that was no accident. Believing him to be dead, the Tides had claimed Talon as their own, protecting him. Seeing that made his heart ache.

"Can you get a shot at Sable from here?" Roar asked.

Perry thought it over. He didn't have his bow, but maybe they could snatch one of the pistols worn by the Horns guarding the clearing. The shot was a good hundred yards—easy when he was using his own gear. But he was less familiar with the Dweller guns.

"Aria's right next to him," he said finally. "I can't risk it. Not with a weapon I don't know well."

Sable had seated her to his right. Aria's father sat on his other side.

"Can't you make a bow?" Soren asked.

Roar glanced at Perry, rolling his eyes. "Sure, Soren. Let's come back in a few days."

Perry turned back to the clearing. Approaching Sable like this wasn't ideal, but enough people had died, and the look in Aria's eyes worried him. Instinct told him it was time.

He thought through every scenario a few times, then explained what he needed to Soren and Roar.

When he was finished, Soren stood and nodded. "Got it," he said, jogging off.

Then Roar hopped to his feet. "Shoot straight, Per."

As he turned to leave, Perry caught him by the arm. "Roar—" He didn't know what else to say. He had so little left, and if this plan didn't work—

"It's going to work, Perry." Roar tipped his chin toward the clearing. "Let's finish the bastard." He jogged off, steps silent as he worked his way to the opposite side of the clearing.

As he watched Roar stalk through the trees, Perry had never been more grateful for his sharp eyes. His heart pounded as Roar drew closer to his target, settling into position.

Hidden in the woods behind Kirra.

Perry needed to use her, just as she'd used him.

The music stopped abruptly—that meant Soren had done his part. He'd made his way to the musicians, found Jupiter, and told him to stop playing.

Roar came next. Across the clearing, he raised his hand,

signaling. He was ready.

Perry's focus turned to the Horn soldier nearest to him. He pulled himself to his feet, legs coiled as he counted down

Three.

Two.

One.

He sprang from his hiding place, knowing Roar was doing the same across the clearing. His legs churned over the soft earth as he ran to the Horn soldier.

"Sable!"

Roar's shout broke the silence like a thunderclap. Hundreds of heads turned toward his voice—away from Perry as he grabbed the soldier by the neck, laying a forearm over the man's mouth to stifle his protests. Perry hauled him into the darkness, back behind the cover of the shrub. Then he took the man's pistol, lifted the weapon, and delivered a quick strike to the temple. The soldier's head snapped to the side and he dropped, unconscious. Perry jumped up and sprinted the short distance to the clearing.

Everywhere, people rose to their feet, craning to see Roar, who held Kirra by the throat, using her body as a shield.

Perry dove into the crowd, sinking into his legs to minimize his height. Twig saw him and gasped, opening his mouth to say something. Perry shook his head, holding his finger to his lips.

Twig nodded.

A few more eyes darted Perry's way. Old Will. Brooke and Clara. A murmur rose up around him but it faded quickly.

The message passed through the crowd like a silent ripple: he was there—but he was to be concealed. The Tides understood. They gave no outward sign that he was among them. They kept the surprise from their faces, but he scented their tempers. He knew exactly how overcome they were to see him alive. The force of their emotion added to his resolve.

As he wove past Straggler and Old Will toward the high table at the center, Roar's voice was the only sound he heard.

"Call them off, Sable! Tell your men to stand down, or I'll kill her!"

Perry reached the edge of the crowd. The wooden dais stretched before him, Sable only a dozen paces away.

And Aria.

"Call your men off and I'll let her go!" Roar yelled. "This is between us! It's about Liv."

Sable took a pistol from Aria's father and stood, pushing back from the table. "I can't say I'm surprised to see you."

Gasps erupted from across the clearing as the crowd surged back, clearing the field between them.

"You have a debt to pay." Roar's voice sounded rough, hoarse with anger. His diversion was working; all eyes remained fixed on him.

Perry lifted the gun and aimed at Sable, searching for a clear shot. He found it. A kill shot, right to the back of his head. Steadying his breath, he exerted steady pressure on the trigger.

Aria shifted, suddenly in the way.

Perry let up, his heart climbing to his throat, but he wasted no time. He crept around the dais in search of another angle, knowing he had only seconds before the Horns spotted him.

"Sable, do something!" Kirra pleaded, struggling against Roar.

"No one else has to get hurt," Roar yelled. "Only you. You need to pay for what you did!"

Sable raised the pistol in a quick, precise motion. "I disagree," he said.

Then he fired.

51

ARIA

The gunshot shook the air. An instant later, Roar and Kirra collapsed to the earth.

Aria reacted without thinking, throwing herself into Sable. She rammed into his shoulder and they crashed to the platform. The hard edge of a plank bit into her back, Sable's weight smashing her down. They rolled off together, onto the grass.

She twisted as they fell, grabbing the pistol in his hand. Her fingers found the trigger and squeezed. She heard the weapon fire just as Sable's fist struck her across the temple.

Pain burst deep in her skull, a blaze that shot all the way down her spine, and everything went dark. The only thing she knew was that she still gripped the gun.

But then it tore from her fingers as unseen hands closed on her arms and wrenched her upright. They pulled with such force that her neck snapped forward, her chin hitting her breastbone.

Aria lifted her head. She couldn't see—not the earth beneath her feet or the people around her. She blinked hard, trying to recover her vision. Trying to stay on her feet.

When her eyes cleared, she thought she'd died. That she'd shot herself while trying to kill Sable. It was the only explanation for why Perry stood only ten paces away, on the platform, pointing a gun at Sable.

Perry stepped down to the ground. Shouts exploded around the clearing. A dozen of Sable's guards aimed their weapons at Perry.

He went still, his gaze flicking to Aria. Then he lowered the gun.

"Wise choice, Peregrine," Sable said at her side. "If you kill me, my men will kill you, and then, quite probably, the killing will keep going for quite some time. I'm glad you recognize that."

As he spoke, Aria noticed that he was empty-handed. She had disarmed him. She'd also taken off part of his ear.

Sable paused, wincing as he gave a small shake of his head, like he'd just become aware of the pain. He pressed at the bleeding wound and saw the blood on his fingers, then let out a raw groan of pure anger. "Take his gun, Loran," he ordered.

Perry never took his eyes off Sable as Loran took the weapon from him.

Aria knew what was coming. She had seen this before.

She'd lived this nightmare once already, on a balcony high over the Snake River. She felt like she was falling again. Like in seconds, she'd plunge into frigid black water.

"I have to admit," he said, letting out a small laugh. "I *am* surprised to see you, Peregrine. My own fault for not being thorough. Not a mistake I'll make again." He glanced over his shoulder, at Loran. "I'll take that pistol. And then you might consider holding your daughter. I wouldn't want her to catch a stray shot."

Loran didn't move. Aria didn't understand. Hadn't he heard the command?

Seconds passed. Finally, Sable looked at him. "Loran, the gun."

Loran shook his head. "You wanted to keep the old ways alive. You said so yourself when we came here." He held up the pistol. "We never used these to settle a challenge before. Did the Tides, Peregrine?"

Every eye in the clearing turned to Perry.

He shook his head. "No. Never did." Then he dove forward, flying at Sable.

52

PEREGRINE

As Perry tackled Sable to the ground, he waged a small debate with himself.

Make Sable suffer, or finish him instantly?

A little of both, he decided.

Sable fought him, pushing against Perry, but he was weaker and slower. Pinning him took no effort.

As Sable fell on his back, Perry punched him across the jaw. Sable's head rocked to the side, his eyes losing focus as the blow stunned him. Perry grabbed the jeweled Blood Lord chain around his neck and gave the links a hard twist, tightening them.

Sable groaned and sputtered, thrashing beneath him, but Perry held him fast. He'd been in this position before, very nearly, with his brother. That had been harder. Much harder than this.

"You were right, Sable." Perry twisted tighter, the gemstones cold against his fingers. "We are alike. Neither one of us deserves to wear this." He twisted again.

Sable's eyes bulged, and his skin turned blue.

"Perry!"

Perry heard Aria's yell, just as the glint of steel flashed in the corner of his eye. He shifted away, but felt the blade slice into his side.

A hidden weapon. He should have known.

The knife grazed Perry's ribs. It was a glancing blow—Sable too weak to put any force behind the strike—the pain that bit into him shallow, nothing compared to what Perry had been through.

"That's not enough, Sable," he growled. "You don't *have* enough." He cinched the links tighter and held on.

Sable convulsed, his eyes rolling back, the tone of his skin going from pale blue to white.

Finally, he went still.

Perry released the chain and climbed to his feet. He decided on the spot: This was it. His final act as Blood Lord of the Tides.

He pulled his own chain over his neck and dropped it on Sable's body.

He spent the next hours defusing the tension in the clearing with Aria, Marron, and Loran. The Horns put down their weapons with little protest when they learned they weren't in danger of retaliation. Aria's father proved to be key to their disarmament. Perry quickly saw that Loran commanded more loyalty and respect from Sable's people than Sable ever had.

Then the questions began as discussions turned to next steps. Who would lead? How would they meet basic needs?

Nothing was decided, but one note was heard over and again: the answers would come eventually and peaceably. Dweller. Outsider. Horn or Tide. They were of the same mind. They'd had enough of strife. It was time to shed the skin of the old world and move forward.

Later that night, when most everyone had settled into sleep, Perry caught Roar's eye and they did what they'd done their entire lives, taking the trail to the beach to grab a few minutes of quiet.

This time was different.

Aria came with them. Talon and Willow, too.

Then Brooke and Soren. Molly and Bear and Marron.

It went on, a small crowd leaving the slumbering camp behind, and migrating down to the wide beach fringed by waves far gentler than those at the Tides.

Hyde and Hayden fetched wood. Jupiter brought down a guitar. Soon there was a fire and laughter. A real celebration.

"I told you we'd do it, Per," Roar said.

"It was closer than I wanted it to be. I thought you'd really been shot."

"*I* thought I'd gotten shot."

"So did I," Aria said. "You fell so dramatically."

Caleb nodded. "He did. He fell with a flourish."

Roar laughed. "What can I say? I'm just good at most things."

As their joking continued, Perry's thoughts turned to Kirra. Roar hadn't been shot, but she had. It wasn't right to celebrate her death, but Sable's . . .

Perry felt no remorse for what he'd done. He wished he could be nobler about it, but he couldn't be. He knew regret, having slain Vale. Perry would carry that burden for the rest of his life. But Sable's death brought him nothing but relief.

Looking at the faces around him, he ached to see his sister's. Liv should have been there, teasing Roar. Laughing louder than anyone at his jokes. Across the fire, Twig and the brothers sat quiet and somber, no doubt feeling the absence of Gren and Reef. They had all been brothers. A circle of Six—now broken, also because of Sable.

Perry's gaze moved to Willow, who sat between Molly and Bear with Talon. Flea slept curled at her feet, but she looked lonely, and Perry knew who she missed.

They had made it here, but the price had been steep.

Aria's hand slipped into his. She looked into his eyes, the firelight illuminating her face. "How are you doing?" she asked.

"Me?" Perry ran his fingers over the bruise Sable had left on her forehead. It would fade, and the cut Sable had given him on the ribs would heal. Perry hardly felt it now. What he felt was the girl he loved, tucked to his side. "I'm doing amazing."

She smiled, recognizing her answer to the same question a few days ago. "Really?"

He nodded. When they found some time alone, he'd tell her about all the triumph and sorrow that stretched at the walls of his heart. For now, he just said, "Really."

A conversation across the fire caught his attention. Marron was talking to Molly and a few Dwellers about forming a leadership council. They planned to begin recruiting members in the morning.

Perry gave Aria's shoulder a squeeze, tipping his chin. "You should be part of that council."

"I want to be," she said, and then fell quiet for a moment. "Maybe I'll ask Loran if he wants to be in it, too."

It was a great idea. Perry couldn't think of a better way for Aria to build a relationship with her father, and he knew how much she wanted that.

Aria's gaze went to his neck, where the chain no longer rested. "What about you?"

"You'll do a better job than I ever did. You already have. And I have important plans for tomorrow."

"Important plans?"

"That's right." He winked at Talon, who was drifting to sleep next to Molly. "I'm going fishing."

Aria's gray eyes brightened. "Using what kind of bait? Earthworms? Night crawlers?"

"Are you ever going to forget that?"

"No. Never."

"Fine." He leaned in and whispered, "Then I love you, my

little Night Crawler." He kissed her then, because he could. Lingered over her lips, because he couldn't stop himself.

Aria drew away first, leaving him out of his mind with desire. He'd been about two seconds from whisking her away somewhere, and she seemed to know it. She smiled at him, her eyes full of heat and promises; then she turned to Soren.

"Nothing to say?" she asked him. "No retching noises or snide remarks?"

"What—no." The words came out together. Soren crossed his arms and lifted his shoulders. "Nothing."

Beside him, Brooke shook her head. "That's a first."

Soren glanced at her, trying—and failing—to hold back a smile. "Can't I just sit here, relishing the fire?"

"You're *relishing* the fire?" Brooke laughed.

Soren frowned, looking confused. "What? Why is that funny?"

Perry noticed they sat a little closer than they needed to, and Brooke seemed happy.

Roar stood unexpectedly and headed into the darkness. Perry wondered if he'd seen the same, the beginnings of a pair, and been reminded of Liv.

But Roar only rounded the fire and grabbed the guitar from Jupiter. He came back and looked at Aria, smiling as he plucked the strings. Perry recognized the opening of the Hunter's Song.

Aria straightened, rubbing her hands together in exaggerated eagerness. "My *favorite*."

"Me too," said Roar.

Perry grinned. It was *his* favorite—not theirs.

"Light of dawn in the hunter's eyes," Aria sang. "Home unfurls inside his mind."

Roar joined in, their voices harmonizing perfectly, and it was a good thing—the best thing—hearing the two people who knew him best sing to him. The lyrics told the story of a hunter's return, and they'd always swept Perry up; he'd hummed them a thousand times while walking the Tide Valley. He would never go back there, but tonight was still a return—to the life he wanted again.

They were safe. He could rest now. He smiled to himself. He could *hunt*.

"Peregrine," Molly said sometime later, when the group had fallen quiet. Talon snored softly with his head in her lap. "Sable made an announcement to us earlier. He told us this place was going to be called Cape Rim. I think we can do better."

"I *know* we can," he said. "What would you call it, Molly?"

"I've been thinking about it, and it seems to me we wouldn't be here if it weren't for Cinder."

"Oh . . . ," Marron said. "That's lovely."

Aria looked up, her violet scent filling him with steadiness. "What do you think?"

Perry looked down to the waves, and then farther out to the dark horizon, where he saw only stars. "I think it's a great name."

53

ARIA

"**A**re you done?" Roar said. "Because that took forever."

Aria stepped out of the Belswan Hover and jogged down the ramp to join him. "It took an hour, Roar."

Behind her, the rest of the council members were still talking. Her father argued with Soren—a dynamic that was already familiar—while Marron and Molly interjected calmly from time to time. The meeting had ended, but there was so much to decide. Their discussions never really ended.

"That's what I said. Forever." Roar fell into step with her as they headed back to the settlement. "How was your swim?"

"Good. It's helping." In the weeks since they'd arrived, she and Perry had been swimming together in the mornings. They left early, before anyone else stirred, and hadn't missed a day yet. The exercise was helping her arm heal—her hand was almost back to normal—but the best part was spending time alone with him.

Yesterday when they'd finished, he'd told her that the water made him feel close to the Tides territory. Aria loved knowing his thoughts. With every one she learned, she fell for him more deeply. It was the best kind of falling, and she wondered if it would ever end.

"I get the feeling you're not smiling because of my irresistible charm," Roar said, pulling her out of her daze.

"I think you're spending too much time with Soren. You're starting to sound like him."

Roar smiled. "Well, Soren doesn't sound like Soren anymore, so someone had to step in."

Aria laughed. It was true. Between Hess's death, and whatever was brewing between Soren and Brooke, the edges had been smoothed from his attitude. Now Soren was only occasionally offensive.

She and Roar talked nonsense as they walked the trail, their conversation easy and light as always. As they approached the settlement, Aria heard the pound of hammers and voices calling back and forth. Though she'd grown accustomed to the din over the past weeks, it always filled her with hope. It meant homes being built.

Part of her work on the council was to develop long-term plans for the city of Cinder. Plans for paved roads, a hospital, a gathering hall. Those would all come eventually. For now, they needed shelter. A comfortable place to lay their heads at night.

"I don't see him," Roar said, eyes scanning as they arrived.

"I don't either." Around them was a symphony of people digging, lifting, erecting walls and roofs, while Flea trotted around like he was supervising. "He took Talon exploring after our swim this morning. I'm sure they'll be back soon." It was another part of Perry's day—time with Talon, hunting, hiking. Whatever they decided.

Aria sat on a half-wall, built with nails poured from the new forge, and with lumber cut from higher elevation and floated downriver. Eventually, the wall would rise to become one side of a house.

This particular house would have a loft with a minor flaw. A crack in the roof that showed just a sliver of the blue sky above. Aria had made plans in secret with Marron. It was going to be a surprise.

Roar sat beside her. "So you want to just wait for them here?"

"Sure." She bumped his shoulder with her own and smiled. "It's a good place to wait. This is home."

ACKNOWLEDGMENTS

This book marks the end of years of effort by many people. Thank you first and foremost to Barbara Lalicki for her unerring guidance and belief in this story. I couldn't have asked for a better editor. These books would not exist without Rosemary Brosnan and Andrew Harwell, both of whom were constant sources of support, encouragement, and editorial wisdom.

My gratitude goes to Susan Katz and Kate Jackson for taking a chance on Peregrine and Aria, to Kim VandeWater and Olivia deLeon for all their efforts to promote the trilogy, and to Melinda Weigel and Karen Sherman for bringing polish and accuracy to my words.

I am ever thankful to my agents, Josh and Tracey Adams, for steering me through the business aspects of the writing life with humor and dedication. Thanks also to Stephen Moore for all his efforts.

I have turned many times to Lorin Oberweger, Eric

Elfman, Jackie Garlick, and Lia Keyes for advice through the writing of this trilogy. Talia Vance, Donna Cooner, Katy Longshore, and Bret Ballou have been there for me since the beginning. To all of you I say: thank you, and are you up for another series?

My family deserves far more of my appreciation and love than I can fit on this page, but here goes anyway. Mom and Dad. Gui and Ci. Pedro and Maji. Toni and Mike. Shawn, Tracy, Nancy, Terri. Taylor, Morgan, Ju, Bea. Luca and Rocky. Michael. I love you. Thanks for putting up with me these past years while I spent far more time with Aria and Perry than I did with you.

Finally, thank *you* for letting me tell you a story about a girl and a boy who did something extraordinary. Your turn now. Find your heading, your Still Blue, and get there. I know you can.